Jeff Strand

JEFF STRAND

Wolf Hunt

DARK REGIONS PRESS
2011

FIRST TRADE PAPERBACK EDITION

WOLF HUNT
Text © 2011 by Jeff Strand
Cover Art © 2011 by Frank Walls

Editor, Norman Rubenstein
Publisher, Joe Morey

Cover and interior design by
David G. Barnett/Fat Cat Graphic Design
www.fatcatgraphicdesign.com

ISBN: 978-1-888993-09-7

Dark Regions Press
PO Box 1264
Colusa, CA 95932

CHAPTER ONE: Meet George and Lou

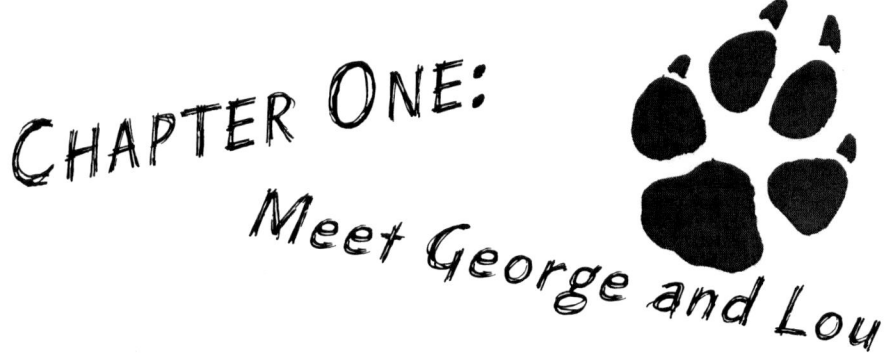

"Okay, it says here that you stole..." George Orton glanced down at his notebook, then flipped through a few pages. "Where did I write that down? Bear with me for a second...yeah, here it is. Sixty-three thousand dollars." He whistled. "Wow. That's a lot of skimming off the top."

The old man's eyes glistened. "I have a family. I have five grandkids. Please don't hurt me."

"Hurt you? For sixty-three thousand you should be begging me not to *kill* you, right?"

"Please don't kill me," said the old man, Douglas, in a whisper. "I'll double whatever he's paying you."

"Hmmmm. Let me check my notes." George glanced down at his notebook again. "Ah, here we go. 'If he tries to bribe you, break an extra finger.' Look at that, you just created more work for me."

"Please—"

"Not to mention that you probably intended to pay that bribe out of the money you stole, so in a few hours I'd have men at my house wanting to break *my* thumbs. Don't get me wrong, I like the idea of getting double pay for this job, but you're asking me to put future earning potential at risk. That's an unfair thing to ask of somebody you've just met."

Douglas' voice cracked. "There has to be a way we can work this out."

"There's really nothing to work out. Were we sent here to break your thumbs? Yes. Will your thumbs be broken when we leave? Yes indeed. Does it have to be the worst experience of your life? Not necessarily."

"I'm sure that—"

"Discussion over. I want you to understand, Doug, that I'm no sadist. I'm here to do a job like any other working man. If it were up to me, there would be no snapping of bones in the next few minutes. But it's not up to me. So now that we've established what is most definitely going to happen, let's see if we can work together to make it go as smoothly as possible."

Douglas looked over at George's partner, Lou Flynn, as if for help. Lou shrugged and leaned back in the recliner, the briefcase of recovered cash resting in his lap. The old man had been skimming for the past few months but hadn't spent a cent, which made things a lot easier for everybody.

Really, the old man should've felt lucky that it was George's turn to handle the uncomfortable part of the business. Lou was pretty good with knives, but he cringed at the act of breaking bones, which meant that he didn't always get it done on the first try. Yeah, Lou was doing an excellent job of presenting a casual front, pretending to be sitting there all cold and emotionless, but George knew that he was feeling sick to his stomach.

Apparently realizing that no help was forthcoming, Douglas looked back at George. A tear trickled down his cheek. "Yes, sir."

"Good to hear. Do you have a cover story?"

"Excuse me?"

"For your family. You're not going to tell them that a couple of hired thugs came over and broke your thumbs for stealing from a drug lord, are you?"

"I guess not."

"Are you clumsy?"

"I...I can be."

"So, theoretically, you could have tripped, put out your hands to break your fall, hit the floor, and snapped your thumbs, correct?"

"I'm not sure."

George sighed. "Work with me, Doug. This is for your benefit. I'm trying to protect your marriage. You want your grandkids to know that you're a scumbag sleazeball criminal? You're way too old to start your life from scratch, so you need to commit to the story, make it believable. Let's practice."

"I fell...and, uh, hit the floor..."

"That's total crap. You need conviction, and you also need a sheepish demeanor. Look me in the eye and start it off with something like 'You'll never believe this,' and then hold up your thumbs. That'll make it seem like you aren't trying to hide anything. It's kind of a ridiculous story, so your performance needs to be spot-on."

Douglas cleared his throat. "You'll never believe this…but I was walking through the living room…"

"Hold up your thumbs."

Douglas held up his thumbs. "I was walking through the living room, and I tripped on a dog bone—"

"Chew toy sounds better."

"A chew toy. I fell and tried to break my fall, and I hurt my thumbs."

"Nobody's going to punish the dog for making you trip, right?"

"No."

"Good." The Yorkshire terrier had been shut in the bedroom after George and Lou arrived. "Let's hear it a few more times."

The old man recited his story five more times, refining it upon George's suggestions. "You'd buy that, wouldn't you?" George asked Lou.

Lou shrugged. "I suppose so."

"That'll have to do." Douglas seemed like a decent enough guy, and he'd clearly learned his lesson, so George didn't want to see him lose his family over this whole mess. "So, Doug, are you ready?"

"Isn't there a way out of this?"

"Oh, come on now, we were doing so well. Why would you want to backtrack like that? Give me your hand."

Douglas hesitated for several seconds. "Which one?"

"Doesn't matter. We're doing them both."

After a few more seconds of hesitation, Douglas held out his left hand. George took it gently in his own, then wrapped his right fist around Douglas' thumb.

"Just close your eyes and breathe deeply. Think about something else. Do you like skiing?"

"No, sir."

"Fishing?"

"Yes, sir."

"Imagine that you're fishing. Picture yourself on the bank of a calm lake, sitting in your favorite lawn chair, watching a bobber float. You've got a cold beer in your hand. It tastes good, doesn't it? Ahhhh, nothing better than a nice cold frosty beer. Do you taste it?"

Douglas' shoulders trembled and he was on the verge of sobbing.

"Nod if you taste it."

Douglas nodded. In one sudden motion, George jerked his thumb backwards until there was a loud *snap*.

The old man screamed in pain. George grabbed his other hand and quickly broke his right thumb as well. Douglas' scream intensified, becoming so high-pitched that George might have almost found it amusing were this not a serious, professional matter.

George waited patiently for a couple of minutes until Douglas stopped shrieking and thrashing. "It's all over now," he said. "I know it hurt. But, hey, in another time and place they would've chopped your hand off for stealing a loaf of bread, so a pair of broken thumbs for sixty-three thousand dollars isn't a bad deal. A better deal if you'd actually got to *keep* the money, but you know what I mean. So are you cool with your cover story?"

Douglas nodded and wept.

"Technically, I'm supposed to break another finger for your attempt to bribe me, but I like you and I'm going to pretend it didn't happen. You should feel lucky—I'm not always this nice. We won't tell if you don't. We'll get out of your hair now. Please don't take any more drug money that doesn't belong to you, okay?"

«««—»»»

"Jeez, I hate that sound," said Lou as they pulled out of Douglas' driveway. "I'd almost rather have his fingers get cut off, know what I mean?"

"I don't think he'd agree with you."

Lou shivered. "It's just disturbing."

"I thought he took it pretty well."

"They usually do, when it's your turn. Maybe we should stick with that dynamic. I kinda like being the quiet creepy one."

George chuckled. "Nice dynamic. You supervise and I do the manual labor. Screw that."

"I'm not saying I won't *ever* rough them up. You're just a better communicator is all." He shifted uncomfortably in his seat. "I hate this car."

"Me too." George and Lou were both big guys, and the car wasn't designed for big guys. George stood six-five, and though he wasn't quite the all-muscle physical specimen at age forty-three that he'd been at age twenty, he was still in fine shape. Lou stood an inch taller and had let himself go a little bit, but even with a potbelly, he was one intimidating son of a bitch.

They both had black hair. George wore a neatly trimmed mustache and goatee, while Lou favored a full beard, which he was in the process of re-growing out like a mountain man, since he'd reluctantly trimmed it before a classy job a couple of weeks ago. Normally they wore black suits, but it was too damn hot and muggy down here in Florida, and so they wore only their white dress shirts. Red tie for George, no tie for Lou, sweat stains for both.

George's cell phone rang. "It's Ricky," he said.

"Tell that scrawny punk to get us a bigger goddamn car next time."

George pressed the "talk" button and put the phone to his ear. "Get us a bigger goddamn car next time, scrawny punk."

"I love you too, George," said Ricky. He made a kissy sound into the phone. "So did the old guy cry like a baby?"

"There were tears."

"Oh, yeah, I bet there were, I bet there were. Did you leave his fingers at a freakish angle?"

"Why'd you call, Ricky?"

"I pulled some strings and got you a top-notch assignment."

In Ricky-speak, that translated to *I've got a crap job that nobody else wants.* "What is it?"

"I can't talk about it over the phone. Let's just say that I hope you've got some silver bullets handy."

"What are we doing, killing a werewolf?"

There was a long pause on the other end. "Look, George, pretend to be surprised, okay? I wasn't supposed to give the werewolf part away."

"You're serious? Some whack-nut really wants us to kill a werewolf?"

"What werewolf?" Lou asked. George waved at him to shut up.

"It's an easy job," Ricky insisted. "There ain't no such thing as werewolves, I know you know that, but this guy Bateman, he swears he's got one in captivity, and he needs you to drive it up to this other guy Dewey."

"Dewey. Like the decimal system?"

"Yeah. And you should make that joke when you see him. Guys in his position, they get a real big kick out of people making fun of their names."

"I wasn't making fun of it. I was clarifying it."

"Anyway, it's not even a half-day job. You'll be on the red-eye back to New York tonight."

"Are we seriously expected to drive with a wolf in the car?"

"Nah, he's in human form. And it'll be a van. Lots of legroom. But I'm not supposed to be telling you this, so act surprised."

"So it's some crazy guy who *thinks* he's a werewolf? I'm not so keen on sharing a van with the mentally ill. He's not going to be howling and crap like that, is he?"

"Just forget I said anything," said Ricky. "I'll text you the address. Be there in an hour." Ricky hung up before George could protest.

"What werewolf?" Lou asked.

"I don't know. I think Ricky's screwing with us."

"Remember a few months ago when we had to lean on that guy who wore the dog collar around his neck because he thought his head was gonna fall off?"

George scowled. "Don't remind me. What a joke that was. Maybe we need to treat Ricky with a little more respect so we can get a higher class of assignments."

"Respect would just confuse him. He enjoys our suffering."

"He's going to be doing a lot of suffering of his own if he was lying about this being a quick job. I'm serious—I'll pop his nose like a water balloon. I've gotta get out of this state."

Chapter Two: Wolf in a Cage

They stopped for an early lunch of drive-thru chicken sandwiches and fries, then followed the GPS directions to a small warehouse in downtown Miami. A kid in sunglasses who looked about nineteen stood outside waiting for them. He raised the sliding metal door and waved their car through.

The warehouse was mostly empty, except for a van, two cars, and about a dozen wooden crates stacked against the far wall. George parked next to a red Porsche that had was dirty and a bit dinged up—a criminal act, as far as George was concerned—and then he and Lou got out as a middle-aged man in an ill-fitting business suit approached, flanked on each side by a goon in black.

"Are you Bateman?" George asked.

"I am." Bateman smiled, revealing yellow teeth that marred an otherwise handsome face. "You two come highly recommended. Which one is George and which one is Lou?"

"I'm Lou," said Lou, tapping his chest.

"And you're George?" Bateman asked.

"Yes, sir." *Nice process of elimination.*

"I've got a task for you gentlemen," said Bateman. "It's a simple transport job and shouldn't cause any problems, but I need good men like yourselves on it. Extremely valuable cargo is involved."

"We know how to protect cargo," George assured him.

"That's what I hear." Bateman gestured to a black van that was parked about twenty feet away. "Follow me."

"It's too damn hot to be in a black van," Lou whispered to George as the five of them walked over to the vehicle.

George couldn't see anything through the tinted windows, but one of the thugs opened up the rear doors, revealing a metal cage with thick bars that filled most of the back of the van. A man sat inside, leaning against the cage wall, looking scared and miserable.

Lou sucked in a deep breath.

George hated assignments that involved this kind of crap, but kept his expression devoid of emotion. It was important to always behave in a professional manner around the guy who signed the checks…or at least authorized the non-traceable cash payments.

Bateman gestured to the man. "Do you know what that is?"

George shrugged. "Somebody who fucked with the wrong guy?"

"That is a lycanthrope. A werewolf."

"I see."

"By the light of the full moon, that weak-looking, frail man will transform into a vicious beast. The legends are true, gentlemen. Werewolves live among us. Their numbers are small, and few believe in their existence, but we've been given an unprecedented opportunity to study one." Bateman shrugged. "Or, if you don't believe me, then you're just driving some poor caged-up bastard from Miami to Tampa. Either way, you get paid."

George glanced at the other two goons, hoping to get some clue as to whether this was all a big gag or not, but their faces were unreadable.

"I'm not in the habit of questioning my employers," George said. "But…a *werewolf*? Really? Isn't that just movie stuff?"

"I don't blame you for being skeptical. I'd worry about your sanity if you weren't. Rest assured that you're being trusted with an astounding discovery, and I'm confident that you'll deliver him to my associate safely."

"What if he sprouts fur and fangs while we're on the road?"

"That won't be an issue. The full moon is two weeks away."

"Ah, okay," said George, not sure why he was embarrassed. "I don't really keep track of the lunar cycles."

"The rules are simple. Even though he's not a transformation risk, do not, under any circumstances, let him out of the cage. Do not, under any circumstances, let anything happen to him. Keep your hands away from the cage. That means do not offer him any food, do not offer him anything to drink, do not offer him any reading material to pass the time during the ride, and do not reach in there to slap him if he won't stop talking. I don't think I have to tell you that getting stopped by the police would create an awkward situation, so don't break any traffic laws. Any questions?"

"Is anybody after him?"

"To the best of our knowledge, no. But I'm sure that you'll proceed with all due diligence."

"Of course." George looked over at Lou. "You have anything?"

Lou thought for a moment. "What if he's gotta use the restroom?"

"Then the cage will get messy."

George grimaced. "Really? Isn't this a five-hour drive?"

"I think you can handle an unpleasant odor for a few hours. We'll give you a can of Lysol." Bateman raised his voice and turned his attention to the man in the cage. "However, if he wishes to be treated with more kindness upon his arrival, he may want to consider keeping his bodily functions under control."

The man glared at him but said nothing.

"What's his name?" George asked.

"Ivan."

"All right. I guess we're taking Ivan the Werewolf for a ride."

«««—»»»

They quickly worked out the remaining details, moved their suitcases to the van (behind the seats but still out of Ivan's reach), left the too-small car in the warehouse, and drove the van out onto the downtown street. It was Lou's turn to drive, so George slid the briefcase of recovered cash under his seat, then turned around and looked into the back of the van.

Ivan appeared to be in his early thirties. He was thin, with a pasty complexion and long, straight hair—to be honest, he gave off more of a vampire vibe than a werewolf one. He wore a blue dress shirt that was probably expensive but looked like it had been worn for several unpleasant days.

Driving around with a guy in a cage was a contemptible thing, but business was business. George and Lou had the luxury of turning down the worst of their job offers—they didn't do anything that involved kids, and never committed murder—but transporting a man in a cage across the state was depravity within their moral boundaries.

"This is messed up," Lou noted.

George turned back around in his seat. "You won't hear me argue."

"I mean, who believes in that werewolf nonsense? 'By the light of the full moon…' What a load of crap. What are we in, the 1600's?"

"Is that when people believed in werewolves?"

"I dunno. Maybe I'm thinking of witches. But, c'mon, look at the world we live in." Lou tapped the GPS that rested on the dashboard. "This thing has street-by-street directions for anyplace in the world we wanna go. In a world where humans can accomplish this kind of technology, what kind of person still believes in the supernatural?"

George grinned. "Maybe that GPS *is* supernatural. Maybe only the devil knows all of those streets. Or it could be ghost-powered."

"I'm trying to make a serious point here. Why would you want to derail that?"

"I'm sorry, I'm sorry. But I don't think Bateman believes in that werewolf stuff for one second."

"You think it's a cover?"

"Yeah. Either our friend back there has got a stomach full of heroin and they're playing a practical joke, or they're trying to distract us from something else that's going on. There's definitely something screwy here, so we need to be careful."

Lou nodded. "I agree."

"You could just ask me," said Ivan. It was the first time he'd spoken.

George turned around in his seat to face their prisoner. "What?"

"You could just ask me if I'm a werewolf. That would be the polite and reasonable thing to do, instead of speculating amongst yourselves."

"Fair enough. Are you a werewolf?"

"No, I'm not a fucking werewolf! What the hell? Are you two really that stupid? You're seriously going to drive me to Tampa so that some pretend-scientist can slice me up?"

"Hey, I don't care what you are. They could say you were the Easter Bunny and it wouldn't change anything. This is just a transport job."

"Oh, sure. Transport job. He told you that I'm a *werewolf*, George. You know, those magical people who transform into scary wolves during the full moon, and can only be killed by silver bullets, and gobble up little children. Those people who are, you know, *non-existent*! Doesn't it bother you to be working for that kind of insanity?"

"I don't think you heard me. You're just cargo."

"Well, that's lovely. Nice humanistic attitude you've got there. Do much slave trading in your spare time?"

"Hey, if you want to be allowed to talk, you'd better watch the lip."

"You can't stop me from talking. I'm valuable merchandise."

"Look, Ivan the Werewolf, I'm about as nice of a guy as you're liable to encounter in this kind of situation, but don't get the mistaken impression that I will let myself be disrespected. There's only one way that this drive will end, and that's with you being delivered to our destination. No other outcome is possible. However, there are several different moods that can hang over our afternoon until then, and I want you to think long and hard about whether you want to have a pleasant drive or an unpleasant one."

Ivan pouted for a few moments. "You're taking me to a guy named Mr. Dewey, right?"

"Dewey's his last name? I thought it was his first. But yeah, that's who we're going to see."

"You know what he wants, don't you?"

"No idea. A pet?"

"You think that's funny? You think the idea of turning me into some madman's pet is just a joke? Do you even have a soul?"

"You're right, that was inappropriate," George admitted, legitimately feeling as if he'd stepped over the line. "Believe me, I sympathize with your plight. It sucks."

"He doesn't want a pet. Do you know what he wants?"

"What?"

"He wants me to bite him."

"Seriously?"

"Yeah. Can you imagine that? The sick, twisted lunatic wants me to turn him into a werewolf. I mean, to believe in werewolves in the first place you've got to have a gigantic screw loose, but to want to become one…?"

"That *is* peculiar," George agreed.

"What do you think is going to happen to me when I bite Mr. Dewey and it doesn't do anything? Do you think he's going to say 'Oh, goodness gracious, my mistake!' and let me go, or do you think he's going to kill me? My death is going to be on your conscience. Can you handle that?"

"I'm not that familiar with the werewolf legend, but you'd have to change into a wolf first, right? He wouldn't just make you give him a nibble on the hand as a human."

Ivan sighed with frustration. "Fine, so when I don't change into a wolf, *then* he'll kill me. Are you okay with that? No problems working for somebody so severely wrong in the head? I don't know about you, but if I heard about somebody whose brain is so diseased that he's kidnapping innocent human beings in hopes of getting a werewolf bite, I'd stay as far away from him as possible."

"I guess you're smarter than we are, then."

"I guess so. I have to go to the bathroom."

"Hold it."

"I can't."

"Think about the desert."

"Do you have one of those things on your palm?" Lou asked.

"What things?"

"The star thing."

"A pentagram?"

"Yeah."

Ivan held up his palm, which Lou checked out in the rear-view mirror. "No. And would you like to know why I don't have a pentagram on my palm?"

"Because you're not a werewolf?"

"Exactly! Because I'm not a werewolf! I manage a temp agency! This is bullshit!"

"Again," said George, "the only way this is going to end is with you being delivered as promised. Pleasant or unpleasant. The choice is yours. Most people go with pleasant."

"They're calling me a werewolf, but you're the ones who are inhuman!" Ivan said. "You're the monsters, not me!"

"That's deep," Lou noted.

"If you do this, it'll haunt you for the rest of your life. You will always be somebody who took an innocent guy to his death for being a werewolf. That doesn't go away. No matter how long you live, you'll never not be that person. Thirty years from now, when I'm long since tortured and dead, you'll still be the guys who were told that a man in a cage was a werewolf—a *werewolf*—and delivered him into the hands of a deranged maniac who believed in that kind of nonsense. Do you really want all those years of sleepless nights?"

"Thirty years from now, one or both of us will probably be dead, too," said George. "Our work is pretty dangerous. I'm actually surprised Lou is still around. He really doesn't take care of his body."

"Not only will you be the men who drove an innocent person to his death, but you'll be the men who casually dismissed him when he tried to explain the insanity of the situation. Even if I were a werewolf, you'd be the villains here."

"Okay, you've talked enough," said George. "Shut up for a while."

"Oh, I'm sorry, are my desperate pleas for my life annoying you? I wouldn't want to be an inconvenience. I certainly hope that my shrieks of pain when they're dissecting me don't cause an unpleasant sensation in your eardrums—I don't know if my mutilated body could live with itself!"

George turned on the stereo, cranking up some classic Metallica to drown him out.

Chapter Three: Lycanthrope Chatter

"Holy crap, look at all of those things." Lou pointed out the window at where eight or nine alligators were sunning themselves along the edge of the water. The wretched creatures were all along Tamiami Trail—Lou had stopped counting about an hour ago when he reached one hundred, much to George's relief—but that was the most they'd seen at once. The fact that they were on the other side of a fence didn't provide much comfort.

"That's why I'd never live in Florida," said George.

"The gators?"

"Yeah."

"I don't think anybody ever gets eaten by them. Maybe in extreme cases, if somebody's dumb enough to go messing with them, but aside from that I think gator attacks are pretty rare."

"Still, I wouldn't want to live around them."

"We've got rats in New York."

"Rats don't bite people's legs off."

"If you lived in Florida, I can almost guarantee you'd never get your leg bit off by an alligator, whereas in New York City, I can almost guarantee you *will* get your car crapped on by a pigeon. Which is worse?"

"I'd rather take the one-hundred-percent chance on pigeon crap than the one-percent chance on an alligator bite."

"I think it's way less than one-percent."

"Any percent is unacceptable."

"It's probably not even one in a million. So what's that…one percent would be one in a hundred, so you'd times it by, uh…ten thousand?" Lou frowned as if mentally checking his math. "One ten-thousandth of a percent chance of getting a leg bit off by an alligator. That's pretty slim."

"They also have hurricanes."

"Again, low odds."

"And it's too damn hot." George had grown up in Cleveland, and moved to New York City in his late twenties. As far as he was concerned, the entire bottom half of the United States could just fall off into the ocean.

"I completely agree about the heat. That's what should keep you away from Florida—the climate, not the alligators and hurricanes."

"Are you two entertaining yourselves?" asked Ivan.

George turned around and glared at him. "Yeah, it's called a conversation. Do you have a problem with it?"

"No, no, by all means, continue your insipid conversation."

"We're driving across this miserable state on a road that has nothing to look at but alligators. Why shouldn't we talk about alligators? If we drive past an anti-abortion billboard, we'll be sure to have a spirited philosophical debate for your entertainment, but for now it's alligators and pigeon crap. Are you going to be okay with that?"

"Sure. Go right ahead."

George grinned. "You didn't think I'd know what 'insipid' meant, did you?"

"Nope. Surprised the hell out of me."

"Well I do. Fuck you, werewolf."

Ivan settled back against the bars of his cage. "You know, if I *was* a werewolf, this cage wouldn't hold me. I'd be picking my teeth with your ribs in about thirty seconds."

"Is that so?"

"Yep."

"Then I'd deserve it, because I would've let my guard down and failed to take the necessary precautions. If you do that, you deserve to have your ribs used as toothpicks. But Lou and I, we don't let our guard down like that. Would you like an example?"

"By all means."

"Right now, I want nothing more than to smack that smirk right the hell off your face. Not torture you, not beat you bloody—just smack you really, really hard. If we pulled off to the side of the road, I am ninety-nine point nine-nine percent sure that I could get in this smack with no danger to myself, and then we could proceed on our merry little way. But even though it would give me intense pleasure to do this, I'm not going to. Instead, we're going to continue to drive your werewolf ass to Tampa, just like we're supposed to."

"Then I salute you," said Ivan, saluting him. "A lesser man would have succumbed, but not the mighty George."

"You've become kind of sarcastic all of a sudden."

"Hey, if I can't appeal to your common sense or your sense of decency, I might as well be a dick for the rest of the ride. How are we doing on gas?"

"No need to worry yourself about the gas situation. We've got everything under control."

"I'd hate to be stranded out here. I know how concerned you are about the alligators."

George glanced at the GPS. "We're going to get gas in a few minutes at someplace called Hachiholata. Nice Indian name."

"Native American," said Lou. "Indians are from India."

"I thought 'native' was offensive?"

"No, 'native' is offensive to people in the jungle with spears, like if you say 'the natives are restless.' Native American is fine. Did you know that the word 'midget' is offensive?"

"To Native Americans?"

"Very funny. To a little person, the word 'midget' is as offensive as the n-word to a black person. Can you believe that? You hear midget, midget, midget all the time, and it's like saying n-word, n-word, n-word. If a politician said the n-word, his career would be over, but he could probably say 'midget'—hell, he could probably tell a midget *joke*—and he'd be fine."

"Can other midgets say midget?"

"I don't know. But I don't say it. It's not their fault they were born like that."

"So anyway," George said to Ivan, "we're stopping for gas in a few minutes. Does that make you feel better?"

"It does indeed. Can we get a burger while we're there?"

"No."

"Come on, I'm starving."

"No."

"You can just toss it through the bars."

"No."

"What am I going to do, throw a deadly bun at you?"

"You can't have a burger. Drop it."

"It's pretty sad that a couple of big strong guys like you are scared of a man in a cage."

"We're not scared of you."

"Yeah, you are. You're scared that if you toss me a hamburger and fries I'll somehow use them to my advantage. That, my friend, is fear. You have to be pretty damn afraid of somebody for them to intimidate you with a sack of fast food."

"What about those overcooked fries? Those tiny sharp hard ones at the bottom of the bag? You palm one of those, we let our guard down—*smack*! French fry in the eyeball."

Ivan stared at him for a long moment. "You know, I can't tell if you're kidding or not."

"I'm kidding, but you still don't get any food."

"See? Fear. Knee-shaking, bone-chilling fear. It's okay, we all have our phobias—it's not your fault that yours is a helpless man in a cage. I'm going to take it as a compliment."

"Is this supposed to be the part where my masculinity is so threatened that I give you a burger just to prove I'm not scared?"

"I wasn't thinking about your masculinity, necessarily, but that was the general idea, yeah."

"I'll make you a deal, werewolf. If you can go ten full minutes without talking, we'll buy you a value meal."

"Seriously?"

"Well, I *was* serious, but you just talked."

"Prick."

"Now I'm going to buy the biggest, juiciest burger they've got, with mayo and ketchup and onions and bacon and maybe even bleu cheese, and I'm going to eat it right in front of you. Do you prefer fries or onion rings?"

"Onion rings."

"I'm going to get those, too. Big greasy ones, with just the right amount of breading. Some places use way too much breading, so it's like you're eating fried dough, but I'll make sure that these onion rings are perfect." George felt kind of guilty after he said that. He normally didn't behave like this, but something about Ivan just annoyed the living hell out of him.

Ivan smiled. "You both realize that you're going to die today, right?"

"I beg your pardon?"

"You heard me. We're all having a grand old time right now, busting each other's chops, kidding around like best buddies, but what you two don't realize is that you're in hell. You're burning in hell right now and you can't even feel the flames. If you walked right up to the devil and tugged on his horns, your soul could not be more damned than it is right now."

"I don't think that's how damnation works," said George. "I think God has to do it or you have to make some kind of deal for vast wealth or something." He nudged Lou. "Did you make any deals with the devil recently that I should be made aware of?"

"If I had, we sure wouldn't be spending our day driving this loudmouth across Florida."

George looked back at Ivan. "Sorry. Your intimidation tactic didn't work."

"A pity."

"Intimidation is a big part of how I make my living, so let me give you some pointers. First of all—and this is a big one, Ivan, so write it down—when you're trying to intimidate your opponent, the most important thing to remember is to not be locked in a cage in his van. If you fail to follow that rule, your chances at a successful intimidation attempt drop to just about nil. Did you write it down?"

"Unfortunately, I don't have a writing utensil."

"Well, then just try to remember it. Your 'hell' speech works much better when you're not in a cage, that's all I'm saying."

"You're a confident man, George. I admire that. I enjoy licking up blood that comes from a confident man."

"That's gross."

Ivan nodded. "Yes, it is. Also irrelevant, since what I'm really going to do is set off this explosive device that's strapped to my left leg."

George felt a sudden flash of panic. He couldn't help it. Then he immediately relaxed—the little creep was just messing with him. "Oh, really?"

"Yes."

"Bateman captured you and caged you up without realizing that you had a bomb on your leg?"

"You've had me in the car for two hours without realizing it."

George looked at Ivan's leg. There didn't *seem* to be a bulge, but...

"I call bullshit."

"Or maybe Bateman knows about it. Maybe we just haven't reached the designated detonation point yet."

"Or perhaps you're conversing out of your ass."

"Aren't you going to order me to pull up my pant leg?"

"Nope."

"Not going to pull a gun on me?"

"I might pull a gun on you if you don't shut up, but I'm not going to do it to make you pull up your pant leg."

The female voice of the GPS announced that they had one mile left until their exit.

"Make you a deal. Buy me a burger and I won't blow us all to smithereens. That's a fair deal, right? A combo #1 and your scorched head doesn't land three towns away."

George turned back around in his seat. He had to admit that Ivan's endless chatter was preferable to the sobbing and begging and screaming that he and Lou sometimes had to endure, and probably better than the whining that Ivan had subjected them to at the beginning of the drive, yet it was still pretty grating. And they had another three hours to go. He wished they had a tranquilizer dart.

They pulled off at the next exit. They could've gone up to Interstate 75 and then quickly found an easy-on, easy-off place to get gas, but whenever possible George and Lou preferred to fill up at mom-and-pop gas stations. Less chance of security cameras. And they liked to support small businesses.

"Welcome to Hachiholata," said Lou, as they stopped at a red light.

The town, if you could even call it a town, was quite a bit smaller than George had expected—just a two-lane road lined by a few non-chain businesses. He didn't even see a McDonalds, and traffic was almost non-existent.

"Looks like a peaceful place," Lou noted. "I could retire here."

"What? You hate Florida!"

"I mean I could retire in a place like this that wasn't in Florida."

"Well, we've got a long way to go before retirement. And when I do, it's sure as hell not going to be—wow, look at that dog."

George pointed out his side window. A dog—a collie, one of those Lassie dogs—was about a block away, running toward the van, barking furiously. A yellow leash dragged on the ground behind it, though George didn't see any sign of the owner.

"He looks mad," Lou noted.

The light was still red. The dog continued racing toward them, moving at an alarming pace, with the van clearly its target. "Make sure you don't run him over when you go," George said. "Jeez, he's really not slowing down…"

The dog *slammed* into the side of the van. George's heart gave a jolt and he let out a cry of surprise.

"What the hell?" Lou asked, sounding even more startled than George felt. "How do you hit a dog when you're not even moving?"

The dog slammed into the side of the van again, still barking. George quickly adjusted the side-view mirror, and saw the dog throw its entire body into the van, face-first, over and over, leaving behind smears of blood. The van rocked a little with each blow.

"Fucker's rabid!" George shouted. "Get us out of here!"

The light had already turned green, so Lou gunned the engine and they sped through the intersection. George spun around and saw the dog, broken and pitiful, limping after them.

"Holy shit!" said Lou. "Have you ever seen a dog do that before?"

"Never." As a rule, George didn't have sympathy for anything that attacked him, but he felt terrible for the poor beast. "Should we go back and put it out of its misery?"

Lou looked incredulous. "You mean run it over all the way?"

"No, I mean shoot it or something."

"Yeah, let's whip out some guns and shoot a rabid dog when we've got Ivan in the back. That won't attract any attention. Real smart, George."

"You don't have to be sarcastic."

"I'm not sarcastic. I'm freaked out!"

George looked back at their prisoner. Ivan sat silently in his cage, his expression unreadable, almost serene. George considered telling him to shut up anyway, but didn't.

"What do we do now?" Lou asked.

"Same thing we were going to do before. Get some gas and deliver the werewolf to Tampa. Let's not lose our heads over a Cujo."

"You're right, you're right."

"I hope its owner is able to fix it up."

Lou looked as if he wanted to make another sarcastic comment, then just shook his head. "There's a gas station up there."

They pulled into the gas station, Hachiholata Gas & Gulp, which had four pumps and a small convenience store. Their rule for the past nine years was that whoever drove, the other guy had to pump the gas, so George got out of the van. There were several dents in the side of the vehicle along with the blood. George wondered if Bateman would be pissed. He didn't seem to care enough about his Porsche to keep it in pristine shape, so he probably wouldn't get all upset over a few dents on a dumpy old van.

George swiped his untraceable credit card and began to pump the gas.

He picked up the gas station's squeegee and dipped it into the cleaning fluid, which was gray and murky and probably hadn't been changed in weeks. He wiped off the blood with the squeegee, rinsing twice before he was done, and finished off the task with a paper towel.

That was totally surreal. Maybe the dog knew they had a werewolf in captivity and was trying to pull off a rescue mission. A little shared-species courtesy.

Nah. Only a rabid dog would bash itself bloody like that. He hoped its owner found it in time to get it to the vet, although he didn't think the dog had much of a chance even if it wasn't diseased. At times like these, George wished he weren't a criminal, so he could safely put a dog out of its misery without having to explain why he had an unregistered firearm.

Another car pulled into the gas station, a small blue one that George and Lou probably couldn't have fit inside without ripping out the front seat. The driver, a hot young brunette in shorts and a tight t-shirt, got out of the car, gave George a friendly, not quite flirtatious smile, and began to pump her own gas.

George opened up the passenger-side door. "Do you want a Snickers?" he asked Lou.

"Nah."

"I'll take one," said Ivan.

George ignored him and closed the door. Maybe it was more of a Three Musketeers moment. He needed something light and fluffy.

There was a sudden growling to his left. George looked over at the source and saw a dog, this one a scary-ass-looking Doberman, come around the side of the van.

More growling behind him. George turned around, and the second dog charged at him. A fucking *rat terrier*?

The Doberman launched into a ferocious barking fit, spittle flying from its jaws, and charged as well.

Chapter Four: Dogfight

With a Doberman attacking him from the front and a rat terrier attacking from the rear, George decided in a split-second that if he wished to avoid being savagely mauled, he should probably focus on the Doberman. He quickly yanked the fuel pump out of the van and doused the dog in the face. It let out a loud yip and violently shook its body, shaking off gasoline as if it had just jumped out of an unwanted bath.

George kicked the snarling rat terrier out of the way.

Even more barking. Another frickin' Doberman was running toward him. And behind it, some large brown-and-white dog of a breed that George couldn't identify. What the hell was going on?

He kicked the rat terrier again. It latched onto his leg, biting but not breaking through the fabric of his pants. He didn't want to douse a dog with gasoline unless absolutely necessary, so he swung his leg as hard as he could, hurling the dog into the air. It landed on its side, yipped, got back up, and rushed at him again, so he sprayed it.

There wasn't time to get back inside the van before the other two dogs reached him, so he held the fuel pump like a pistol. He had a real one in a holster under his shirt, and this was one of those moments where he wasn't particularly concerned about the locals knowing he had a gun, but shooting around spilled gasoline was never a good idea, even if the resulting explosion would most likely take care of his psycho dog problem.

He heard Lou's door open. "Stay in there!" George shouted.

He sprayed the second Doberman, getting the unfortunate canine right in the eyes. Its wail of pain hurt George's ears and his conscience, but the dog didn't veer from its prey. It leapt into the air, striking George in the chest and knocking him down onto the cement.

He threw his arm over his eyes to protect them, blinking away tears as the gasoline fumes hit him hard. The dog's head jerked around as if it were having an epileptic fit, but it got a good solid bite on George's chest. He punched the dog in the face with his left fist, then bashed it on the side of the head with the fuel pump.

Had it broken the skin? Did he now have rabies? Did they still treat that with several painful shots in the stomach?

The woman screamed, though George couldn't see what happened to her.

He *could* see, however, that Lou was standing a few feet away, holding his own pistol.

George tried to wave him away, but the Doberman's jaws clamped onto his wrist. "Don't shoot! Gas!"

Lou, thank God, behaved intelligently and did not shoot. He grabbed the dog by its leather collar and strained to drag it off of George. The Doberman let go of George's wrist but its nails raked across his chest as his partner slowly pulled the thrashing animal away. Then Lou slammed it against the van. Once, twice, three times, four times, five times, and then the Doberman stopped struggling.

George had to kick the rat terrier again.

The brunette's car door was open and she was halfway inside, but the brown-and-white dog was inside with her, tearing at her flesh as she shrieked in terror.

George quickly got up, forcing himself not to look at his wrist. Another small dog, some kind of mutt, came at him. George's tendencies toward being pro-animal-rights were not as passionate now as they'd been sixty seconds ago, and he blasted the little bastard with enough gas that it ran off-course and smacked into the van's back tire instead of him.

The woman flailed and kicked at the dog, but she couldn't get it out of her car. George's moral code allowed for breaking an old man's fingers, and for driving an accused werewolf across the state in a cage, and for use of gasoline as a blinding agent against dogs when necessary, but it did not allow for watching an innocent woman get savaged by an out-of-control animal.

"You get in the car," said Lou, waving him back as he hurried toward the woman. "I've got this."

"What the hell is going on?" a square-faced, middle-aged man demanded, voice filled with panic. He'd come out of the convenience store and held a rifle.

"Get back inside!" George shouted.

But the man's moral code, much like George's, apparently did not include a clause about hiding in a store when somebody was being attacked. He took a few steps toward the woman's car, then stopped and took aim at a new dog that was running toward them, having come from behind the store. Another Doberman. Who the hell owned all of these Dobermans?

He fired. A perfect head shot. The Doberman tumbled forward.

Lou reached the blue car. He grabbed the dog by its long tail with both hands and gave a sharp tug. The dog twisted around, bashing its head against the steering wheel and honking the horn, then scrambled out of the car, lunging at Lou's throat.

Lou slammed his hands together, boxing the dog's ears. It yelped but didn't stop fighting. As Lou quickly backed away, the dog snapped at his legs.

Yet another goddamn dog—was there a dog factory in the area or something?—came running toward the gas station, followed by two more. All big ones. One of them was dragging a leash.

The gas station attendant fired the rifle. Either his first shot had been total luck, or he was getting too scared to shoot straight, because this one didn't even come close. He fired again. Another complete miss.

George's fuel hose wasn't long enough to reach the dog that was attacking his partner, which didn't matter because Lou stood between the dog and a possible gasoline stream. George dropped the pump and rushed forward, kicking the dog in the side, hard enough to produce a *crunch*.

The brown-and-white dog stumbled away, then launched itself against the car, bashing itself against the metal over and over.

George looked at the woman. Her shoulder was a mess. The gas station attendant fired again, this time hitting one of the oncoming Dobermans in the ear. That didn't stop the animal. The top half of its ear dangled in a bloody flap, and the attendant adjusted his grip on the rifle, holding it like a club.

"Behind you!" the woman shouted at George.

George didn't even have time to turn around before the dog knocked him to the ground. He couldn't see the creature, could just hear its growling and feel its hot breath on his neck. He elbowed it in the face, which probably hurt his elbow worse than its face. Some froth got into his eyes.

George frantically tried to blink it out, as Lou grabbed the dog under its front arms and pulled it away. The dog snarled and twisted around and bit at

Lou's nose, while Lou struggled to get the thrashing animal away from George.

"Help!" the attendant shouted.

George pushed himself up again. The attendant lay on the ground, kicking at the dogs that had brought him down. He swung with his rifle, but one of the dogs sunk its teeth deep into his forearm, creating a spray of red, and he lost his grip on the weapon.

"Pull your legs in the car," George told the woman, putting his hand on the door. She seemed to be in shock and didn't respond. Instead of acknowledging his command, she was staring off behind—

George looked to see what she was staring at. A pit bull. Running right at him. Fast.

Again, there wasn't enough time to get the van door open, or even to grab the fuel pump. George, less concerned with dignity than survival, quickly climbed up onto the hood of the van, just as the pit bull's teeth snapped at his ankle. George had a lot of good physical attributes, but few would call him nimble, and the process of scrambling up onto the hood of the van was a sloppy one.

While the pit bull was distracted with George, Lou managed to run around to the other side of the van. George heard a squeal of pain as Lou apparently kicked a miniature dog, and then Lou successfully got into the driver's side of the van and slammed the door shut behind him.

The pit bull jumped for George's tender and succulent (he assumed) flesh. It didn't get his ankle, but it did get his pants leg. George grabbed for the first thing he saw—a windshield wiper—to steady himself as the dog tried to pull him off the van.

He pounded on the windshield. "Start the car! Start the frickin' car!"

As George tried to shake the pit bull off his leg, he helplessly watched the gas station attendant's desperate fight for life. One dog was at his legs, the other was at his shoulder, as if they were working together to rip him in half. The attendant still had a lot of struggle left in him, but the dogs were winning.

Awful way to go.

Lou started the engine. As he backed up the van, George's already precarious grip slipped away, and he tumbled off the front of the vehicle, crushing a tiny dog beneath him as he landed on his ass. The pit bull went for his face.

He punched it away, but the blow barely seemed to phase the animal.

George extended his thumbs and thrust at its eyes. He missed by a few inches—and missed getting his thumbs bit off by even less. He elbowed the dog just like he'd elbowed the other one. It had the same lack of effect.

"Hold it steady!" said Lou from above.

George looked up. Lou had rolled down the passenger-side window and was pointing his gun at the dog.

"Don't—!"

Lou squeezed the trigger, firing a bullet into the dog's forechest. The dog flopped off of George and lay on the cement, flailing and whimpering.

"Don't shoot!" George shouted. "There's gas everywhere!"

"It was killing you!"

"It wasn't killing me, it was attacking me! Don't fire bullets when there's gasoline spilled on the ground!"

"The gas station guy did!"

"He wasn't near the actual gas!"

"I saved your life!"

"Put the gun away!"

George got up yet again, though this time it was quite a bit more difficult.

"Move!" Lou said.

Before George could move, Lou fired another bullet, shooting a medium-sized black dog that had been racing at George.

"I said stop shooting!"

"Then get the hell out of danger!"

George turned to check on the woman. She hadn't shut her car door. In fact, she was no longer in the vehicle. She was running toward the gas station attendant, which seemed like the exact opposite direction in which a young woman who'd already been mauled by a dog should be running.

The attendant wasn't struggling as much, but he was still alive. The woman had something in her hand.

Lou reached through the open window and smacked George on the arm. "Get in the goddamn car!"

That was an excellent recommendation. Lou scooted back into the driver's seat as George opened the passenger door, got inside, and slammed the door.

As the woman rushed over to the attendant, the dog that was ripping apart his legs let go of its bloody prey and turned on its new victim. She blasted it with a dose of what was looked like pepper spray, and the dog howled and ran off in the other direction.

Before she could get the other dog, it tore a huge strip of flesh out of the attendant's throat. George winced and slapped his hand over his mouth. Even if he wanted to be a hero, that poor bastard would be dead within seconds.

The woman sprayed the dog. It yelped, but the pain wasn't enough to keep it from tearing out a second piece of the attendant's throat.

Lou sped forward. The van bounced as he ran over one of the dead dogs. "Get the lady!" George said.

Lou drove up next to her, George opened his door, and she jumped inside the van, squeezing onto George's lap. He pulled the door closed most of the way, then threw it open again, bashing yet another Doberman in the face. Then he closed the door and, tires squealing, they sped out of the gas station and back onto the road.

The woman began to sob. "You'll be okay," George assured her. "We'll get you to the emergency room. They'll fix you up."

"Did you see what they did to that man? He…he…I don't think we can help him."

"That was the weirdest thing I've ever seen," said Lou. "They couldn't all go rabid at once like that, could they? I mean, do you think they escaped from a medical center or something?"

"No idea. Not a clue. Jesus." George hurt in several places and wanted to check out the extent of his injuries, but he couldn't do it with the woman in his lap. He did glance at his wrist, which had a couple of puncture wounds, but the blood was seeping instead of spraying so he figured he'd be okay.

Clang! Clang! Clang!

George cursed under his breath. Ivan kicked at the bars of his cage once more, and then smiled at the sound of the woman's gasp. "My name is Ivan. Lou is driving. You're sitting on George's lap. They're driving me to my death. Because you know this, I assume you have to die, too."

George pointed a warning finger at him. "Shut up."

"Oh, I'm done. No, wait, I missed the part about you thinking I'm a werewolf."

"I said, shut up."

"What are you going to do, come back here and beat me up in front of a witness? That doesn't seem very smart. When you kill her, are you going to snap her neck quickly or drag her death out, slowly?"

"One more time—"

"I think you should drag it out slowly."

"*Enough!*" George shouted. Then he closed his eyes and rubbed his forehead, trying to get rid of the sudden migraine. He hadn't had one of those in over a year, and he'd been in a lot of stressful situations in the past year.

"Don't take it out on me," said Ivan. "I'm not the one who let her into the car, Mr. Intellect."

George took a deep breath, willing himself to remain calm. The situation was screwed up enough already without him letting Ivan send him into a rage. He had to ignore the werewolf, keep himself from losing his mind, assure the woman that she was in no danger, and think this whole thing through.

They drove in silence for a few seconds. The woman looked as if she wanted to lunge for the door handle. They'd almost definitely let her go free fairly soon, hopefully outside of a hospital, but George couldn't have her making any wild escape attempts until this was all figured out. He reached over and locked the door.

"So what now?" she asked.

Chapter Five: Questioning What The Hell Just Happened

"How's your shoulder?" George asked.

"It's fine," the woman insisted. "Just let me go, okay? I won't say anything, I promise."

"What's your name?"

"Seriously, who am I going to tell? You saved my life. I wouldn't turn you in."

"Ma'am, just tell me your name."

She hesitated. "Michele." The way she said it, George thought she might be giving him a fake name, but that didn't matter—he just needed something to call her.

"Michele, we're not going to hurt you. We're FBI agents, and the man behind us is a federal prisoner. We're just transporting him to a maximum security facility."

"The FBI doesn't transport people in cages."

"Okay, look, forget about the guy in the cage for a minute. We're not going to hurt you, and we're not kidnapping you. We're going to take you to a hospital."

"If you're not kidnapping me, then let me go."

George's headache got even more intense. "Fine. We're kidnapping you for now. But we're not going to hurt you."

"You'll be locked in here with me pretty soon," Ivan said. "Assuming they decide it's okay for you to live."

"Can we muzzle him?" Lou asked.

"No! That's exactly what he wants us to try to do! Let's just get situated and figure this out." George gently slid Michele off his lap, putting her

35

between him and Lou. Though he liked having cute young women on his lap, now wasn't the time. It was a tight, uncomfortable fit on the seat with them squished together, but he didn't plan to keep her around for much longer.

"Are you going to bleed to death?" George asked.

Michele shook her head. The shoulder of her shirt was soaked with blood, but though the wound was grisly, it didn't seem to be that deep. "If you're going to force me to ride with you, do you at least have some Band-Aids?"

"Yeah, we've got some stuff. If you reach behind the seat there's a brown suitcase." George pressed his wrist against his pants as Michele reached back and got his bag. He ran the index finger of his other hand over his chest. The bite wasn't too bad, and the lines where the dog's nails had raked across his chest felt more like scrapes than gashes. The traces of gasoline didn't exactly feel pleasant on his wounds, but he was a tough guy, he could handle it. George gestured to the upcoming exit. "Go ahead and get back on Tamiami Trail for now."

Lou nodded and took the exit.

George opened the suitcase, dug through his dirty clothes, and took out the first aid kit. He handed the suitcase back to Michele and she returned it to its spot behind the seat. The first aid kit was fairly small, but it had enough supplies to take care of various on-the-job injuries one might sustain when one's job involved dealing with unsavory and occasionally violent individuals. George took out a handful of bandages, gave half to Michele, and they began to tend to their wounds.

There were so many things to discuss, George wasn't sure where even to begin, so he started with the first one that popped into his mind: "Lou, why the hell did you shoot when I told you not to?"

"Because you had a great big dog trying to rip your guts out."

"What if there'd been a spark?"

"Dogs don't produce sparks when bullets go in them."

"What if you'd missed?"

"I wasn't gonna miss."

"Lou, you're a shit shot!"

"Watch your mouth around a lady. The dog was five feet away. I wasn't gonna miss. I'd rather take the chance of blowing us all up than letting you get eaten. If I hadn't fired the gun, you'd be sitting there with only one arm and one leg whining at me going 'Why didn't you shoot it? Why didn't you shoot it?'"

George considered that for a moment. "Okay, I probably would be. But the next time a flammable substance is all over the ground, don't shoot, got it?"

"Screw you. The next time gas is involved, I'm going to find a frickin' flamethrower."

"Is this really the most important thing you two have to argue about?" Michele asked.

"I'm sorry. Lou, I'm sorry. But when I make an important judgment call like that, it's very frustrating to have you—"

"You can't keep talking after the apology."

George closed his eyes and rubbed his forehead again.

"How are your bites?" Lou asked.

"They're fine. They hurt like hell, but they're fine." He inspected his wrist wound again. It was badly swollen but the flow of blood had almost stopped. Apparently the dog had been polite enough not to sink its teeth into an artery. "I can't believe I killed those dogs. I wouldn't even spank Quincy for going potty off the paper."

"You did what you had to do."

"Did I?"

"Oh, no, no, no, no," said Lou. "If you're going to have a dark night of the soul over those dogs, save it for when I'm not around."

They'd had countless lively debates over the years, but George and Lou rarely bickered like this. Of course, they rarely found themselves in a situation so far out of their control.

"I apologize," said George, wrapping a large bandage around his wrist. "I'm not going to say anything else. And I thank you for shooting the dogs."

"No problem."

George turned his attention to Michele. "Do you know anything about what made those dogs go berserk?"

"I don't have the slightest idea."

"I didn't think so." With Michele on the seat, there really wasn't room for him to turn around to face Ivan, so George adjusted the rear-view mirror to give himself a good look at their captive. "Ivan, what do you know about this?"

"Why, whatever would I know?"

"You can drop the smart-ass tone. Tell me what just happened out there."

"Baffling, wasn't it? All those dogs going nuts. What an odd occurrence. I guess Lou was right, there must have been some sort of problem at a local medical facility, causing a bunch of rabid dogs to escape and go on a rampage. Unfortunate timing for you two, huh? I'm glad I was safely locked in this cage. You should probably report this incident to your superiors."

"Maybe he's right," said Lou.

"He's not right." George tried to look menacing, although that was difficult when he and Ivan were just looking at each other with a tiny mirror. "We get hired to drive a werewolf across the state. That's weird enough. Then we stop for gas, and every dog in town comes after us—dogs that were *not* rabid, because some of them had obviously just pulled away from their owners."

Ivan smiled. "A riddle wrapped in a puzzle cloaked in an enigma."

"What do you know about this?"

"Well, George, I suppose the first possibility is that I have friends who train vicious dogs for a living, and that I cleverly surmised that you would need to stop at that particular town to get fuel for your van, after I cleverly surmised that you wouldn't be taking the most efficient route to get from Miami to Tampa. Pretty brilliant of me, although to make this plan *truly* foolproof I'd need an army of dogs waiting in all of the neighboring towns. Let's stop someplace else for another tank of gas and see if that's the case."

"I want to know how you made that happen."

"It wasn't me. That would lack credibility."

"I'm dead serious, Ivan. How did you make those dogs lose their minds? Or do you just give off some kind of scent or something?"

"I can't believe you're trying to pin this on me. That's as silly as the idea of me being a werewolf."

"Look, asshole, wolves are dogs—"

"Oooooh, look who knows his biology!"

"—and there's no way this is a coincidence."

"Well, then, if it's not a coincidence, I must have the power to control dogs, or at least make them go nuts. Is that what you want to hear?"

"If it's the truth."

Ivan let out a high-pitched, incredulous laugh. "Listen to you! Has the big bad thug-for-hire opened his mind to the possibility of the paranormal?"

"I didn't say that."

"Oh, but two hours ago, if I'd told you that you shouldn't mess with me because I've got the power to send a bunch of killer dogs after you, you would have just made fun of me. You would've been all 'Oh, dude, if you're trying to scare me with your doggie powers, don't do it from inside a cage,' right?"

"You were the one insisting that the whole werewolf thing was ridiculous."

"Yes, but I was the one who had something to lose by being a werewolf. You came at it from neutral ground. Now you're a believer, and all it took were a few nasty dog bites. I'm proud of you, George. This has opened a whole new world of excitement for you."

"I didn't say I was a believer."

"You implied it. That's all I need to declare victory."

George glanced at Michele. "I don't really believe he's a werewolf."

Michele said nothing. She still looked more concerned about being murdered by kidnappers than whether anybody believed in lycanthropes.

"Let's take a vote," said Ivan. "I believe I'm a werewolf. George reluctantly believes I'm a werewolf. What about you, Lou?"

"I believe that you need to stop talking."

"Or what?"

"Or else."

"That's the best you've got? Really? You know what, I'm embarrassed to be your prisoner. Flat-out humiliated. It was cool for a while, when I thought that a couple of scary mob guys had me, but you two buffoons? I might as well be in the hands of the—"

"Enough!"

"Don't you want to know what non-threatening group I was going to compare you to?"

"One more word," said George. "Just one more word, and I *will* come back there and beat the snot out of you."

"Bet you won't. So what about you, Michele? We've got two votes in favor and one non-committal. Do you think I could possibly be a werewolf?"

"I don't know."

"It's not about what you know, it's about what you think. I'm the only one who knows for certain. So do you think I'm a werewolf?"

"Sure, whatever."

"Three votes in favor. That's a majority, even if Lou changes his cowardly cop-out vote to 'no.' Looks like I'm a fuckin' werewolf with the power of dog control, ladies and gentlemen. Now what are we going to do about that?"

"Not a thing," said George. "The plan stays the same."

"The plan to deliver me to Mr. Dewey in Tampa so I can bite and transform him? Come on, guys, there's no need to be discrete around our new friend Michele, is there? After all, you're planning to kill her."

"Nobody is getting killed."

"Nobody except poor Michele."

"Don't listen to him," George told her.

"Right, don't listen to the guy in the cage," Ivan said. "Clearly there can be no wrongdoing in a situation that involves people in cages. Maybe you'll be lucky and their plans revolve around slavery instead of murder, but either way, I'm not getting a strong 'drop you off at the hospital and everything will be all right' vibe from this, are you?"

"Seriously, don't listen to him," said George. "We're going to let you go."

"Then why haven't you done it already?" Ivan asked. "She asked to be let go as soon as she saw me. True gentlemen would have honored the poor doomed victim's request."

"We've got shit to figure out first."

"Then figure it out. It sounds like I'm the only one trying to figure things out, to be completely honest. Oooooh, I hope if you decide to rape her, you take it outside—there are some things I just don't enjoy watching."

"We should just let her out," said Lou. "She won't tell."

"Of course she won't," said Ivan. "It's not like she's seen anything *memorable*."

"Get off at the next exit," George told Lou.

"Why?"

"Because we need some answers."

"No, no, this is an 'ignorance is bliss' deal. Let's leave this alone."

"I'm not comfortable with not knowing what's going on when things are this severely screwed up. We left behind a bunch of dead dogs and a dead gas station guy—that'll be on the news. We need a full understanding of what we're dealing with."

"We shouldn't have brought the girl."

"Yeah, I know. We weren't thinking right."

"I never said to bring her in the first place."

"Okay, fine, *I* wasn't thinking right. The dog teeth in my skin messed with my thought process. Are you happy?"

"Just saying."

"They're going to *kiiiiiiiiillllllll* you," Ivan sang out from the back.

"We should call Ricky, at least," said Lou. "Let him know what happened."

George sighed. "Yeah, you're right. Damn it."

He took out his cell phone and pulled up Ricky The Prick from his "recent contacts" list. Ricky answered on the first ring. "Hiya, sweetie. How's the werewolf doing?"

"He's fine. But we had a pretty big problem."

"Fleas? Hairballs?"

"Ricky, don't make me—"

"All right, all right. Jeez, you sound tense. What's the problem?"

"We stopped to get gas, and about a dozen dogs attacked us. Like they'd gone crazy. One of them bashed itself half to death against the van."

"You for real?"

"Yeah. Lou had to shoot two of them. The guy who worked there, they ripped his goddamn neck open."

"No kidding? He died?"

"Unless you can live with most of your throat gone."

"Wow. I've never seen somebody get mauled to death by dogs before. I mean, I've seen videos, but never in real life. You guys all right?"

"I'm kind of bit up, but I'll be okay."

"You should put some antiseptic on the bites."

"Thanks. I'll do that. Any idea why a bunch of dogs would suddenly attack us like that?"

"Who do you think you're calling, National Geographic? How would I know?"

"We think the werewolf was responsible."

"Uh, by 'werewolf' you mean the guy that nutcase Bateman *thinks* is a werewolf, right?"

"Yeah, him."

"This is a joke, isn't it? You're trying to get back at me for giving you the crappy werewolf assignment. Y'know, there are a lot of worse places you can be. A guy at a sewage treatment plant isn't paying his protection money. Can you believe that? A sewage treatment plant. How do you get protection money out of them in the first place? The world is crazy. You could be on your way to the turd processing factory right now, so don't—"

"Are you done?"

"I don't think I was supposed to say anything about the sewage place. Don't tell anybody, okay?"

"Enough, Ricky! We need to know if we should keep going where we're going, or if we should get off the road for a while until things blow over."

"Oh, you should definitely keep going. They want the werewolf this evening at the latest. Where did you say the dogs were?"

"It's a small town called Hachiholata or something like that."

"Can you spell it for me?"

"H-A-C..." George trailed off. "No, I can't spell it for you! Just find it!"

"All right, all right, I'll follow what's going on there. Worst case, we'll try to get you a new van that nobody will be looking for, though I'm not sure we have any people in that area who can make that happen. For now, just assume that everything's cool. I'll call you back."

"Are you going to contact Bateman?"

"Oh, hell no. Just keep going. I'll take care of everything."

"Thanks," said George. He hung up and tucked the cell phone back into his pocket.

"I noticed that you didn't mention your new hostage," said Ivan.

George ignored him. "Still take the next exit," he told Lou.

"Why?"

"Because this wolf is going to talk."

Chapter Six: An Unwise Decision

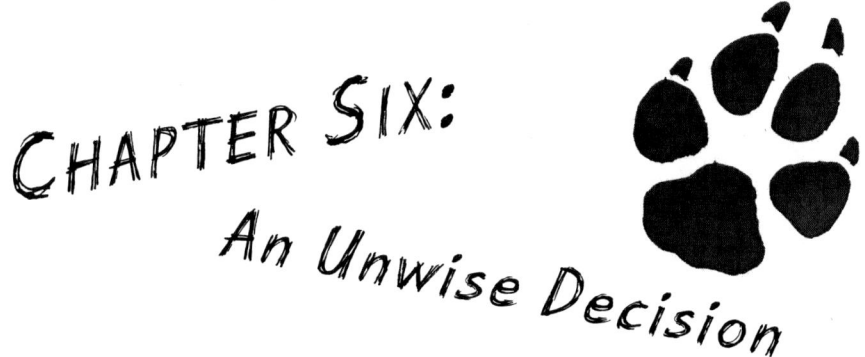

"That seems like it could turn out bad," said Lou.

"We're not going to let him out of the cage," George insisted. "We're not even going to get close to it. I'm just going to make him talk."

"Why does he need to talk? Why do we need to know anything? I'm perfectly happy not having a clue in the world about what's going on."

"Well, I need some answers. We were not sufficiently briefed before we took this job. There's a big frickin' difference between transporting an annoying guy in a cage and transporting a guy who can command dogs to do his bidding…or, you know, his scent makes them crazy and violent, or whatever it is that he did. If he can mess with animals like that, who knows what else he can do? Maybe he's…I don't know, an abomination or something, and we should destroy him for the good of mankind."

"I liked it better when we didn't care if he was a werewolf or not."

Truth be told, so did George. He usually didn't want to know the details. He'd committed plenty of immoral acts without understanding the true motive behind them.

But this was different. A lot different. This wasn't about stolen cash or sleeping with the wrong person's wife or making a poor business decision that needed to be rectified with knives. This was an unexplained phenomenon. Or, if it *had* been explained, then Ivan really was a werewolf, which was completely absurd but a matter that needed to be further investigated.

Sure, George had absolutely no intention of doing anything to put the job or his personal safety at risk, but Ivan didn't need to know that.

"Are you having trouble adjusting to your new view of the world?" Ivan asked. "It's always a little devastating when decades of preconceived notions about the way things really work are shattered all at once. But just wait until you meet the aliens."

"Let me explain something to you," said George. "Do you understand the concept of 'everybody fucks up once in a while'?"

"Yeah, I think I do."

"Good. This is how it relates to current events. When Lou and I do a job, we're expected to complete it successfully. That's what we get paid for. But no matter how good you are—and we're good, believe me—there's going to be the occasional job that goes bad. Somebody's not where they're supposed to be, somebody who's not supposed to be there shows up, your car breaks down…there are lots of reasons why a job might not work out properly. The people in charge understand this."

"Yeah, right. If you don't deliver me to Tampa, you'll be at the bottom of a lake by midnight."

"Oh, we're going to deliver you, don't get me wrong. But if we deliver you with your arms and legs broken, we'll get yelled at, and possibly forfeit our fee, but nobody's going to kill us. Now, I don't want to get yelled at, and I certainly want to get paid for all the crap I've gone through today, but I've reached a level of frustration where busting you up might be worth it."

"Cool. I'm glad I could bring you to that level."

"George, are you sure you wanna do this?" Lou asked. There was a knowing look in his eyes. He was playing along.

George nodded. "Oh yeah."

"All right. Promise me you won't do any permanent damage."

"Do you see what they're doing?" Ivan asked Michele. "They're going to break my legs. I wonder how they're going to do it? Tire iron to the kneecaps, I guess. That's what I would do if I were them, to make sure it hurts enough."

"You don't really believe that he's a werewolf, do you?" Michele asked George.

"I might."

"But that's crazy."

George pointed to her shoulder. "How do you explain that?"

"A pack of feral dogs. A chemical in the air. A ridiculously elaborate assassination attempt on you. There's a huge number of things I'd need to cross off my list before I got to 'werewolf.'"

"Well, hopefully he'll help us cross them off."

"You know, George," said Lou, "we really should get rid of the girl. The longer we keep her around, the more she's gonna see, and the worse things are gonna get."

"So you think we should just drop her off somewhere?"

"Maybe."

"What if she talks?"

"What's driving around with her gonna do to change that? Are we so charming that an hour in the van with us is gonna keep her from going to the cops?"

George sighed. "I don't know."

"I don't want you to let me go," said Michele.

"What?"

"I'm staying with you. I want in."

"*What?*"

"I want ten percent of what you're getting."

"You don't even know what we're getting," said George.

"Did you see the shitty car I was driving? I'll be happy with ten percent of anything. Look, I already know what's going on with you guys, so you might as well keep me around and pay me off."

George and Lou exchanged a look of disbelief. "And why wouldn't we just kill you?" George asked.

"If you wanted me dead, you could've just left me back at the gas station. Instead, you brought me with you, knowing full well that we were leaving behind my car, which has my purse in it, which means that people will know that I'm missing, which means that they'll look for other clues, which means that they'll find some blood on the pavement, which means that they've got DNA evidence on you. It'll take a while, because there's so much blood to sort through, but why would a couple of smart men like you want to link yourselves to a murder when you could just keep a cooperative girl around for a tiny payoff?"

George grimaced. He tried to think of a bigger blunder they'd ever made in their careers in crime than letting Michele into the van. None immediately came to mind. Still, bad guys or not, they couldn't have just watched her get ripped apart by dogs while she was trying to save the attendant from getting ripped apart by dogs. Obviously, they should've expelled her from the vehicle as soon as they'd driven away from the gas station, but Ivan had opened his big mouth right away, and George wasn't thinking straight, and he had a hot chick on his lap, so how could he be expected to make an intelligent decision?

That said, they were supposed to be professionals. He gave Lou a sheepish look. "When did we become such retards?"

"Don't say retards. That's offensive to developmentally disabled people. We're just the regular kind of stupid."

"Fair enough. What do you think?"

Lou shrugged. "Better than disposing of a body."

"All right," George told Michele. "You've got yourself a deal. Ten percent."

"Ten percent of your combined take, not just ten percent of what one of you is getting."

"Of course."

Michele extended her hand. George shook it. He had to admit, he now liked her on a much deeper level than just her physical attractiveness.

"You guys are going for that?" Ivan asked. "Seriously? Well, shit, if I knew it was that easy to negotiate, we could've saved ourselves a couple of hours. Let me go and I'll make it worth your while. How much do you want?"

"One hundred bazillion dollars," said Lou.

Ivan sneered. "How about twenty bucks and a gently used porno mag, you fuckin' Neanderthal?"

"Watch the potty mouth," said George. "My partner doesn't appreciate foul language around women."

"Yeah, well, your partner can go fuck a duck-fucked pony from Fucksville."

"I don't even know what that means, but I'm going to quote it every chance I get."

"Fuck you."

"What's the matter, werewolf? You don't sound quite as arrogant as you were before."

"Well, I'm either terrified, or I'm faking it because I have some sinister plan ready to go into effect. You'd better hope it's the first one, because I'm really in the mood to exsanguinate a couple of minor-league thugs and their new hooker."

"Is that another word that I'm not supposed to know what it means?"

"What word? Hooker? Surely you know that one."

"Hey, George, I think you're getting a bit worked up," said Lou. "Just ignore him."

"Oh, no, he's not getting ignored. Not at all. There's our exit."

Lou gave him the *I knew that* look that George had seen a hundred times. George cracked his knuckles. He encountered a lot of scumbags in his line of work, but there was something about Ivan that he truly disliked. He wasn't going to hurt him, or even touch him, but the werewolf was going to lose the attitude, no question about it.

This town seemed quite a bit larger than the last one, although there still wasn't much there. Every other establishment on Main Street seemed to be an antique shop. George hated antique shops.

"Find us someplace isolated," George said. Lou gave him another *I knew that* look.

It took about a mile and a couple of turns to find a dirt road with a misspelled sign in green spray paint that said *"No Tresspassing."* Lou turned onto the road, and after rounding a corner there was more than enough tree cover to keep any witnesses from seeing what they were doing from the paved road.

Lou parked and shut off the engine.

"You ready to talk?" George asked.

Ivan smiled and gave him a thumbs-up sign, though now his smile seemed kind of forced.

"Please don't cause us any trouble," George told Michele.

"Please don't damage our investment," she said.

George grinned and got out of the van.

«««—»»»

Michele's day had started with a pregnancy scare. She'd thought it would improve from there.

The stick had not turned blue, thank God. The non-father, Aaron, was the only guy to whom she'd ever provided pity sex. He'd been *so* distressed when his girlfriend broke up with him, and his prospects of landing another girl in a timely manner were bleak, and Michele wasn't exactly getting it on a regular basis, so she'd slept with him.

The "during" part had been pretty good, despite the fact that he kept singing during sex, but when she woke up in the morning Michele really wished she'd gone with the original plan of spending her evening with some microwave popcorn and a DVD. She'd carefully extricated herself from their spooning and hid in the bathroom for an hour, trying to will herself not to take the cowardly way out and sneak out of the apartment before Aaron woke up.

When he did wake up, beaming, she'd sat on the edge of his bed and explained that it had been a one-time "friends with benefits" thing. He'd cried. For ten minutes he'd sobbed into his pillow about how his heart had been broken a second time in twenty-four hours, and finally Michele decided that her best plan of action was to go away.

He kept calling and sending her text messages and e-mails. He changed his Facebook relationship status to "It's complicated." She kept trying to explain that she'd lost herself in the moment and wasn't looking for a boyfriend. Finally, a week after their night together, she'd gotten completely fed up with the situation and used the term "pity fuck." He quit calling, texting, and e-mailing. He changed his Facebook relationship status to "Single."

Michele felt terrible. She hated losing a friend.

This morning, after a mildly restless sleep that came from being nervous about the fact that her period hadn't started quite yet, she'd awakened feeling sick to her stomach, rushed into the bathroom, and vomited.

She couldn't be pregnant. They'd used protection *and* she was on the pill. One-night-stand pregnancy came from drunken flings, not pity sex.

She'd prayed to God that it was just food poisoning. She'd thawed the chicken out on the counter. You weren't supposed to do that. She knew that, and now she was suffering for her careless meal preparation.

She'd driven forty-five minutes away to ensure that she didn't run into anybody she knew while buying the pregnancy test. Then, with the bag and receipt in her hand, she'd suddenly decided that she had to know *now*, and so she found herself in a Walgreens restroom, peeing on a stick.

When the test showed that she wasn't pregnant, she'd cried with relief.

Then she'd cried with disappointment.

She certainly didn't want to have Aaron's kid, and the test being negative was a one-hundred-percent good thing. She was emotionally wrecked from all of the stress and that's why she was crying like this. That's all it was. She'd had a rough day.

On the way out of the store, she'd bought some flowers to make herself feel better. Carnations. Even if buying herself flowers was mildly pathetic, it did cheer her up.

And then, while fueling up, a bunch of dogs went berserk and she got stuck in a van with a couple of mobsters.

If she believed in karma, she would've thought that she was being punished for breaking Aaron's heart with their ill-advised intercourse. Or that her habit of pulling on the family dog Tin-Tin's tail when she was three had finally come back to haunt her. But she didn't believe in that stuff, so it was just bad luck. Wrong place at the wrong time.

She felt like she should be siding with the guy in the cage, but he just seemed...well, *evil*. Instantly unlikable. If Ivan approached her at a bar, she'd be creeped out and refuse to touch any drinks he bought her. Though he obviously wasn't a werewolf, he probably deserved to be locked up in there—she could imagine him wandering the streets, offering lollipops to little girls if they promised not to tell.

Of course, George and Lou were clearly not kind-hearted, caring people, and she genuinely believed that they might kill her if they felt backed into a corner. She could definitely see them walking her out into the woods, apologizing softly, then putting a bullet in the back of her head. They'd feel awful about it, but they'd do what needed to be done.

Swearing not to tell anybody wasn't going to work. *Of course* she'd tell. There was no possible way she wouldn't run to the police and describe the two thugs in their black van, and they knew it. They weren't going to simply let her go.

But if they thought that she thought they had a deal, there'd be no reason to come to their senses and kill her. They could stop constantly worrying about her. And then she could find an opportunity to escape. Now that they'd stopped the van, maybe an opportunity was approaching.

And—she couldn't deny it—this was all kind of exciting. A werewolf? Where was this going to lead?

George shut the passenger-side door of the van and walked around to the back. She could jump out right now and make a break for it.

No, too risky. She didn't want to get shot.

But with George distracted by whatever he was planning to do with Ivan, she'd definitely keep her eye on Lou.

Chapter Seven: Don't Mess with Wolves in Cages

George opened the rear doors of the van. Ivan seemed to be trying very, very hard to look amused by the whole situation.

"You know, you have to actually open up the cage if you want to beat me with a tire iron," Ivan said. "Don't get me wrong, I'm all in favor of you making a fatal mistake, but that seems pretty extreme."

"I'm not opening the cage," said George. He waited for a few moments, letting the tension build, then took his pistol out of the holster.

"So you're going to shoot the cargo?"

"Question for you. How long do you think it takes to bleed to death from a kneecap that was shattered by a bullet?"

"No idea."

"More than three hours. So you'll still be alive when we deliver you."

"Okay."

"How long do you think it takes to bleed to death from two kneecaps that were shattered by bullets?"

"More than three hours?"

"Exactly. And where do you think is one of the most painful places to get shot?"

"We both know that you're not going to shoot me."

"Oh, trust me, I know no such thing. I hope it doesn't come to that, but if it does, I'll take my scolding like a man. If there was ever a time in your life when you should be cooperative, it's now."

"Do you really think that threatening me with a gun is going to get you accurate information?"

George nodded. "I'm a good judge of when somebody is telling me the truth."

"You mean like when I said I had a bomb strapped to my leg?"

George chose to ignore that. "When somebody is scared, it's easy to tell if they're lying. And I don't care how cocky you are, having a gun pointed at you is a scary thing."

"And what are you going to say when they ask why you shot me?"

"I'll say that you told me you had a bomb strapped to your leg, and that you wouldn't show me, and that I felt I had no other way to keep their precious werewolf from blowing himself up."

Ivan's smile vanished.

George pointed the gun at him and gave Ivan his coldest stare. "What do you know about those dogs?"

"I didn't do anything to them."

"That's not what I asked."

"Point the gun someplace else and I'll tell you."

"Do I need to start counting?"

"Okay, fine. Fine." Ivan looked a bit flustered, though he was clearly struggling to maintain a calm demeanor. "When I get stressed out, it has a weird effect on dogs. I don't know why. It's been like that since I was a teenager."

"This bad?"

"No, never this bad, but I've never been this stressed before! I don't know what it is; maybe I've got some…" He trailed off. "I don't even know. That's how this whole werewolf thing started, but I swear there's nothing to it beyond that."

"That doesn't seem like enough to create a werewolf theory."

"I told people that I was a werewolf, all right? I used it to impress some chicks in a club. You know, those ones who are all wet over Team Jacob. You tell them you're a werewolf, you watch a dog flip out, and you're in their panties. I don't think any of them really believed it, it was all just role-playing, but word got back to Bateman and he sure as hell believed it."

"So you're officially saying that you're not a werewolf?"

"Why do I even need to officially deny something like that? How am I supposed to prove it? What should I do, *not* transform into a wolf? The full moon is two weeks away; I couldn't change if I wanted to. You've got me in a no-win situation here, George."

"If you've got dog blood in you or something, how could that work from so far away, inside a van?"

"I don't know! If I understood it, I'd be doing a lot more with the power than just trying to get laid. It's just some weird effect I have on dogs that I can't control. Nothing more."

"You're stressed now. Why aren't any dogs coming after us?"

"How the hell should I know? Maybe the residents of this town are cat people! I'm not a werewolf, for Christ's sake!" He scooted over to the end of the cage and held up his palm. "Like your partner said, no pentagram. If I was a werewolf, I wouldn't care that you've got a gun on me, because I'm sure you don't have silver bullets in there. What are the other signs?"

"I'm not sure," George admitted.

Ivan extended his arm all the way out of the cage. The barrel of George's pistol was still a couple of feet out of his grasp. "I don't have hairy palms. I don't have an unusually long middle finger. It's all a huge misunderstanding."

"Put your arm back in the cage," said George.

"I don't know what you want from me! Do you need me to break my arm to show that there aren't werewolf bones underneath? Is that what I need to do?" Ivan bashed his arm against the cage, hard enough to make George wince.

Ivan bashed his arm again. His eyes were crazed, like he'd totally lost it.

George lowered his gun. "Hey, knock that off."

"I'll split my arm open! Then you'll see!" Ivan struck the bars again, right on the elbow, and George was surprised that the bone didn't break through the skin. It hurt just to see it.

"I mean it. Stop that." For a half-second, George was about to make a move to restrain him, then he caught himself. Ivan could snap both of his own arms off if he wanted, but George wasn't going to get close enough to the cage for Ivan to grab him. Not a chance.

One more slam, this one against the top of the cage, and George thought he might have heard a bone crack. He wondered if Lou was feeling queasy. "Is that what you want?" Ivan asked, extending his arm all the way, but still coming up a foot short of George's neck. "Is that what you want?"

"This needs to stop," George said. This was getting out of control. It was time to just shut the doors again and drive out of here.

Then Ivan's arm changed. Instantly.

One second it was a regular human arm, the next second it had doubled in bulk and sprouted thick dark brown fur. And in that second it had lengthened and made up the distance between Ivan's fingers and George's neck.

George could barely even register what had happened.

Now he had a set of claws digging into his throat.

"Drop the gun!" Ivan shouted. The rest of his body remained human, though his voice had gone down about an octave. "Drop it now or I'll rip open your neck!"

George dropped the gun. He wasn't sure if he was actually following Ivan's orders, or if he was just too shocked to keep a hold of his weapon.

"Stay where you are, Lou!" said Ivan, not looking back. George couldn't tell if Lou could see exactly what had happened or not. "I'll kill him! One squeeze and he's dead!"

George wanted to shout "Do what he says!" —but he couldn't breathe. How had this happened? How the hell had—

Lou fired a shot into Ivan's back.

Michele screamed.

Ivan grimaced, and blood misted in the air, but he didn't release his grip on George's throat. His other arm transformed, so quickly that George could barely see it change, and then he grabbed the front of George's shirt and yanked on it, slamming George's face into the cage.

"Tell him not to shoot me again!"

George couldn't speak.

"I have nothing to lose!" Ivan shouted. "I'll kill him! You fire that gun again and his death is on you!"

"Okay, okay," said Lou. "Just stay calm."

"Give the gun to the girl! Now!"

Lou handed the gun to Michele. She took it, but seemed unsure whether she should point it at Lou or Ivan.

"Nobody has to die," said Ivan. "We can get through this and go our separate ways. You just need to let me out of the cage."

George managed to find his voice. "We don't have the key."

Ivan raked the talon of his index finger down George's cheek, causing him to cry out in pain. He could already feel the blood trickling down his face. "You're not delivering a cage without a key. I will pop your fuckin' eye if you don't stop playing around."

"It's in the glove compartment," said Lou.

"Get it." Ivan slammed George against the bars again. "I bet you're feeling a little bit silly, huh? Maybe you'll think twice before you mess with another werewolf. You know what, I should just do it. I should just rip your throat out. It would be worth never getting out of this cage to watch you choke on your own blood."

"Don't…"

"Say please."

"*Please.*"

"Oooooh, that almost sounds like you're begging for your life! I like that. I like that a lot. Do it some more, motherfucker!"

"I've got it," Lou announced.

"Then get over here!" Ivan licked his lips. "Georgie, you really don't know how much I want to take a big bite out of you. I just think you look delicious right now. Mmmmmmm."

George had no response. He was still trying to process the fact that not only might he be moments away from death, but there was a living, breathing goddamn werewolf right in front of him. There were countless ways for a guy like him to die, but like *this*? What could they even put on his tombstone?

Lou hurried around to the back of the van, breathing heavily in panic. He held up the key to show Ivan.

"Don't show it to me! Use it!"

Lou didn't hesitate. He shoved the key into the lock and turned it sideways.

Ivan immediately released his grip on George's neck and shoved the cage door wide open. It smashed into George and knocked him to the ground. Ivan jumped out of the cage, landing on his feet and transforming as soon as he hit the dirt.

His pants and shirt split apart, exposing a newly muscular and fur-covered body. He grew at least two feet in height, and claws burst through his shoes.

Ivan's face took longer to change completely—several seconds rather than almost instantly. Along with the sprouting brown fur, his jaws extended, his nose transformed into a snout, and his ears changed into the pointed ears of a wolf.

Ivan stood before them, still humanoid, but a very definite wolfman. Then he put back his head and howled, even though it was broad daylight and there was no moon to howl at.

He jerked back as a bullet punched into his chest. Michele fired again, hitting him in the stomach. Though she was a surprisingly good shot, the overall effect seemed to simply be to piss him off. He took a menacing step forward, and her third shot missed completely. She pulled the trigger several more times, but the gun just clicked.

Lou said "shit." George just thought it.

The werewolf smiled, revealing plenty of sharp teeth, and let out a low growl. He looked as if he wanted to make some sort of taunting comment, yet said nothing. Maybe he couldn't talk in this form.

He howled again, then—moving on two legs instead of all fours—ran down the path in the direction they'd come.

George, Lou, and Michele all watched him go, staring in horror and amazement.

"Get in the van!" George shouted, slamming the rear doors of the van shut. "Get in the van now!" He ran around to the driver's side door, which Lou had left open. Lou and Michele didn't seem to be moving. "Did you hear me? Let's go! Let's go! Let's go!"

"Where are we going?" Lou asked.

"Get in!"

Lou nodded. He and Michele ran over to the passenger's side. Michele got in first.

"You don't have to go," George told her. "We're setting you free."

"I'm not staying out there with that thing on the loose!"

"Fair enough."

She scooted over as Lou joined her on the seat. It was an even tighter fit than when she and George had shared it, but comfort was not a huge priority right now. George started the engine.

"What are we doing?" Lou asked.

"What the hell do you think we're doing? We're getting that werewolf back!"

Chapter Eight: The Chase

"Why the hell would we go after him?" Lou asked, sounding more than a little unhinged.

"Because we've got a job to do! And if we fail at that, we're at least going to run that fucker over! He may be able to withstand bullets but he'll sure crunch under our tires!"

Lou shut his door. "We can't follow a werewolf in a van! He'll just run off into the woods!"

"He might."

"And he'll kill us!"

George drove forward and began to make a three-point turn. "If he wanted to kill us, he would've done it while we were standing there with our jaws hanging open. He could've killed all three of us, shredded us on the spot, but he didn't." George didn't actually know this, but it sounded reasonable.

"Good! I'm glad he didn't! When a werewolf like that doesn't kill you, you count your blessings; you don't give it another chance! We shouldn't be following him, we should be driving to the nearest bar, or finding a church to join or something!"

"I agree with Lou," Michele said.

George got the van turned around and floored the accelerator. "I said you could get out."

"Do you have any more bullets?" Michele asked, as they drove off the dirt road and back onto the paved one.

"We've got a couple of spare clips. Lou, reload her."

Lou reached for the gun. Michele hesitated, as if unsure whether she should give up the weapon.

"It's empty," Lou said. "You might as well hand it over."

Michele gave him the gun.

"Don't give it back to her," George said.

Lou reached under the seat, then snapped in a new clip. "I know."

"There he is!" George shouted, pointing through the windshield.

Ivan was a long way ahead, at least five or six blocks. Bastard was fast. It looked like he was still in his wolfman form. George wondered if he could change from wolf to human as quickly as he could change from human to wolf.

How could Ivan do that? Werewolves were supposed to scream in pain and thrash around and slowly transform by the light of the full moon. George couldn't conceive of a biological process that allowed somebody to change immediately, at will, with such control that he could transform a single appendage. It was completely freaky. It was *wrong*, damn it!

The van was closing the distance pretty quickly.

There were a few houses along the road, but they hadn't passed any cars yet in either direction and nobody seemed to be hanging out in their front yard.

"Watch out!" Lou shouted.

George swerved out of the way of the garbage can that lay on its side in the middle of the road. Goddamn garbage collectors.

"He wants us to follow him," said Lou. "He wouldn't be running alongside the road otherwise. We should let him go."

George wondered if his partner was right. Ivan was clearly leading them on a fun little chase for his own amusement. They didn't have to put themselves at risk like this. They could take the hit to their reputation. They'd still get work.

But he shook his head. "No. We're not letting that prick outsmart us again."

"He didn't outsmart us. You outdumbed him."

"Fine, I got overconfident and it bit me in the ass."

"Yes. It did." Lou nodded. "It certainly did."

"Well, it's his turn to get overconfident. Now we know exactly what we're dealing with. No more is-he-or-isn't-he questions. He won't trick us again."

An overweight couple sat on a porch swing. The man stood up in surprise as Ivan ran past him. Fortunately for the couple, Ivan didn't veer from his course. The woman stood up as well as the van sped past.

Ivan glanced back over his shoulder, then immediately picked up his pace, at least doubling his speed. George ground his foot against the already-floored accelerator.

Lou cleared his throat. "I just wanna make it very clear—"

"Your objection's noted. We won't get ourselves killed over this, I promise."

"I don't think you can promise that."

George knew he was being reckless, but he didn't care. Well, that wasn't true—he cared, but not enough to give up the hunt. He couldn't stand the idea of that smirking creep thinking that he'd made George look like an idiot. The bastard was having himself a big hearty werewolf chuckle as they chased him, thinking how goddamn clever he'd been. He'd regret it. Ivan the Werewolf was going to be delivered to Mr. Dewey, even if it was in bite-sized pieces.

The werewolf rounded a corner and disappeared from sight.

"Slow down!" said Lou. "Don't topple the van!"

George wanted to ask his partner to please shut up because he did indeed realize that he needed to slow down before making this very sharp right turn, but decided to just remain silent. Let Lou bark out orders. It would keep him distracted.

He made the turn without toppling over the van and sped down the new street. Ivan was a couple of blocks ahead. He turned to the right and again vanished from their view.

"He's just going in circles!" said Lou.

"It's not a circle yet!"

George spun the steering wheel to the right and they rounded the corner. A car was parked on the side of the street. Ivan leapt up onto it, ran over the top, then jumped back onto the street without missing a beat. Showing off. Fine. He could do somersaults for all George cared.

Ivan began to run down the center of the street, not seeming to care who saw him. If that's how he wanted to be, no problem, then George didn't care who saw them run his wolf ass over.

"So what's the plan if we catch up to him?" Lou asked.

"If you can think of one, shout it out. Right now I just don't want to lose him."

Ivan was slowing down a bit. Was he getting tired? George imagined a great big red target on the werewolf's back as the distance ahead of them dwindled to just a few van-lengths.

Now one van-length. If George gunned the engine, Ivan would be part of their front fender. *Werewolf go splat.*

And then...Ivan sped up again, racing away from the van and turning another corner.

"Damn it!" George pounded his fist against the dashboard.

"It's just a game to him," Lou said. "Following him is ridiculous."

"You know what?" George asked, applying the brake. "You're absolutely right."

Let the werewolf go. Take the heat. Why drive around after him, which was obviously what Ivan *wanted* them to do, and fall into another trap? Why risk his, Lou's, and Michele's lives just to salvage his own bruised ego? Why be a complete and total suicidal idiot about this?

George Orton was no quitter. When a job needed to get done, he saw it through to the end. Abandoning a task because it was too difficult was something reserved for pathetic losers. He lived his entire life by that code.

That said, when there was a *supernatural beast* involved, fuck it. Smart people quit.

"Let's get out of this place," said George. "We'll let Ricky explain what happened and just lay low for a while."

"I like that plan," said Lou. "That's pure genius."

"Are you in favor?" George asked Michele.

"I get a vote?"

"Not one that counts, but I figured I'd ask."

"Yes, I'm very much in favor of not following the werewolf around."

"Fine. It's settled." George considered offering Lou an extremely large sum of money in exchange for calling Ricky to deliver the news, but no. He'd been the one to screw up, and wanted to make sure that a chant of "I told him not to do it!" was not part of the initial confession.

Ivan, several blocks ahead, ran back into their line of sight and stopped in the middle of the road, facing them.

"Oh, look," said George. "The little fellow is mad that we're not playing Follow the Leader anymore."

Ivan began to walk toward them. Without a break in his stride, he transformed back into a human, just as quickly as he'd become a wolfman. His shredded clothes hung off his body.

"I have to admit, that fashion statement works for him," said George. "Not a lot of people could pull that off."

"We're still driving away, right?" Lou asked.

"Yeah, yeah, absolutely."

George watched Ivan's continued approach. Ivan was moving quickly, but not yet running. He was now close enough that George could see the smug grin on his face. Bastard.

"So if I wait for him to get closer, and then floor the gas pedal, do you think he'll change back into a wolf and then jump on the roof of the van?" George asked.

"Yes," said Lou.

"Definitely," said Michele.

They were probably right. And, having just made what he considered to be a wise decision, George wasn't inclined to put them back in danger…but if Ivan was right in front of them, in human form, just walking…

"We need to get out of here," said Michele.

George shook his head. "I'm not running away from him."

"But we just decided—"

"We decided not to chase him. That's not the same as running away."

Ivan continued walking. He cracked his knuckles, as if preparing himself to deliver a substantial ass beating.

"What could we do that he won't expect?" George asked. "Lou, maybe if you shoot him a couple of times while I try to hit him with the van…?"

"We can't start shooting! It's a residential neighborhood!"

"We've been driving around chasing a werewolf! We've already attracted some attention!"

"That doesn't mean we should attract *more*! We still need to think about the future, George! We need to get out of here, ditch the van, ditch the girl, and keep ourselves out of an interrogation room!"

Ivan was now only about fifty feet from the van. Still moving at the same pace. Still had the same grin.

When he was twenty feet away, George floored the gas pedal. The tires squealed, and the van shot forward. George tried to focus on Ivan as if staring at him through a giant magnifying glass, watching intently for the slightest hint of movement that might indicate if he was going to dodge to the right or to the left, so that George could turn in that direction and bash him.

Ivan transformed again, his entire body at once. With one jump, he was on the hood of the van, and with a second he was on the roof.

George slammed on the brakes, trying to dislodge him. The werewolf didn't go anywhere. There was a loud metallic *thump* on the roof as Ivan punched or kicked it, followed by two more. Apparently he couldn't punch through the top of a van in one blow. That was a plus, at least.

"He's on the roof!" Lou shouted.

"I know he's on the goddamn roof!"

George floored the accelerator yet again, then slammed the brake a second later. He tried that several more times, jerking the van forward a few feet at a time in a desperate attempt to get the werewolf off.

There were three more quick thumps on the roof, but light ones, like a polite knock.

Lou saw what was about to happen before George did, but was still only able to get as far as "Oh sh—" before a pair of oversized wolfman feet came down upon the windshield and the entire thing exploded, spraying safety glass everywhere. Michele screamed and threw her hands over her face. Glass rained down on George's lap and he let go of the steering wheel in panic. The van veered to the right.

Ivan leapt onto the front hood. Lou scrambled to use his gun, but Ivan lunged forward and plucked it out of his hand. He gave them a fanged grin, and then jumped back onto the roof.

The van bounced up onto the curb and George quickly grabbed the steering wheel again and straightened their course.

"He's got my gun!" Lou shouted.

"Quit saying things that I already know!"

George applied the brakes. "You two, go back and get in the cage. He can't bend the bars or he'd have done it before, so you'll be safe in there!"

"We won't be safe! Now we're up against a werewolf with a gun!"

"You'll be safer than you are now!"

"Everybody just calm down!" Michele brushed some glass out of her hair. They sat in silence for a long, tense moment. "Ivan?"

No response.

"Ivan? It's Michele. I understand that you have a problem with these guys, and that's totally cool, and you're completely justified in anything you want to do to them, but I'm an innocent bystander in this whole thing, so if you could let me go, that would be really nice!"

They waited. Ivan said nothing, and there were no sounds to indicate movement above.

"Ivan? I know you can hear me. I think it's terrible that they locked you in there. It was wrong of them. There's no excuse. If you could just give me some sort of sign that it's okay for me to get out of the van..."

Now there was some movement, the sounds of weight shifting above them. Finally, Ivan spoke: "I just want to be *liked*, you know?"

George groaned. The werewolf still had the energy to be a smart-ass. This was not good. "Hey, Ivan," he said, "it's crazy for you to stay up on the roof like that. Somebody's going to see and call animal control. You win! You proved that you're far superior, and I look like a total douche. We aren't going to follow you anymore. Just run off and make your escape."

"But, George, you said that the only way this was going to end was with me being delivered to Tampa."

"I misspoke."

"Well, you can't give up yet. I'm not ready for this to be over. I was bored out of my mind for those two hours in a cage, so you owe me at least two hours of entertainment. You know what I should do? I should murder somebody."

He leapt off the roof and onto the street, human now. He turned to look at them, then put a finger to his lips and said "Shhhh. Don't tell."

Then he began to stroll down the sidewalk. Didn't even jog. Didn't look back to see what they were doing.

"I hate that son of a bitch," said George. "I hate him more than I've ever hated another person. Look at that goddamn swagger."

"Shouldn't you be less pissed and more grateful to be alive?" Lou asked.

"I will never stop being pissed. He has now created a 'lifetime of seeking vengeance' scenario."

Ivan stopped at a small brown home. An affordable, practical car was in the driveway, and the front yard was littered with toys. Ivan shrugged—an exaggerated shrug, obviously meant for them to see—and then walked up to the front door.

George's stomach sunk. "Aw, crap. He's really going to do something." He hurriedly got out of the van.

"You're going after him?" Lou asked.

"Of course I'm going after him! Be ready to drive away fast. If you hear sirens, get out of here and don't worry about me. If I don't come out in a few minutes...I don't know, you work it out."

George ran toward the house as Ivan opened the front door and stepped inside.

Chapter Nine: Home Invasion

George had always been prone to extreme perspiration, but he couldn't remember ever having been this drenched in sweat. He felt hot and sticky and miserable, he reeked of gasoline, and lots of glass chunks were still stuck to his clothes. The dog bite on his chest stung, and his wrist hurt even worse, and overall this had been one spectacularly crappy day.

He didn't anticipate that it was going to get better in the next few minutes. Revenge or not, he most definitely was *not* looking forward to going after Ivan without even the safety of being in the van. But he'd be forever haunted if Ivan killed the little kid who owned those toys because of his mistake.

And he did have his gun. Not that bullets had done any good thus far, but it still felt slightly reassuring to have a weapon, even a useless one.

Ivan had left the front door ajar. George pulled it open and stepped inside. The house was messy but not dirty. More toys, mostly action figures, were all over the floor, and a television in the living room blared one of those daytime courtroom shows that George hated in concept but that were surprisingly addictive. The place smelled like air freshener.

A muffled scream.

Gun raised, George ran through the dining room into the kitchen. Ivan had his arm around a blonde in her early thirties, his hand over her mouth and Lou's pistol pressed against the side of her head. Ivan remained fully human, and looked amused by her efforts to struggle.

"Hey, George, look what I caught!" he said with a smile.

George pointed the gun at him. "Let her go."

"Sorry, doesn't scare me at all." Ivan pulled Lou's gun away from the woman's head, removed his hand from her mouth, then bashed her against the counter, hard. He yanked her back to a standing position and put the gun to her head again. "Stop squirming," he told her.

She let out a sob. *"Don't hurt me…"*

"Stop squirming or I'll smash you against the counter until I break out every tooth in your head."

"C'mon, Ivan, let her go." George tried to keep his voice calm and polite, like a hostage negotiator. "She had nothing to do with this."

"Well, that's part of the fun, isn't it? Innocent people harmed? Collateral damage?" He backed up a few steps, toward the refrigerator and another counter, dragging the woman with him. "I hate guns. Guns are for thugs and cowards." He tossed the gun onto the counter, slid a butcher knife out of a wooden rack, and immediately pressed it against the woman's throat. "Oh, yeah. Much better."

"The cops are on their way," George said.

"Excellent. Maybe I'll kill her and let them find you here with her corpse."

"So what do I need to do to get you to let her go? Just tell me."

"Hmmmmmm." Ivan pretended to consider that. "I'm not sure. This is an interesting new side of you, George. All concerned about innocent women and stuff. If I had time I could probably come up with something, but at the moment, nah, nothing springs to mind. I think I'm going to kill her."

The woman's entire body shook as she sobbed.

"What's your name, sweetie?"

"Diane."

"Diane, huh? I don't see a ring on your finger, Diane. Are you married?"

"No."

"Kids, though, right? How many?"

"Two."

"How old are they?" She didn't answer, so Ivan pressed the blade harder against her neck. "How old are they?" he repeated, almost growling the words.

"Five and seven."

"What are their names?"

George stepped forward. "Ivan, don't—"

"You need to stay exactly where you are and keep your mouth shut!" Ivan lowered his voice and took on a soothing tone as he spoke to Diane. "Ignore the rude man who interrupted our conversation. What are the names of your children?"

"Robin and Gabriel."

"Robin. Girl or boy?"

"Boy."

"Two boys, huh? I bet they're a handful. Where are they now?"

"School."

"Oh, yeah, it's Wednesday, so that makes sense. Silly question. It must be a challenge to raise two young boys on your own. You're not a welfare mother, are you?"

"No."

"Why aren't you at work?"

"*Please...*"

"Diane, answer my question. Why aren't you at work?"

"I have the day off."

"Okay, fair answer. You figured you'd get in some alone time, run a few errands, clean up the house, and take a mental health day, huh?"

"Yes."

"Things would sure be tough for Robin and Gabriel if they didn't have a mother, wouldn't they? I bet they'd cry their little eyes out. I hope you have relatives who would take them in, or else the poor kids may end up bouncing from one foster home to the next. They can't always keep orphaned siblings together, you know. Oh, they try, they give it their best, but there's only so much you can do."

George felt like he was going to vomit. What the hell was he supposed to do? Rush him? Try to shoot him in the face? It was absolutely killing him to stand there helplessly, but what else could he do?

"Hey, George, I'll make you a deal. You throw that gun over here, toss it into the sink, and I'll let her go. I won't even slice off an ear. Maybe I'll slice off part of an ear, but not the full ear, I promise."

"No way."

"Okay, okay, I won't cut off anything. No mutilation. You won't get that offer again, and you've got five seconds to decide."

George put on the safety, then tossed the gun across the kitchen into the sink. Bullets didn't seem to hurt Ivan anyway, so it wasn't as if he was worse off.

"Nice toss," said Ivan. "Just for the record, I wasn't worried about getting shot, but I don't want you squandering bullets and attracting the cops while we're having sooooo much fun."

"I said, the cops are already on their way."

"And I believe you're fibbing. I at least know that *you* didn't call them. Hey, George, do you know who else in this room likes to lie? I'll give you a clue. It's not the woman."

Oh God...

"That's right. Well, Diane, it's been lovely chatting with you, but now I need to create a couple of orphans."

He slowly slid the blade across her throat. Diane's eyes widened, her legs buckled, and Ivan let her fall to the floor, clutching at her neck and making horrible choking sounds.

"You sick fuck!" George shouted. He took another step forward—he couldn't help himself—and Ivan held up the bloody knife in a defensive position.

"Don't do it, George. You'll get it a lot worse than she did." He crouched down next to her. "See how I didn't cut all that deep? I could've cut all the way to the bone, but then she would've bled out too quickly. This way it lingers a little more." He ran a finger through the gash in her neck and held it up for George's inspection.

"She didn't do anything to you!"

"No, but you did."

Diane's body twitched as the pool of blood on the tile expanded. George had witnessed some terrible things in his life, even a few cold-blooded murders, but those were brutal, emotionless killings designed to punish or send a message. He'd never seen anything like the sense of malicious glee that was on Ivan's face right now. The guy couldn't be happier if he were a ten-year-old at an amusement park.

Diane coughed, sending blood trickling down both sides of her mouth.

Ivan held the butcher knife over her, moving it back and forth. "I think I should stab her again. What do you think, George?"

"If you do, I'll kill you."

Ivan shrugged. "Eh, empty threat." He stood up and picked George's gun out of the sink, then pointed it at him. "I don't want to shoot you. You won't be much fun if I do." He crouched back down next to Diane. "Wow, lots of blood in the human body, huh? You don't think there's that much just looking at somebody, but we leak pretty good."

George forced himself not to scream in rage. "You've made your point."

"Oh, I'm so far from having made my point that it isn't even funny." Ivan slammed the knife into Diane's stomach, burying it all the way to the hilt. Most of her strength was gone by this point, but she still let out a gasp of pain through the gurgling blood. He wrenched the knife out of her, considered his next target for a moment, then slammed the knife deep into her thigh.

George clenched his fists so tightly that his fingernails dug into the skin.

"Pretty frustrated, aren't you?" Ivan asked, yanking the blade out of her leg. "I would be too, in your shitty situation. You should beg me to let her go. That would be pretty entertaining, since she's basically dead at this point."

Ivan stabbed her five more times, running the length of her body, each *thunk* making George cringe. Then Ivan stood up and rolled her onto her back with his foot. Diane lay splayed out on the kitchen floor, eyes open, unquestionably dead.

"You're pathetic," said George, his mouth completely dry.

"Pathetic? That's the adjective you're going to throw out? Pathetic? You had to stand there and watch me murder a mother of two. Your best buddy apparently isn't even going to check on you. George, dude, at this particular moment, I am most definitely *not* the one who's pathetic."

"Then why don't you come after me, instead of an innocent woman?"

"It's not an either/or deal. I can do both."

That comment scared George a lot more than he wanted to admit, but he stood firm and held up his fists. "Then let's do it."

"No rush, no rush." Ivan put a hand to his ear. "Hear that? No sirens. Amazing what you can get away with during a weekday, isn't it? Let me tell you a little about me. Secret origins kind of stuff. I *love* to kill people. Absolutely love it. Always have. It's the usual serial killer deal—I caught a frog when I was in grade school, and spent the afternoon playing around with it, putting it in a Lego maze and that kind of thing. Tried to make it eat a grasshopper. Great afternoon. Then my mom called me in for dinner, and I knew she wouldn't let me bring the frog inside, so I was going to let it go, but instead I took out my pocketknife and cut off its arms and legs. Frogs are a bitch to hold down while you're doing that. Loved watching it writhe. I spent the whole meal wondering how my poor dismembered frog was doing, and I didn't even have dessert. That's right, hot fudge sundaes on the table and all I cared about was that frog."

George wiped some sweat from his forehead. He'd really hoped that Lou would come in, guns blazing, even though Lou didn't currently have a gun. His partner had to be doing *something*, right?

"I went back outside, looked in the shoebox where I'd left that frog, and he was still alive. Oh, he wasn't doing much, just sort of opening and closing his mouth, but he was alive. So I dissected him. I couldn't tell you what the frog parts were called or what their biological functions were, but I saw all of them."

"Am I supposed to respect this?" George asked.

"I don't care if you respect it or it disgusts you or gives you a big fat boner. I just want you to listen. I killed a lot more frogs after that. I mean a *lot* more. If the Supreme Being turns out to be a frog, I am more fucked than Hitler. From there I moved up to mammals. Mammals were even more fun. Bagged my first human when I was twenty-one. A hooker. I wish I'd been more inventive, but no, it was the typical 'crack whore who won't be missed' scenario. Wanna know how I did it?"

"Actually, I don't."

"Oh, come on."

"How did you do it?"

"Blowtorch. It's extremely inefficient."

"So how many people have you killed?"

"Americans, not that many, probably not even a dozen. But I spent some time in Africa, and, oh, I racked up a body count there. Same thing in Mexico. You go to the poor parts of the world, and you can live like a king and slaughter like a dictator. It's pretty fantastic."

"Yeah."

"I love how you're reduced to saying things like 'Yeah.' Very weak. Question, would it weird you out if I started licking up Diane's blood? Because I don't want to be nasty or anything, but it's smelling really good to me right now, and I'd love to just bury my face in her neck and slurp away."

"Don't let me stop you."

"I probably shouldn't indulge. You seem like the kind of person who would attack a guy when he's licking blood from a mutilated corpse."

"What about the whole werewolf thing?" George asked.

"Oh my God, it's more awesome than you can imagine. I mean, I know it's supposed to be a curse and everything, but if you'd be killing people *anyway*, it's the best thing in the world. Not everyone takes to it. Lot of suicides in the werewolf community. They're always fighting the change instead of embracing it."

"So clearly the full moon is bullshit."

Ivan shook his head. "Pretty much. I mean, the full moon causes the transformation whether you want it or not, but there are a lot of other factors. Most werewolves—and I don't want to imply that there are hundreds; we're actually a very rare species—they're terrified of what they are. But if you relish the change, and you practice, practice, practice, you can do it whenever you want. Hurts like hell, but you can learn to even like that part. I love it."

"How'd you get caught?"

"I let myself get caught."

"Yeah, right."

"Okay, maybe that part wasn't entirely intentional. But I sure got out, didn't I?"

"What happens next, Ivan? Are you trying to make me the first person in the world to get talked to death by a werewolf?"

"Ooooh, we're back to being saucy again, huh? Didn't take you long to get over your horror. I want to fight it out. No guns, no butcher knives, no wolves, just you and me, man to man."

"You're going to stay human?"

"Yep."

"For how long?"

"Until you're lying on the floor with a broken jaw. I know, you're thinking that you'll get one good punch in and I'll instantly wuss out and change, but you're wrong. Let's see who's the better man."

"Fine," George said. "Let's do this."

"Excellent." Ivan dropped the butcher knife. It hit Diane's face and stuck there. Then he set George's gun back in the sink. "I recommend that we move out of the kitchen, so that nobody slips on the blood."

Chapter Ten: Thug Versus Wolfman

"Works for me." George walked into the dining room. Though he was so scared that he was practically trembling, he forced himself to remain optimistic. He was going to get out of this with a dead werewolf at his feet and his dignity restored. Ivan was positive that he had the upper hand, and technically he *did*, but it would only take one moment of arrogance and carelessness for George to make his move.

Ivan had joked about "one good punch," which was exactly what George planned to do. Werewolf or not, superhuman or not, you didn't immediately recover from a nose-breaking blow. If it didn't send shards of bone rocketing into Ivan's brain, George would pound on him until his own knuckles were bloody and Ivan's face was nothing but frothing pulp.

Ivan followed him. The two men stood about five feet apart.

George rushed forward, throwing a sideways punch at Ivan's nose, hoping to make it *splatter*. Ivan pulled back out of the way, and George cursed as he hit nothing but air.

Ivan punched him in the stomach, so hard that George dropped to his knees, gasping for breath. The pain was so incredible that he was honestly surprised Ivan's hand hadn't burst right through his stomach and come out his back.

He knew he needed to get back up, quickly, but his guts felt like they'd been completely squashed. Even if he was a wolfman, how could such a skinny guy hit so goddamn hard?

"Done already?" Ivan asked. "This was barely worth me wasting time with the frog story."

George forced himself to at least get up off his knees, though he remained doubled over with his arms crossed over his stomach. He pulled his arms away, raised his fists, and stood up straight.

Ivan punched him in the face. His head shot back with almost neck-snapping force, and he stumbled backwards against the dining room table. He fell to the floor.

C'mon, Lou, where the hell's the cavalry? At this point, he'd almost welcome a visit by the cops. Better to spend twenty years in the clink than to let Ivan beat him to death.

"I'm going to give you one more chance to get up and fight like a…you know, it doesn't even have to be like a man, just not like a crippled old lady. Can you do that for me, George? Because if you can't, I'm going to change into a wolf and start eating you."

George reached up and grabbed the back of one of the chairs. He used it to steady himself as he pulled himself up.

"I don't even like the taste of human flesh that much," said Ivan. "I'm into a lot of demented things, but cannibalism isn't one of them. And I do consider it cannibalism, even if I'm in my wolf state."

"Weren't you just talking about licking up blood?" George asked, bracing himself against the table and trying hard not to throw up.

"That's different."

"How?"

"It's drinking instead of eating. If there's no meat involved, it's not cannibalism. Everybody knows that. Not that I'm morally opposed to cannibalism. It's just not for me."

George needed to focus his rage. He had a hell of a lot of rage available to focus. *Just imagine the sense of euphoria you'll feel when that bastard's head explodes into a billion sloppy chunks. Work with the pain and fury. Harness it. Make it your bitch.*

He quickly picked up the chair and smashed it into the side of Ivan's head, like a pro wrestler. Neither the chair nor Ivan's head broke apart, but Ivan let out a loud grunt and stumbled away, clearly stunned, which was satisfying enough.

Not wanting to lose his momentum, George rushed him and swung the chair a second time. Ivan dodged, but George got him on the reverse swing, bashing the wood into his chest and cracking one of the chair legs.

Ivan's right arm transformed. George took another swing. This time, Ivan grabbed a hold of the chair and yanked it out of his grasp, then threw it against the wall, where it broke into several pieces and clattered to the floor.

"Didn't take long to violate the no-weapons agreement, huh?" Though Ivan's tone was sarcastic, his eyes flashed with anger. The hit with the chair had obviously hurt. Ivan the Werewolf wasn't invulnerable after all.

He had, of course, just taken a brutal chair hit to the head without his skull fracturing, so George was still in plenty of danger.

"I thought you weren't going to change," he said.

"You cheated first."

And George was going to cheat again. He bolted back for the kitchen. A few close-range gunshots to the face would certainly test the wolfman's resilience.

He leapt over Diane's corpse, slipped on the blood, and fell on his ass.

He scrambled to get back on his feet, but his hand flew out from underneath him as he tried to push himself up on the blood-covered floor. If he were lucky, Ivan would pass out from laughter at George's predicament, giving him a chance to escape.

Ivan's sense of humor was apparently on hold for the moment. He grabbed the back of George's shirt with his clawed werewolf hand and dragged him back through the blood and over the corpse. She still had the butcher knife in her face. George yanked it out as he slid over her.

He twisted himself around and jabbed the knife at Ivan. Missed.

Another jab and the blade went an inch into Ivan's upper leg. He winced, and then backhanded George across the face with his wolf hand. The handle of the knife popped out of George's grasp as he struck the tile yet again. It fell to the floor. Ivan kicked it out of the way, so hard that it slid all the way across the kitchen and onto the carpet of the dining room.

George chose his target, bent his knee, and then slammed his foot into Ivan's groin with as much force as he could summon.

It was a spectacular direct hit. Ivan howled and clutched at his balls.

His head transformed, but it wasn't the rapid transformation from before. Fur sprouted in random patches on his face, and his skull became misshapen. His cry of pain revealed wolf-sized teeth in a human-sized mouth. His nose changed into a snout and then back into a nose, and three of the fingers on his left hand grew talons; unfortunately, they were not positioned in such a way as to further damage his scrotum.

A line of fur raced across his arm and then disappeared.

The leg he'd stabbed changed into a wolfman leg, throwing him off-balance.

Despite his size and constant urging from the coach, George had never played football. He wasn't into team sports. But he sure as hell knew how to do a tackle, and he took advantage of Ivan's distraction to charge him, ramming into his gut and knocking the still-shifting werewolf to the floor.

Ivan's head changed to full wolfman and he bit at George's arm. George pulled away just in time, threw a punch that connected solidly with Ivan's jaw, then got off him and went for the sink.

Ivan grabbed his ankle just as George snatched the gun.

George fired a shot. Even at almost point-blank range, George's aim was slightly off, and the bullet tore across the side of the werewolf's head, ripping a trail of red through his fur.

Ivan released his ankle.

George fired again, hitting him in the forehead. A gout of blood burst from the wound. He emptied the rest of the clip into the werewolf's chest, wanting to shout something clever but settling for a primal scream.

Ivan, bleeding profusely, fell back against the counter. Aside from a two-inch patch around his right eye, he was now a full wolfman.

His werewolf eye glowed red with fury.

George almost threw the empty gun at him, but didn't. Ivan was still very much alive, and George might need the weapon later.

Ivan ran his palms down his face and chest in one fluid motion, wiping off some of the blood. He said something that looked like it was meant to be a sadistic, menacing comment, but came out only as a growl.

Not wanting to lose his advantage, George hurried over and threw a punch at the werewolf, hoping to hit him directly in one of the bullet holes. He didn't quite succeed, but it was a solid blow to the chest. One that had no visible impact.

He punched again. Still nothing, except a bolt of pain in his hand that made him think he might have broken a finger or two.

Ivan drew his hand back, bloody claws glistening. With him in full werewolf mode and pissed off beyond belief, George had no doubt that a full-force swipe could knock his head off, or at least remove most of his face. He ducked underneath Ivan's arm and sprinted through the dining room.

There had to be another weapon in the house. Perhaps not a fire poker or machete, but maybe a broom that he could snap in half or a fire extinguisher.

He ran through the living room into the hallway. The doors on each side were closed, so he ran into the open doorway at the end.

A bedroom. Obviously Diane's. A television on the dresser was set to the same channel as the one in the living room, and a folded-out ironing board stood next to the bed. A blouse was draped over it. An iron, the red light on, rested on the board.

So, what, she'd been about to do some ironing, then went into the kitchen for a snack?

It didn't matter. He grabbed the iron and tugged on the cord to pull it free of the power outlet.

Something moved on the other side of the bed.

A little kid popped his head up, his face stained with tears. He looked about five.

Oh, shit!

Which one was it? Robin? Gabriel? George couldn't remember which one was younger.

George frantically waved for the kid to duck back down.

"Okay, sweetheart, I'll get you a juice box, just promise Mommy you won't touch the iron, all right?"

George moved out of the bedroom, almost pulling the door shut behind him but realizing that it would look suspicious. Ivan stood at the other end of the hallway, still full werewolf. His bullet wounds seemed to be smaller than before—George couldn't actually see them shrinking, but there was unquestionably some sort of rapid healing going on.

Instead of waiting for the werewolf to come after him, George charged forward. He'd replace the smell of air freshener with the scent of burnt dog.

The way he'd envisioned the attack, George would press the hot iron firmly against Ivan's chest, relishing the sizzling sound. But two steps in, he could tell that he wasn't going to get that opportunity, so he adjusted the angle of the iron, holding it so that the pointed end was in front. He swung the iron as he ran, aiming it in an arc toward Ivan's ear, hoping to impale the creature.

Ivan blocked the swing, smashing his clenched, clawed fist into George's forearm. George lost his grip on the iron. It fell, landing with the hot side on George's leg, but bouncing off before it could do more than startle him.

George took a powerful blow to the chin—not quite a decapitation blow or a face-removing one, but certainly enough to rattle his jaw—and careened back against the bedroom door, which swung all the way open.

Ivan looked past him and snarled.

There wasn't any sense looking back. It didn't matter if he'd seen the little boy or not, because either way, George wasn't going to let the werewolf through the doorway.

He was starting to feel pretty lightheaded, though, and his wrist was soaking through the bandage.

He shook off the dizzy spell. No time for that shit.

George just had to get past the werewolf and lead him away from the bedroom. Ivan was interested in killing *him* and not a five-year-old boy, right?

Unfortunately, it was a narrow hallway and they both took up a lot of space. Getting past him was going to be almost impossible.

He could rush back into the bedroom and close the door, but he figured the door would only last a few moments of being pummeled by Ivan, if that. More likely it would explode in a shower of splinters and they'd have nowhere to go.

Screw it. He'd try another tackle.

George lowered his head and ran at Ivan, building up as much speed as he could in those few steps. Ivan shoved him aside, slamming George against the wall and dislodging two framed photographs.

Jaws wide open, Ivan lunged at George's face.

Chapter Eleven: Ferocious

Lou Flynn sat in the driver's seat of the van, trying not to fidget in front of Michele. He wasn't quite sure where their relationship stood at the moment, and he guessed there was a pretty good chance that it might revert back to a "kidnapper and captive" deal, so he wanted to make sure she didn't notice any signs of weakness. He had an almost uncontrollable desire to chew his fingernails, but withstood the urge and just scratched his left knee, pretending that it itched a lot.

He stared at the front door of the home, waiting for George to emerge, victoriously leading the werewolf in handcuffs, or holding its severed head. Better the handcuffs than the severed head, since despite the current danger of having an actual werewolf trying to slaughter them, exterminating their cargo would most likely lead to a whole mess of problems that they weren't ready to handle.

He hated when George said things like "If I'm not back in a few minutes, get out of here." What that really meant was "If I'm not back in a few minutes, sigh with frustration, utter a couple of your favorite expletives, and then embrace your heroic side." George knew that Lou wasn't going to simply drive off and leave him, despite the overwhelming temptation to do so.

"Does he do this a lot?" Michele asked.

"Foolishly chase werewolves?"

"You know what I mean."

Lou shook his head. "Nah. Things usually go pretty smooth."

That was true. It wasn't as if their lives were a series of disasters. Even excluding the supernatural element, the path this job had taken was unlike anything they'd ever experienced. They'd exchanged some gunfire with gangsters, just barely dodged the cops a few times, and once, when he'd been carving a scarlet "A" on a cheating husband's arm, the man had somehow gotten a hold of his switchblade. A quick punch to the nose corrected the situation, but it had been a pretty scary moment.

Overall, most jobs, even the most distasteful ones, went reasonably well.

Lou had decided that he might give this lifestyle another five years, keep building up his nest egg, and then retire. Enjoy life. Travel to places that *he* wanted to go. Find a girlfriend, and then propose to her. Let his beard grow down to his navel.

If he had to die before that, so be it, but he didn't want to die chasing a werewolf. Werewolves should be left alone. He and George should've told Ricky to suck it and made him find somebody else.

"C'mon, George," he said under his breath, still watching the front door. "We shouldn't be here."

"Should you go in there after him?" Michele asked.

"I'll give him a couple more minutes."

"I can wait here. I'll honk if somebody's coming."

"What you mean is, you'll drive away as soon as I get out."

"No, I won't."

"Of course you will. I would."

"You saved my life."

"Right. Which means you probably have a newfound appreciation for not being dead. And I hate to say this, but your ten percent has pretty much been flushed down the can."

"I figured that."

"Do you think there's some kind of reasonable explanation for this? I mean, it's hard to stay a skeptic when a man changes into a wolf-thing right in front of you, but do you think there's *some* way he could've faked it? Penn and Teller, they could probably pull that off, don't you think?"

"Not unless they've turned to sorcery instead of illusion."

"Crap."

"Yeah."

Lou shifted in his seat. "I'm surprised the cops haven't shown up yet. That damn wolf was running down the street in broad daylight. What about those people on the porch?"

"They're probably throwing out all of their weed."

"Could be."

"Or maybe the police don't rush out to respond to werewolf reports."

"Well, the people who called in wouldn't have to *say* it was a werewolf. They could just say it was a big dog."

"But if they did use the word 'werewolf,' that could explain why the police haven't given this a top priority."

Lou nodded. "Yeah, you're right. Also the people who live around here might have day jobs."

There was a crash from inside the house. Lou sat up straight.

Did that noise relate to damage inflicted *by* George, or to him?

"Crap," he said.

Michele said nothing. She looked as if she might be back to considering making a run for it. If she did, Lou probably wouldn't try to stop her, though he had no plans to tell her this.

He sighed.

More crashes.

He had to go in there. No matter how dumb or bordering on suicidal it was, he had to go in there to try to help his partner.

"He's gonna get me killed," Lou muttered, unfastening his seat belt. "Or maimed. It's official: you're seeing me alive for the very last time because of him. Son of a bitch. Excuse my language."

"No problem."

Lou looked over at Michele, took the keys out of the ignition, and pocketed them.

"So you're leaving me with no way to escape if the wolf comes back out?" she asked.

"I'm leaving you with no way to ditch us, correct."

A gunshot rang out from inside the house. Lou hurriedly opened the door and got out of the van. More gunshots went off as he ran toward the front door. Oh, how this sucked. This sucked so thoroughly. It was hard to even quantify the level of suck involved here.

He pressed the button on the handle of his switchblade, snapping out the blade, and then opened the front door and stepped into the living room, hoping to see George stomping up and down on a pile of werewolf mush. Instead, the living room was empty.

A commotion in the hallway.

He ran over there and saw Ivan, fully transformed, looming over George.

Ivan's back was to Lou. Lou's first instinct was to freeze, but he forced himself to ignore the terror and rush at the creature. He slashed diagonally across Ivan's back, left shoulder to the right side of his waist, cutting deep.

The werewolf howled in pain.

Wow. The switchblade seemed to work better than bullets.

Ivan spun around and Lou slashed him again, cutting in the opposite direction. Ivan howled once more, clawing at the long red gash, and then violently shoved Lou out of the way. Lou smashed into a dent in the wall that he thought may have already been made by George, but kept his footing as the werewolf rushed past him, through the living room, and out the front door.

"You hurt him!" George shouted. "You actually hurt the bastard!"

"Are you okay?" Lou quickly reached out his arm. George grabbed it and pulled himself up.

"Yeah, I'm fine! What's important is that he's *not*! Let's go!"

"Where?"

"After him!" George hurried into the living room, and then into the kitchen.

"Where are you going?"

"I'm getting the guns!"

George returned, holding both pistols. He gave one to Lou and hurried for the door. "Come on!"

"But—"

"If he's weakened, maybe we can take him down! He's a deranged psychopathic killer, Lou! We can't let him escape!"

Lou followed George out of the house. Psychopathic killer? Who had Ivan killed? Was the blood on George's clothing not his own?

Michele slammed the door of the van shut. Clearly she'd been trying to make a break for it, but retreated back to the safety of the vehicle when Ivan came outside. The werewolf ran past the van and down the sidewalk, moving with great speed yet at a visibly slower rate than during the previous chase and leaving a small trail of blood.

"In the van!" George shouted.

"Oh, for God's sake!" Lou threw up his arms in protest, but still got in the van. He tossed the keys over Michele to George, who started the engine and sped off.

"We're going to run him down," said George. "We're going to squash him underneath the tires, and then we're going to back up and do it again!"

Ivan ran along the sidewalk, just ahead. George looked wild-eyed, almost deranged and psychopathic himself, and Lou suddenly wondered if he'd survived his brief fight with the werewolf only to perish in a van wreck. "Don't drive on the sidewalk!"

"I'm not going to!" said George, although it kind of looked like he was.

Ivan darted across to the other side of the street, then onto somebody's yard and crossed between two houses. George slammed on the brakes.

Off in the distance, Lou heard sirens. "Damn, it took them long enough," he said. "Okay, George, it's time to get the hell out of here."

"We need to catch him."

"No! Now, I'm usually happy to let you take the lead, and I've let you give orders all day, but we need to *leave*! I'm *not* going to prison for this, do you understand? If you want to keep chasing him, fine, but you're doing it on foot."

George gave him a look of absolute fury, which immediately softened. Now he almost looked like he was going to cry. "Yeah, you're right. We'll go. The cops'll take him down."

"You okay?"

"*Should* I be okay?"

Lou didn't say anything. They kept to the speed limit to avoid attracting police attention, though of course it was entirely possible that the cops were also seeking a black van as a vehicle of interest in the disappearance of Michele. Much to Lou's relief, they ended up making it out of the town and back onto Tamiami Trail without even driving past one of the cops or emergency vehicles.

George stared straight ahead as he drove, looking more spooked than Lou had ever seen him. That was only to be expected—Lou was more spooked than *he'd* ever been, too, and most likely Michele felt the same way. But George's mental state seemed to go beyond simply "Holy shit! That werewolf almost killed me!"

"Do you need to go to the hospital?" Lou asked.

George shook his head.

"We can. I mean, if you're that badly hurt. I can drop you off at the door, or I can come in with you if you need it, or whatever."

"Do you know what he did?" George asked.

"What?"

"He killed the lady who lived in that house. Not just killed her—he made her talk about her family, and then he slashed her up, like it was a great big joke. Remember that hit we saw two years ago in Buffalo?"

"Yeah."

"That guy laughed and it was frickin' chilling, but that was an 'I finally got revenge' laugh. You could sort of understand where he was coming from. This was…it was just like 'Look how much fun I'm having stabbing this woman.' It was playtime."

"Jesus."

"He kept doing it after she was dead. He sat there stabbing her corpse. And her *kid* was in the house."

"Seriously?"

"Yeah. He was hiding in the bedroom. This little kid. He's already terrified, and he's going to walk into the kitchen and find his mom in a great big pool of blood, stabbed to death by a madman. I should have gotten him out of there. Should've taken him to a neighbor or something. He's five, Lou. He shouldn't see that. What's going to happen to him?"

"He should be okay, right? I mean, Ivan's gone."

"I'm not talking about whether or not he gets killed by a goddamn werewolf. I'm talking about him seeing his dead mom!"

"Okay, okay, I dunno what to tell you, George! It's heartbreaking, but we didn't have a choice. We couldn't hang out there any more. Protecting the kid from psychological trauma isn't worth going to prison, right?"

"I guess not."

"No, no, don't use the word 'guess.' This is a definite. I'm not going to jail for a kid."

"Yeah, you're right."

"I am right, and we need to get this perfectly clear: we're not heroes. If you wanna be sad about the kid, I completely understand—it's disturbing as hell. But don't sit there thinking that we should've taken him by the hand and led him over to the nice old lady who lives next door. You got me?"

"I've got you."

"Good. I'm not a cold-hearted monster. I'm gonna have some sleepless nights over this whole thing, but the reason I'll get to have those sleepless nights is that I'm still alive."

"I said I've got you! Quit hammering in the goddamn point!"

"And now I think we should call Ricky."

"Aw, shit."

"Yeah."

"Who's Ricky?" Michele asked.

"If we're lucky, he's going to be the guy who covers our butts." George took his cell phone out of his pocket.

"You want me to do it?" Lou asked.

"Nah, I'll take the heat."

"Don't throw up on the phone."

"I won't."

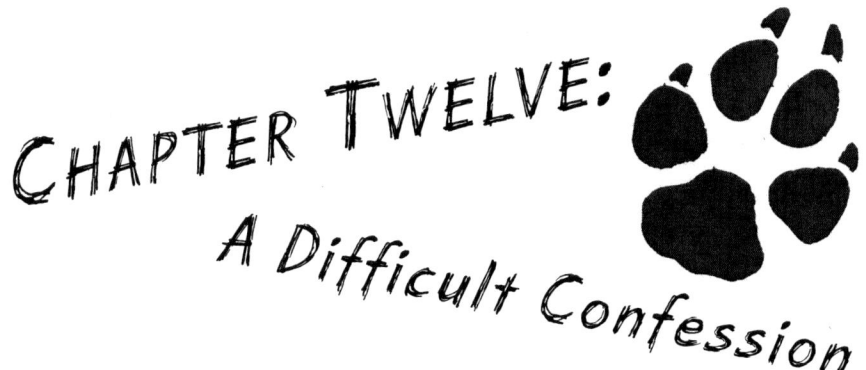

CHAPTER TWELVE: A Difficult Confession

George took a deep breath, exhaled slowly in an effort to calm himself, then called Ricky. He hoped that the little prick didn't give him any crap, because George was positively not in the mood for it.

Ricky answered. "George?"

"Yeah."

"Hey, I was half a second away from calling you. Your dog problem is on the news. I thought you were just yanking me, but I'm looking at it right now. Anyway, I just got off a conference call with Bateman and Dewey. Intense stuff."

"Intense how?"

"Manic depressive intense. Anger and joy. I'm glad I only have to deal with them over the phone. So here's the deal: get off the road ASAP. Find someplace safe to hide out. Get as far off the beaten path as you can. They weren't anticipating any problems like this, so they're going to send out a bunch of reinforcements and collect the furball from you."

"Oh."

"Your voice sounds funny."

"Yeah."

"Just relax. It's all going to be taken care of. Your buddy Ricky makes your headaches go away."

"So, Ricky, what if there was another problem that they hadn't anticipated?"

"What do you mean?"

George could almost feel the new ulcer burning into his stomach lining. "What if we lost our cargo?"

87

"Oh, shit, George. Don't tell me that. Please don't tell me that."

"I'm sorry."

"You lost him? For real?"

"Yeah."

"Oh my God. This is—you've got to be—how the hell do you lose a guy in a cage?"

"He escaped! He changed into a werewolf and escaped!"

There was a long silence, and then Ricky let out a sigh of relief. "Ah, okay, you're just screwing with me. Good one. I almost had a heart attack over that."

"I am absolutely dead serious! He transformed into a wolfman and got out of the cage!" George didn't see any reason to confess to his own starring role in the escape.

"*What?*"

"That's what happened!"

"Listen to me. I've got to report back to Bateman and Dewey, and it's fine if you want to goof around with me, I deserve it, but these men have no sense of humor and I need to know the truth: do you still have Ivan with you?"

"No."

"Shit!"

"I'm sorry."

"Shit! Oh, shit! How could you lose him? You idiot!"

George bristled. Whether he was an idiot or not, he didn't appreciate being called one by a little punk like Ricky. "He changed into a wolf, that's how I lost him! I wasn't expecting it!"

"But everybody told you he was a werewolf! I know for a frickin' fact that it came up in the conversation!"

"I didn't believe it! You didn't believe it either! Why the hell would I believe something like that? If there's a real-life werewolf involved, that's a concept you need to do a better job of selling! You need to give me pictures or video or expert testimony! I thought he was just some skinny guy in a cage! And it's not even the full moon! The full moon was supposed to be a crucial element! I'm sorry things went bad like this, but we were *not* given enough information to successfully carry out this task!"

Ricky sounded as if he were about to hyperventilate. "You have no idea how bad this is. They're going to execute you!"

"Execute us? Nobody said this job had the risk of us getting executed!"

"Every job has the risk of you getting executed! You know that!"

"Why did they pick us to do it? If this was so important, why didn't they get one of their own men?"

"Because you and Lou are good! And because it was supposed to be an easy transport job!"

"Well, it wasn't!"

"Look, George, this is a nightmare scenario, but I'll do everything I can to keep you guys alive. I'll stick out my neck for you. Is there anything else I should know?"

George hesitated. "No."

"Why'd you hesitate?"

"Okay, the werewolf murdered somebody. A lady."

"Aw, damn it."

"And when we were at the gas station, we picked up this girl who was being attacked by the dogs. She 's in the van with us now."

"Are you tugging my dick?"

"No."

"You brought a witness? Are you on crack?"

"The dogs were going to kill her!"

"You didn't have to let them kill her, but that doesn't mean you had to—you know what, I'm not going to have this conversation. I'm going to get back on the phone with a couple of very violent men, and get my ass chewed out while I try to figure out how to unfuck this disaster. Did your werewolf buddy bend the bars?"

"No."

"Then lock the girl in there."

"Are you kidding me?"

"Do I sound like I'm kidding? We're in hardcore damage control mode. This is 'fingernails ripped out before they drown you' bad. You need to put that girl in the cage, hide out, and pray to God that we can clean up the loose ends. Now I have to go."

George flinched as Ricky slammed down the phone in his ear.

"Did that go as bad as it sounded?" Lou asked.

"It did go poorly." George's head was pounding. "It's not our fault, right? How could we know? Even if we believed in the werewolf thing, it's not a full moon. We specifically discussed the full moon issue when we picked him up, right? I made that comment about not following the lunar cycles that closely. It's not our fault, right?"

"Well," said Lou, "you're right that it's not *our* fault…"

In addition to all of his other physical discomfort, George felt his upper lip begin to twitch.

"…but I'm not gonna say anything else about it," said Lou. "It's done and we can't take it back. We're just gonna start from where we are and stick together."

"Thanks, buddy."

"However, I'm hoping that the plan involves finding someplace to hide out until reinforcements arrive."

"It doesn't."

"Crap."

"We can't let him go on a killing spree," said George. "He'll leave a trail of bodies just to prove he's better than us. If we don't stop him, ten bucks says that the police will find our names spelled out with somebody's intestines."

Lou rubbed his forehead. "I've got a headache."

"Mine's worse. If we recapture him, we'll be okay. We'll have to do some apologizing, but they won't kill us."

"Do you know that for sure?"

"No, but I do know that they *will* kill us if that werewolf gets away."

"So what are we gonna go, catch him in a net?"

"Maybe."

"We can't catch a werewolf in a net! That's ridiculous! We can't even run him down in a van!"

"He has weaknesses, Lou. I got him in the crotch and it hurt him bad."

"Wolfman's got nards," said Michele.

"Excuse me?"

"'Wolfman's got nards.' It's a quote from *The Monster Squad*." She seemed to realize that George was not amused. "Sorry. Trying to lighten the mood."

"What's your knife made out of?" George asked Lou.

"Sterling silver."

"Our lead bullets made him bleed but they didn't really slow him down. Your knife, though—that got him. Maybe some of the werewolf lore is accurate. What do you think we could do with pure silver?"

"Do you have any?"

"No. I'm sure we can't just drive to Wal-Mart and pick up a clip of silver bullets, but we can get other stuff. What else can you use to stop a werewolf?"

"We could dig a big pit and cover the top with leaves," said Lou.

George shook his head. "We don't have time for that."

"George, that was a joke. An obvious one. If you're so far gone that you think I was being serious about the big wolf pit, then maybe we're not in the best frame of mind to go on a werewolf hunt."

"Okay, we need some silver," George said, continuing as if he hadn't heard Lou's comment. "Maybe we can make a tip for a spear or something. Jab it through his nards."

"That's actually not a bad idea."

"We need a jewelry store and a sporting goods store. No problem."

"We drove by a bunch of antique stores when we first got here."

"Perfect." George smiled, but then he remembered the little boy who might be crouched next to his dead mother right now, and his smile disappeared. He hoped the kid and his brother wouldn't be separated if they went into foster homes.

"You okay, George?" Lou asked.

"I'm fine. Delightful. Come on, let's go save our lives."

«««—»»»

The first antique shop was an absolute dump of a place. Granted, any shop that sold old crap fit George's definition of "dump," since he had a whole head full of bad memories about his mom and grandmother dragging him around from shop to shop, squealing in delight when they found more rare garbage to display in their curiosity cabinets. He couldn't prove it and didn't want to, but he was pretty sure that the first female orgasm he'd ever witnessed was at the moment his grandmother found an old coffee table. It stayed in her living room for twenty years and wasn't any better than one she could have bought at a furniture store for less money and without Grandpa having to spend six months fixing it up.

The decrepit guy behind the counter had asked if they'd been in a car accident, and George explained that, yes, they had, and that they appreciated his concern. George asked about silver, and the ancient guy had stared at him for a while, trying to think. "No," he finally said, "but I've got some Silver Age comic books. A buck each."

"No, thank you."

"Seventy-five cents."

"Sorry."

They thanked him and left the store. The next one was only two shops down, so they jogged over there and went through the rickety door. A bell tinkled as they entered. An old lady sat on a rocking chair on the other side of the small shop, reading a paperback novel and smoking a cigarette. George didn't like or care about antiques, but he was pretty sure you weren't supposed to smoke around them.

"You're not going to get blood on my stuff, are you?" the old lady asked.

"No, ma'am. We'll be careful."

"Were you in an accident?"

"Yes. None of us are going to die, though. In case you were worried."

"Anything I can help you find?"

"We're looking for silver. Pure silver, if you've got it."

The old woman nodded and tapped some ashes off her cigarette onto the ashtray that rested on the rocking chair arm. "I've got plenty of silver. What do you want?"

"Anything you've got."

"Sounds desperate."

"No, we're just late for a wedding, mostly because of the car accident." He gestured at Lou. "This jackass forgot to pick up a gift."

"Please don't curse in my store."

"Jackass?" George decided to let it go. "Anyway, we need a gift. The bride loves silver."

"All right." The old woman took another drag from her cigarette, then stood up and walked over to the counter, moving at an excruciatingly slow pace. George wanted to ask her to speed it up, since people might be horribly mutilated while she ambled over there, but figured that wasn't such a good idea.

"Do you have a restroom?" Michele asked.

"No."

George gave her a dirty look. She probably assumed that George and Lou wouldn't prevent her from going to the bathroom when this old lady was around to hear their conversation. She really was going to end up in the cage if she wasn't careful.

The old woman hobbled behind the counter, then ducked out of sight. A few moments later, she stood back up and set a wooden box on the counter. She raised the lid, revealing dozens of rings.

"Great, great," said George. "Which ones are silver?"

"The ones colored silver."

As a rule, George didn't hit old ladies, though it was a rule for which he was momentarily inclined to try to find a loophole. He quickly went through the selection, plucking out ten or eleven of the rings.

"By the way, I don't take credit cards," the old lady said.

"You don't?"

"Nope."

"In the twenty-first century, in a store full of high-ticket items, you don't take credit cards?"

"The credit card companies charge me service fees. Nobody ever got charged a service fee for cash."

"Actually, ATM's do usually charge a service fee for cash withdrawals. But that's fine. I'm not going to tell you how to run your place."

"Thank you. I appreciate that."

"What else do you have in silver?"

The old woman looked around. "Over against that wall, there's a silver mirror."

"Good. Lou, go get that." Lou nodded and went over to retrieve the mirror. "What else?"

"Well, let me see...are you Catholic?"

"We're whatever religion worships silver."

"I've got this," said the woman, taking out a silver crucifix that was about six inches long.

George picked it up and examined it. "This Jesus kind of looks like Kenny Rogers."

"Don't blaspheme in my shop, please."

"I apologize. I was just commenting on the fine production values here. How much?"

The lady thought for a moment. "Two hundred dollars."

George looked at Michele. "Is that a good deal?"

"How should I know?"

"Don't women know standard pricing on all precious metals?"

"Sorry, I don't buy a lot of silver crucifixes."

"Two hundred, deal," said George, "under the condition that you never saw us. Plus we'll take the mirror and all of the rings."

"This mirror isn't silver," said Lou, scraping his fingernail along the edge. "It's just painted."

"Stop scraping my merchandise."

"Forget the mirror," said George. "But we'll take all of the rings."

"Must be one big wedding."

"It is."

"Is that thing real silver?" asked Lou, gesturing to a very small cross that dangled from a chain bracelet on her wrist. "I mean, more real than the mirror?"

"Yes, but it's not for sale."

George snorted. "It's not for sale, or you're going to charge us a lot for it?"

"Five hundred dollars."

"We'll stick with the rest of the stuff, thanks."

"No," said Lou. "We'll take it."

The old woman shrugged, removed the bracelet, and handed it to Lou. Lou put it around his own wrist. George rolled his eyes.

"All right. Anything else you're looking for?"

"Do you sell nets?"

"You mean like fishnet stockings?"

"No. God no. Like a big net that you could use to catch a…bear."

"Sorry. There's not a huge market for antique netting."

"Thanks. Pay her, Lou."

Lou held the briefcase with the sixty-three thousand dollars they'd taken from Douglas that morning. They'd decided that leaving it unattended in a van with a broken-out windshield was not the wisest course of action. Stealing from it was probably not the best way to keep their own thumbs unbroken, but they could replace the missing money before they handed over the briefcase, and considering the extreme circumstances it seemed perfectly justified.

Lou popped open the top of the briefcase, keeping the contents hidden from the old woman's view. He snatched out a few bills then closed the briefcase.

"Are you involved in organized crime?" the old woman asked.

George nodded. "Knock twenty bucks off the price of the crucifix, and nothing happens to your business."

Chapter Thirteen: More Prey

"Why'd you do that?" George asked, starting up the van.

Michele was relatively certain that she knew what he was talking about. However, she didn't want to accidentally confess to something else, so she feigned ignorance. "What?"

"You know."

"Really, I don't. And do we have time for guessing games?"

"You asked the old woman about the bathroom."

"So? Am I not allowed to pee?"

George cracked his knuckles, one at a time. Next to her, Michele felt Lou's leg muscles tighten, as if he were cringing. George drove away from the antique shop, looking extremely stern. He was good at it. "You were trying to escape."

"Did you see the place we were in? Did it look like the kind of place to have a secret rear entrance? Let me give you Women 101, George: when we go into a store, we usually have to pee."

"This guy Ricky, who sets up our jobs—he told me to lock you in the cage. I don't want to do that. Right now, we can pretend that we're business partners, but when you try something sneaky, it makes me feel that I need to take an extra level of precaution."

"You don't."

"Are you sure?"

"I'm sure. Just needed to pee. I had to go before the dogs attacked."

She was, of course, lying. The antique store *might* have had a back exit. If not, she would've used the opportunity to steal some kind of weapon. Unfortunately, George had kept her close during the shopping adventure, and she hadn't been given the chance.

To be perfectly honest, the cage seemed like the safest place to be. If Ivan couldn't get out, he probably couldn't get back in, and Michele was very close to raising her hand and politely volunteering to be locked in there. It wouldn't be that uncomfortable.

The problem, of course, would come when they met up with the other bad guys. If she seemed to be on relatively even ground with George and Lou, she might be able to still talk her way out of this. If she was locked in a cage while George and Lou introduced her…well, it was going to be difficult to sell the idea of them being newfound business associates.

She really did have to pee, though.

The positive side to this whole thing, and she did indeed feel that it was a positive side and not merely self-delusion, was that there was an incredible story here. If she survived the werewolf ordeal, she'd be on television twenty-four hours a day for at least the next week. Book rights. Movie rights. She'd donate a generous portion of her proceeds to the gas station attendant's family, and perhaps to the families who'd tragically lost their household pets in the dog attack, but as long as she didn't get killed and her injuries didn't go much further than the slashed-up shoulder, the danger would be worth it.

That said, she'd still try to get the hell away from George and Lou, given the opportunity. She wasn't crazy.

"We have a lot of problems right now," said George. "Please don't cause more for us."

"I won't."

«««—»»»

Ivan Spinner sat in a tree, feeling good about life. He hadn't felt so good half an hour ago, when he climbed up this tree; in fact, he'd been pissed off and even a little ashamed. Why did he run away when that bozo Lou cut him? Yeah, it hurt, but he should have ripped Lou's heart out, stuck it on the end of his talon, and licked it like a Tootsie Roll Pop. It would've been fine to murder Lou. That still left George as his plaything.

Of course, he couldn't forget Michele. He had no ill feelings toward her, but he was certainly going to enjoy devouring her fine ass, even though he wasn't really a cannibal. He'd be romantic about it. He'd tell her he loved her first.

He reached back and touched the cut. It felt almost healed. The one on his chest had faded to a red scratch. Both cuts still hurt, but that was typical—the wounds went away before the pain.

He wished he hadn't been forced to reveal the full scope of his power. Unfortunately, though being a werewolf made his life much easier and a lot more fun and was quite honestly absolutely fucking fantastic, it did *not* allow him to bend bars. He'd been a little worried—not too much, but a little—that George and Lou would take him all the way to Tampa without giving him a chance to escape. Ivan didn't know much about Mr. Dewey and his crew, and though he was relatively certain that he could've gotten away even after George and Lou made their delivery, it was much better to be on the loose here.

He wondered if the werewolf element had made it into the news, or if they thought it was just a regular old human serial killer who'd cut up Diane. He loved the idea of some hillbilly being interviewed: "Why, I saw it, and that thing, it was half-man and half-beast! I ain't done seen nothin' like it in my life, even when I've sucked down a couple quarts of my county-famous moonshine!"

Ivan climbed down from the tree. Logically, he knew that he should make a run for it and move to another part of the world—again—but what was the point of being a werewolf if you couldn't terrorize people? George had probably dropped a great big loaf in his oversized underwear, but Ivan hadn't come close to being satisfied with the thug's comeuppance.

He'd loved George's expression when he slid that blade through Diane's silky neck. Fifty percent horror, fifty percent guilt, mixed into a delicious concoction of misery. George was sitting in that van right now, wailing "It was all my fault! It was all my fault!"

Yeah, George, it sure as hell was.

And this whole killing spree is going to be your fault, too.

Ivan's shirt had fallen off completely, though his pants had held up fairly well thanks to the elastic waist. He could probably break into somebody's house and steal a change of clothing without too much trouble, but, no, it felt like the kind of afternoon where he should murder somebody just for their clothes.

Murder them *slowly*.

Make them die a lingering, horrible, excruciatingly painful death simply because they wore the same size shirt as him.

He sat down next to the tree. It was a pretty desolate piece of road, but three cars had driven by while he was up there, so another one was bound to approach before too much longer.

He wondered if any of his four-legged friends were around. He closed his eyes and put out the call. Nothing heavy-duty like before; just a mild little dog-call to see if any showed up.

Ivan didn't have the slightest idea how this power worked, whether he was sending out some frequency that only dogs could hear, or if one of George's guesses was right and it had something to do with his scent, or if he could control dog brain waves, or whatever. Unlike the transformations, which he'd mastered in a ridiculously short timeframe—okay, eight years, but that was damn good for a werewolf, since most of them *never* learned to control it—he still hadn't quite figured out the whole dog thing. It was sort of like being able to move a pencil with his mind, except that he didn't know if the pencil was going to roll across the table or twirl up into the air and poke out somebody's eye.

He sat there for about five minutes until a small gray Schnauzer walked along the side of the road toward him. No collar. He wondered if it was a stray.

He heard the engine of an approaching car. Sometimes, things just worked out perfectly.

The dog looked at him and let out a sharp bark.

"Fuck you," he told it. He continued to concentrate.

The dog walked into the middle of the road and began to happily move in the direction of the oncoming car.

Poor, poor doggie. Ivan chuckled as the dog, its tongue hanging partly out of its mouth like a complete moron, trotted along toward its doom. *I think I'll name you…Roadkill.*

The car, a white sedan, came around the corner. The driver swerved at the last instant, missing the Schnauzer by the length of its stubby tail, and then careened off the road.

The dog ran off.

Well, shit. He'd hoped to see the dog get creamed *and* to disable the vehicle. Oh well.

Ivan stood up, jogged over to the car, and opened the passenger-side door. The driver, a bald man who was too young to be naturally bald, seemed shaken up but not hurt. He'd been wearing his seatbelt. Smart lad.

"You okay?" Ivan asked.

"Yeah…stupid dog ran right in front of me…" The man sounded kind of dazed. That wasn't any good. Ivan wanted him fully aware of what was about to happen.

"Did you injure yourself?" Ivan asked. "Do you need me to seek the services of a medical professional? If you have one of those new cellular phone devices, I could probably call for assistance." He climbed into the car next to the man, who looked shocked at both Ivan's shredded pants and the fact that he was getting into the car uninvited.

"I don't need—"

"Shut the fuck up," Ivan told him, pulling the door shut. He gave him a wide smile, revealing his werewolf teeth. "Spoooooooky, huh?"

The man immediately reached for his door handle. Ivan decided to go half-werewolf. The one bitch he had about his lycanthropy was that he couldn't talk as a wolfman, so he went for the not-quite-as-hairy, not-quite-as-muscular, but still clearly wolfish and scary look. It was actually kind of demonic.

The man screamed.

Ivan laughed at him, a low, sexy growl of a laugh that the ladies found ever so alluring. Then he showed him his claws. "You try to leave this car and these are going right into you."

The man kept screaming, so Ivan said it again, louder. Then he raked his claws across the man's chest. "Shut up!"

"Oh, God, please don't hurt me!"

"I just *did* hurt you, dumb-ass. Do you like your head?"

"What?"

"I said, do you like your head? It's not a challenging question. Yes or no. Do. You. Like. Your. Head?"

"Yes."

"Then don't make me rip it off and drink from it like a juice box, all right? What size shirt do you wear?"

"A...a large."

"I look better in a medium, but I prefer large for comfort, so that'll work just fine. What's your name?"

"What *are* you?"

"What the fuck do you *think* I am? A Martian? Come on, buddy. I know you're scared, but think before you ask stupid questions. Now apologize to me for wasting my time."

"I'm sorry."

"Apology accepted. I asked you your name."

"Dale."

"Like Chip and Dale? The squirrels?"

"Yes."

"Or Chippendales. Wow. Never thought of that before. I wonder if it was intentional."

"I...I don't know."

"That's okay. I wasn't really asking. Chip and Dale, I guess they aren't squirrels, are they? They're chipmunks. Chip the Chipmunk. That's a pretty lame name for a cartoon character when you take Dale out of it, don't you think? The Disney writers weren't having a good day. Now it's my turn to apologize to you—we're getting pretty far off the subject at hand, which is your shirt size."

"Yes."

"Yes? What were you saying yes to? Were you agreeing that I need to apologize to you?"

"No. I mean—I don't know."

"Why the hell would I apologize to you? I don't owe you a thing, Dale. How dare you? I mean, how *dare* you?"

"I'm sorry!"

"Oh, don't be so gullible, I'm just messing with you. Clearly my whole Chip and Dale bit was wasting your time, and I do owe you an apology, so from the bottom of my werewolf heart, I'm sorry. Now let's talk about me ripping your guts out."

Dale looked as if he wanted to say something, most likely "What?" or "No!" or "Please!" but couldn't find his voice.

"Oh, don't look so surprised," Ivan said. "You knew I was going to kill you as soon as I turned into a scary monster. Do you want to know why I'm going to do it?"

"I..."

"For your clothes. That's it. No other reason. I'm going to end your life, all however many years of it...how old are you?"

"Thirty-two."

"...all thirty-two years of it for your shirt. And I don't even like your shirt. How does that make you feel, Dale?"

Dale threw a punch at him. Ivan deflected the blow with his palm with very little effort, then used the same hand to grab Dale's wrist. Then, with the index finger of his other hand, he slashed a line across the length of Dale's entire arm, opening it up like a zipper. Dale, not surprisingly, screamed.

Sweet. Ivan had thought Dale might be too paralyzed with fear to actually fight back, so this would make things more interesting.

"Did that hurt? I hope so. That's just a sneak preview, by the way. A tasty little sample of the main attraction. I really feel sorry for you and the hellish pain you're going to endure. I'm sure glad *I'm* not the one sitting here in a car with a sadistic werewolf."

"I've got money!" Dale said.

"Lots?"

"Yes."

"How much?"

"Thousands."

"Here?"

"Not with me, but—"

"Sorry. You just failed to save your life. Any other good bribes?"

"You don't have to do this!"

"I realize that. I like that it's optional."

"I'll do anything." Dale finally succumbed to tears. Ivan had expected that part to happen a bit sooner.

"Oh, now, Dale, there's no reason to cry. You say you'll do anything. Would you…take a knife and cut out your own stomach?"

"What?"

"If I gave you a knife, would you cut out your own stomach? I wouldn't make you eat it or anything—although, come on, let's be honest, it would be pretty cool to watch somebody eat his own stomach. I'd just make you cut it out. Do that and I'll let you go."

"I can't do that."

"Then don't say shit like 'I'll do anything' if you don't mean it. Would you slash your own throat? Would you jam a stiletto heel in your heart? Would you give yourself brain surgery? I hate it when people throw out offers that they're not prepared to honor."

Dale began to sob.

"Where were you headed?"

"Home."

"To your wife?"

"No."

"Do you have a girlfriend?"

"No."

"Why not?

"I don't know."

"Is it because you're bald?"

"No."

"When did you last get laid?"

"I don't know."

"Liar. Somebody who looks like you knows exactly how long ago it was. Tell me."

"Three weeks."

"Hey, that's not so bad. I thought it would be six months or something like that. Was she a prostitute?"

"No."

"One of those Internet booty calls?"

"Sort of."

"Sort of? Details, please."

Dale sniffed. "We met online, but I'd seen her in person a couple of times."

"Gotcha. Do you need a Kleenex or something? Your nose is all snotty. You wouldn't want your hot Internet sex bunny to see you like this, would you?"

"No."

"Are you going to see her again?"

"No."

"Because you broke up, or because I'm going to murder you?"

"We weren't really together."

"She was a hooker, wasn't she?"

"I said no."

"Was she a skank?"

"No."

"Do you love her?"

"No."

"Do you love anybody?"

"I don't know."

"Ah, so you *do* love somebody. Well, Dale-without-his-Chip, let's discuss this. Just remember that the longer you keep me engaged in conversation, the longer you get to live, unless I hear a car coming and have to gut you. You never know, the details of your love life might be so fascinating to me that I *forget* to murder you. Wouldn't that be nice? I'd be walking home and think 'Oh, how about that, I completely forgot to murder Dale! How forgetful of me!' You'd enjoy that, right?"

"Yes."

"Who do you love?"

"Karen."

"Does she love you back?"

"No."

"Are you sure?"

"I don't know."

"So who is this darling Karen?"

"Co-worker."

"Is she hot?"

"Yes."

"See, that probably explains why the attraction isn't mutual. Is she blonde, brunette, redhead...?"

"Black hair with red streaks."

"So you're into the dyed hair thing, huh? Nice. Does she have any tattoos?"

"One."

"One that you know about, right?"

"Yes."

"Does Karen live around here?"

Dale vigorously shook his head. "No."

"Are you sure? You're not just saying that to protect her from me?"

"She doesn't live here."

"Well, obviously she doesn't live *here*. The question was whether or not she lives *around* here."

"No."

"I think you're being deceptive. How far away is she? Five minutes? Ten?"

"I don't know."

"It's really not much of a crush if you don't even know where she lives. You should've followed her home. Women love it when you put forth that extra bit of effort. And with enough practice, you can actually build up a resistance to pepper spray. It's true. I love the taste now."

Dale was still crying. It was becoming kind of annoying.

"You know, Dale, we don't have to be enemies. I'm not saying that we should hang out and drink together and become best buddies, but this doesn't have to end in such a negative way. Having a werewolf on your side makes you kind of powerful. Ladies can't resist a nice furry werewolf, if you know what I mean."

"I don't."

"I think you're lying about not knowing where she lives. I think you've done a bit of light stalking in your time. Don't try to deny it—I see that glint of mischief in your eye."

"I never stalked her."

"Okay, fine. No stalking from the Boy Scout. But you know where she lives. We could pay her an unannounced visit. If she doesn't want to let you in, I'll kick the door down. Or, better yet, you just keep the car running while I go get her. We'll take her someplace nice and private. You could do anything you wanted to her. I wouldn't even watch if it made you uncomfortable—I'd just wait in the next room and listen."

"Go to hell."

"Do you understand what's happening here? We're bargaining for your life. That's a pretty major deal. On one hand, I'm threatening you with a horrible death—blood and limbs flying everywhere. That's option one. On the other hand, I'm offering you a completely hedonistic experience, the chance to do whatever you want with your precious little Karen, and she'll be helpless to stop you. Whatever freaky, depraved, brutal, and just plain fun thing you want to do, you can. I might even let you keep her afterward. That's option two. What do you say?"

"I said, go to hell."

"Really? You're not even going to pretend to go along with the plan? I don't know if that's admirable or stupid. Okay, deal's off. Get out of the car."

"What?"

"Get out of the car. Now."

Dale wiped some tears from his eyes. "You're letting me go?"

"No, I'm not letting you go. You had your chance and you turned it down, so get out of the car and run so I can hunt you down and tear you apart. Go on. Shoo."

Dale unfastened his seatbelt. "Please, I—"

"The time for talk is over. You should have at least given me a fake address and then waited for an opportunity to exploit a moment of carelessness. That's what I would've done. Get out. I'm giving you a head start, but I'm not saying how long, so if you're not a complete idiot you'll get moving now."

Dale opened the door, got out of the car, and ran. Ivan watched him go. He was a good runner.

If he didn't have other things to do, Ivan would've made an evening out of this. It was extremely rewarding to chase a victim until he or she literally collapsed from exhaustion. One time he'd even followed a man in an electric wheelchair, just casually circling him in full wolfman form, hoping to go until his battery completely ran out. Unfortunately, they got too close to a populated area and the cripple was screaming too much, so Ivan had to kill him, though he rode around on the wheelchair for a while afterward.

He got out of the car, stretched, then completed his transformation. Became the Beast. It felt exhilarating.

The Beast took off after Dale. Caught up to him in seconds. Swiped his claws across Dale's back, cutting so deep that flesh dangled from all five of his talons.

Dale didn't fall. Impressive.

The Beast let him run a few more steps, watching him bleed, then pounced. Dale hit the ground face-first, letting out a loud grunt and then a muffled shriek.

Poor, unfortunate Dale. If he'd gone along with it, the Beast really would have helped him rape the girl he loved.

He went wild with his claws and teeth, shredding Dale's back. Then he rolled him over and shredded his front side.

He rolled him over again to get any parts he might have missed. There weren't many.

He smiled as he looked down at the remains. A moment later, he frowned.

Shit. Now Dale's clothes were in worse shape than the ones he was wearing.

Chapter Fourteen: Working Things Out

"Is that him?" Lou asked, pointing through the broken windshield.

George applied the brake and leaned forward. "Where?"

"There!"

"The cat?"

"Is that a cat?"

"It's sure as hell not a werewolf."

"It's a possum," said Michele. "They're everywhere."

"I didn't see what it actually was," said Lou. "I just noticed movement."

George muttered something rude. They'd been slowly driving around for more than an hour. They hadn't been able to get a net, but one of the local shops did have a blanket and a travel-sized sewing kit. So Lou had sewn the silver rings onto the blanket in various places, hoping that maybe if they successfully tossed the blanket on top of the werewolf, the silver would keep him from getting out. It was perhaps the furthest thing from a foolproof plan that they'd ever concocted, but unless they drove past a guy with a cart selling hot dogs and silver bullets, their options were limited.

Michele was filing the handle of the silver cross into a point. If by some miracle they were able to get close enough to use it, it would make one hell of a weapon. Sharpened silver cross to the heart. No more werewolf.

"Looks pretty good, don't you think?" asked Michele, holding it up for their inspection.

"Yeah." George was originally going to ask Lou to file the cross and Michele to sew the rings, but he didn't want to seem sexist. They'd both done fine work. "Oh, by the way, Lou, I forgot to complement you on your lovely bracelet. It really brings out the color in your eyes."

"It could be useful."

"That tiny thing? Maybe if we stab him with it a few thousand times."

"It makes me feel better to have it."

"Because it's silver or because it's a cross?"

Lou shrugged. "Both. Don't make fun of me."

"I wouldn't even bother."

"Maybe we should get some wooden stakes, too," said Lou.

"That's vampires."

"I know that, but how do we know that the vampire myths didn't come from werewolves? I completely believe in werewolves now, but I don't believe in vampires yet, so isn't it possible that somebody once killed a werewolf with a wooden stake to the heart and over the centuries the story changed to a vampire?"

"That's actually not a bad point," said George. "Maybe we should get some garlic, too. What else kills monsters?"

Lou shrugged. "Direct sunlight?"

"Well, Lou, I'm afraid we already know his weakness isn't direct sunlight, because we've seen him out in the direct goddamn sun!"

"We're brainstorming! You don't criticize ideas in a brainstorming session!"

"Fine, fine. Write 'direct sunlight' on the chalkboard. Jesus. What else?"

"In *The War of the Worlds*, they defeated the aliens with the common cold."

"Are you kidding me?"

"Yeah. I was just seeing if you would criticize it. How about holy water?"

"Good, good. We'll pick some up if we drive by a church."

"Also," said Michele, "he might need to return to his coffin before sunrise."

"Let me make this very clear," George told her. "Lou gets to behave like a third-grader because he's my partner. You do not have that option. I want serious suggestions."

"I'm so terribly sorry to have offended you," said Michele. "I guess I was just trying to draw attention away from the fact that our brilliant plan to recapture the werewolf is to just drive around hoping he'll be conveniently wandering around. It's a good one. I see why you make the big bucks."

"Better this than sitting around with our thumbs up our rectums waiting for the reinforcements," said George. "You never know, he may be looking for us, too."

"Oh, that's reassuring."

"You seem to think that because we've done arts and crafts together that we're not going to put you in that cage. That line of thinking is incorrect."

"Sorry. I just happen to believe that brainstorming ways to kill vampires in hopes that these ways might also work on werewolves is silly."

"Not just vampires. All monsters."

"Either way, it's silly. We should get more bullets."

"Bullets don't kill it."

"So far they haven't. But a whole shitload of bullets at once might kill it. Or even a grenade."

"Do you own a grenade?"

"No, but I'm not the mobster."

"We're not mobsters. We perform unpleasant tasks that are usually illegal, but we don't have any mafia connections. And when we pack for a trip to break an old man's thumbs, we typically leave the grenades at home."

"Can't you get them? Don't you have connections?"

"Not in the middle of the frickin' swamp! You think I can just call somebody and have them drop a little care package with a parachute out of a plane?"

"They killed King Kong by shooting him off the Empire State Building," said Lou. "We could try that."

"You're an asshole."

«««—»»»

Frank Bateman had gone three weeks and four days without a cigarette. The last one was after he drowned his son's chemistry teacher. Technically, his men had been the ones to tie the rocks around Mr. Amrita's feet and drop him into the lake, but it had bothered Bateman. He liked Mr. Amrita. He seemed to genuinely care about his students and brought an infectious enthusiasm to the subject matter. Hell, after the first parent/teacher conference, Bateman had almost been compelled to break out his old chemistry set from when he was a kid and start mixing some liquids.

But when he'd explained to Mr. Amrita that it was unacceptable for Bryan to get less than a C in the class, apparently the implications of that message had not sunk in properly. That's what Bateman got for trying to be subtle. There was no doubt that Bryan deserved the D, since he was a lazy video game-playing dumb-ass who probably cheated just to get the D, but that wasn't the point. The point was that Bryan needed a halfway decent grade point average if he was going to get into a good school, and Mr. Amrita stood in the way of that.

Bateman had met them out there by the lake and explained the situation. Some would say that it didn't matter, since the poor chemistry teacher was going to die anyway, but Bateman felt that a man always deserved to know why he was being put to death. It was a respect thing. Mr. Amrita had done the usual begging and crying, which was fine. He was scared and Bateman understood that. No shame in fearing death.

He'd waited in the car while Gallows and Bonez (not their real names) rowed Mr. Amrita out to the middle of the lake and dropped him in.

Then he'd gone home and told Bryan that if his chemistry grade wasn't at least a C on his next report card, he'd smash the fucking Xbox to pieces with a sledgehammer and Bryan wouldn't get another one. After that, Bateman went out onto the back porch and had a cigarette.

He'd been nice and relaxed since then, until he got the call that the werewolf was loose.

Very disappointing. And unnerving.

He probably should've used top men for this, but George Orton and Lou Flynn had an excellent reputation, they just happened to be in the area, and they worked cheap. The last part was the most important. Bateman didn't live his current lifestyle by throwing money away, and it should have been a straightforward, easy job. Now he had to pay out the ass for bounty hunters, and the deal with Mr. Dewey was a flat fee arrangement, although Bateman planned to try to renegotiate, considering that the whole idea about the werewolf not transforming except during the full moon was apparently an extreme bit of misinformation.

Dewey was seriously pissed about Ivan getting away, but seriously thrilled with the new discovery about Ivan's power. Bateman was much more pissed than thrilled.

All he could say was, thank Christ they'd put in the chip. They could pinpoint Ivan's location anywhere he went. His arm had healed right up before he regained consciousness, so he didn't even know about it.

Bateman's non-emergency "civilian" cell phone rang. Unknown caller. "Hello?"

"Hello. It's your former captive. I assume you got word that I escaped?"

Bateman sat up straight at his desk. "Where are you?"

"I'm around. Here and there. But I'd like to register a formal complaint about their treatment of me. George in particular was very rude."

"Why are you really calling? I take it you're not going to be nice and turn yourself in?"

"No, but you'd like that, wouldn't you? I need to get a hold of George and he apparently has an unlisted number."

"I'm not giving you shit."

"Seriously? From your point of view, you actually think that putting me in touch with George is a bad thing? I'm all in favor of making things difficult for people, but don't be stubborn just to be stubborn."

"I don't have his number."

"What? Why not?"

"Because we don't do direct contact for jobs like this."

"Well, that's inefficient and stupid. I guess put me in touch with that guy Ricky instead."

«««—»»»

"Aw, crap, that's Ricky," said George. Maybe it would be good news. *Hey, we found the werewolf at the movies. Something with Sandra Bullock. He didn't put up a fight. Everybody's enjoying a good laugh at the whole thing, so you and Lou can just upgrade to first class and bask in luxury on your flight home.* He answered. "Yeah?"

"It's Ricky."

"I know. Any updates?"

"Yeah, I've sort of got your werewolf on a conference call."

"Hello, George." George's grip on the phone tightened at the sound of Ivan's voice. It was a tiny phone, so he relaxed his hand so as not to break it.

"What do you want?"

"World peace. No, scratch that, world destruction. But at the moment I just want to chat."

"So chat. Where are you?"

"I was about to ask you the same thing. Hey, Ricky, did George tell you about how I made him so mad that he opened up the cage?"

"That's not how it happened," George said.

"He opened the cage and dragged me out by my feet. Said my attitude needed adjusting. Lou sat there and watched him."

"I don't care about any of this," said Ricky.

"You should. He was going to beat me bloody. If it weren't for his temper, I'd still be on my way to Tampa."

"Is this why you called?" George asked. "To make shit up?"

"No. Well, that's part of it, but that's not the whole reason. Hey, Ricky, I'm going to need you to drop off the call. Wait, you're the host, so before you do that give me George's number in case we get disconnected."

Ricky gave it to him and then hung up. George was surprised he didn't protest.

"You still there, George?"

"Yeah."

"Oh, good. So I was thinking that we should meet up."

"I'm all in favor of that. But why do you want to do it?"

"Because being a werewolf doesn't pay that well, and I heard you and Lou chatting about the briefcase of drug money, back when you thought that I'd never, ever, ever get out of the cage. I could hide away for a couple of years with sixty-three thousand dollars."

"It's less than that. We spent some on jewelry."

Ivan chuckled. "You're a funny guy, George. So I'm offering you the chance to meet with me, give me the money, and have your problems diminish."

"If we give you the money you'll lock yourself back up in the cage? That doesn't even make sense."

"I didn't say that your problems will go away completely. But if you hand over the cash, I'll disappear. You'll never hear from me again. Otherwise, there will be a bloodbath beyond anything your criminal mind can imagine. I'm talking about dead women and dead babies. Dead grandmas, dead grandpas, dead aunts and uncles, dead moms, dead dads, dead sisters, dead brothers...I will kill and kill and kill, and I will write 'George Orton Was Here' in the blood of every victim."

"The cops will take you down."

"You think so? Maybe. I might only get to murder twenty newborns instead of thirty. I guess if you can only kill twenty babies, why even bother, right?"

"I don't believe you."

"That's fine. I wouldn't believe me, either. But this is a one-time offer. Once the Everglades genocide begins, I'm not going to take a time-out to see if you've changed your mind."

George knew the skinny bastard was up to something, but he also believed that Ivan would make good on his threat. If they were going to drive around looking for him, they might as well meet him somewhere. "All right."

"Superb choice."

"Where should we meet?"

"I'm in Naples. How far away are you?"

George punched in some information on the GPS. "About fifteen minutes."

"I'll call you back in fifteen minutes. Lie to Ricky when he asks what's going on. If I get any kind of feeling that you're not playing fair, the deal is off." He hung up.

Chapter Fifteen: No Time for a Good Plan

"What are we going to do with her?" Lou asked.

"I don't know."

"You could let me go," Michele said, helpfully.

Though they had a perfectly good cage to lock her in, the broken windshield meant that she could scream for help and attract attention. They could gag her, in theory, and you couldn't really see the cage from outside the vehicle, but the broken windshield would also make the van very enticing to thieves if they left it unattended.

They *could* just let her go, except that if they did succeed in recapturing Ivan, they'd wish that Michele wasn't free and blabbing to the police. It was a big loose end they didn't need. But what else could they do? Bring her to the meeting with Ivan and get her killed?

"I didn't run before," she said.

"Actually, you did."

The phone rang. Fifteen minutes on the dot. "Yeah?" George answered.

"Where are you?"

"We're in Naples. Just passed a Seven-Eleven."

"Well, that's helpful. Put the Cotton Mouse Tavern into your magic machine."

George entered the name in the GPS. "Nine minutes away."

"Then be there in seven. Find us a cozy booth."

At 2:47, exactly when the GPS said he'd get there, George pulled into the parking lot of the Cotton Mouse Tavern, a bar with about three billion neon beer signs on the outside, along with an ugly-ass rat-thing on the roof. There were about eleven or twelve other cars in the lot, none of them fine automobiles.

George parked, shut off the engine, and turned to Michele. "This is our chance to negotiate with this psycho. If he thinks we called the cops, he may start killing people. So I'm not going to lock you up, but I'm going to trust that you'll make the right decision and not cause any trouble that will get anybody killed."

"You're letting me go?" Michele asked.

"Yeah. It's either that or drag you in there with us. You want to tag along?"

"Not really."

"You know, it would've been nice to be consulted on this," said Lou. "I'm just saying."

"Where were we going to talk about it?"

"We could've talked about it right in front of her. What was she gonna do?"

"Are you saying that we shouldn't let her go?"

"No, I've been in favor of letting her go from the beginning. I'd just like to be part of these decisions. We're partners. You're not my boss."

"Then I apologize. But for the past nine years our relationship has generally involved me making the decisions and you cheerfully going along with them. Forgive me for not realizing that suddenly you want to—"

"I get to go, right?" Michele asked.

"Yes," said George.

"Yes," Lou added.

"Thank you. I'm not going to get anybody killed, I promise."

George and Lou got out of the van. Lou carried the briefcase, while George carried the folded-up blanket. Michele followed them, then stood there, looking uncertain.

"I guess it's inappropriate to, I don't know, shake your hand or anything like that."

"It *would* be weird," said George.

"Yeah, that's what I thought. I hope you guys catch the werewolf. I'm rooting for you."

"Thanks."

Michele stood there for another moment, then walked away from the van. George watched her go, wondering if he'd just made a huge mistake.

"Did we just mess up?" Lou asked.

"I don't know. What else were we going to do with her? Hobble her?"

"I kind of liked her. Not just because she was hot."

"Well, damn, you should have asked her out on a date. That might keep her from rushing right to the cops."

"Think I'd have a chance?"

"Not in hell."

"Yeah. Oh well. So in addition to letting her go, are we really going to walk in there and talk to the werewolf?"

"Yep."

"This is a decision we're making on purpose, as opposed to, say, getting in that van and driving for the border?"

"Which border?"

"Whatever one is closest. Canada or Mexico. I don't care."

"You don't have to come with me."

"Yeah, I know. But if I didn't, you'd get all killed and stuff, and then I'd have to deal with funeral arrangements, and your financial affairs are probably completely screwed up."

"They're actually very solid. I've even got a living will. It says that if I can't go to the bathroom on my own, pull the plug. That's my minimum standard for quality of life. So if Ivan doesn't kill me but he turns me into a paraplegic, that's what you need to know."

"Got it. Hey, George?"

"Yeah?"

"We're just standing here talking so we don't have to go in there and face this guy, aren't we?"

"That's why *I'm* standing here, at least."

"We should get it over with."

"Yeah."

They walked into the bar. A jukebox played a country/western song that immediately became George's least favorite song of all time. All of the stools at the bar were taken, though a couple of the booths in the back were unoccupied. An extremely intoxicated sixty-year-old slow-danced (even though it was a fast song) with a twenty-one year-old who had one hand in each of his back pockets. The place smelled like smoke, booze, and desperation.

It wasn't even three o'clock in the afternoon on a Wednesday. Didn't these people have lives? Granted, George's line of work didn't stick to a strict nine-to-five schedule, so who was he to judge?

There was no sign of Ivan.

"Now what?" Lou asked.

"I guess we have a seat."

They weaved through the crowd to the booth furthest in the back and sat down on the same bench, giving the werewolf a place to sit across from them. George brushed some ashes and a wet straw wrapper off the table, put a finger in his left ear to block out the hellish noise, then called Ivan.

"Are you there?" Ivan asked.

"Yeah. Where the hell are you?"

"Making sure you're not setting a trap."

"We're not that clever."

"I see that. I'll be there in a minute."

Ivan hung up. George tucked the phone back into his pocket. A waitress who was neither the appropriate age nor the appropriate body shape for her tight t-shirt walked over to their booth. "What can I get you?"

"Coke," said George.

"Diet," said Lou.

The waitress gave them a look of mild disgust, as if they'd announced their intention to simultaneously urinate on the floor, then rolled her eyes and walked away.

"If you end up dying today, you'll wish you at least had a regular Coke," said George.

"If I live, I'm getting back in shape."

"Fair enough."

Right after their drinks arrived, Ivan walked into the bar. He looked confident. Fearless. Arrogant. Like a complete prick.

He walked through the bar and sat down at their booth, then gestured to their drinks. "Didn't you order me anything?"

"No," said George. "Order your own drink."

"Did you bring the money?"

"Yeah."

"Let me see it."

Lou took the briefcase off his lap and set it on the table. He kept it close, as if worried that Ivan might make a sudden grab for it.

Ivan nodded. "Open it."

Lou popped open the lid. He held the briefcase open just long enough to give Ivan a glimpse of the cash inside, then closed it back up.

"Thank you," said Ivan. "Now burn it."

"I beg your pardon?"

"Take out a lighter and set the money on fire. Right now."

"We really aren't in the mood for any more of your games," George said, leaning across the table in what he hoped was a threatening manner. "Now are you here for the cash, or are you here to waste our time?"

"Well, I'm *definitely* not here to waste your time, George. And we all know that this could never be as simple as you bribing me to go away, because I've already proven that I'm not a man of my word. Remember when I kept insisting that I wasn't a werewolf? Good times."

"So what's it going to take for us to make a deal?"

"Oh, there won't be a deal. Just a massacre." Ivan looked around the bar. "How many people do you think are in here? Twenty-five? Thirty?"

"About that."

"How many do you think I can kill? I think I can get eight before this place completely clears out. What's your guess? Higher or lower?"

"We're not playing around, Ivan."

"You're not? Then why are you here? You actually think you're going to stop me?"

"We might."

"Okay, I'll make you another deal. Both of you take your drinks and slowly pour them on your heads, and I'll surrender."

"I'm not kidding," said George. "We're done with the games."

"We've barely even started the games. What have we done so far that qualifies as a game? You chased me around that neighborhood, but that wasn't really a game, that was just a chase. Doesn't count. There weren't any games played at poor Diane's house—personally, I consider that cold-blooded murder. If you thought it was a fun game, well, you're just not a very nice person. Are you two playing games without me?"

George gently kicked Lou under the table. They did not have an elaborate plan to trap Ivan. They'd tried to come up with one, but all of their ideas seemed like plans that could go terribly wrong. So they'd settled for the following scheme: if they decided that they had no other choice, George would give Lou the signal by gently kicking him under the table, at which point they would pull out their guns and pump several rounds into Ivan's face. Hopefully that would surprise and weaken him enough for them to throw the blanket with the silver rings over his head and drag him out to the cage. If he got a chance, Lou would also try to stab him.

It was far from subtle, and it wasn't something they really wanted to do in front of a tavern full of witnesses, but they didn't have much of a choice at this point.

They pulled out their guns.

Moving faster than George would have ever expected possible in his human form, Ivan slid below the table. He was an arrogant prick, but apparently not such an arrogant prick that he hadn't anticipated that he might be in physical danger. As he disappeared from sight, George and Lou shoved their guns underneath the table and squeezed the triggers. They were blind shots but almost point-blank ones.

The table went flying into the air, sailing across the bar and crashing into the dancing couple, knocking them to the ground with what looked like a spatter of blood, though George caught this only in his peripheral vision and couldn't be sure.

He and Lou opened fire on the fully transformed wolfman, pumping bullets into his face and chest. The "shoot and shoot and shoot" portion of their plan was working nicely.

Blood sprayed and Ivan recoiled with each shot, throwing up his clawed hands to defend himself. One shot got him directly under the left eye. Another broke off most of a talon. At least three got him in the heart.

In the background—the faint, distant background—George heard people screaming. Lots of commotion.

Lou's gun ran out of ammunition a couple of seconds before George's did. They both kept pulling the trigger for a few clicks after bullets stopped firing, staring at the blood-soaked monster that stood before them.

Ivan let out a howl of animalistic fury.

No way were they going to get the blanket on him. George didn't even make a move for it. Better not to let Ivan know they had it.

Lou, who'd taken out the silver cross so quickly that George didn't even see him do it, put their emergency backup plan into action: he lunged forward with the weapon, thrusting it toward Ivan's heart.

Ivan swiped at Lou's hand, striking it with such force that George thought he might have snapped Lou's wrist. The cross flew across the bar, striking the wall and falling to the floor. Lou was lucky that the same thing didn't happen to his hand.

Though Lou cried out in pain, it didn't slow him down. He punched Ivan in the chest, hitting him hard enough to create a shower of crimson from Ivan's blood-soaked fur.

George threw his own punch, aiming for Ivan's neck but hitting him in the shoulder. The bastard was solid as hell, and George felt as if his knuckles burst inside his skin. Both George and Lou could throw mean punches, but though their blows clearly hurt Ivan, they didn't knock him down.

God, he wished they'd had silver bullets. What kind of irresponsible scumbag would send you on a trip with a werewolf and not provide silver bullets?

Ivan balled his hand into a fist and punched Lou in the face, sending the big guy crashing into the bench, against the wall, and onto the floor. At least Ivan hadn't tried to kill him—had he used his claws, Lou's face would be splattered across the bar next to the silver cross.

The werewolf slammed its hands against George's arms, pinning them to his sides. He tried to knee Ivan in the groin but though his knee connected with its target it was just a glancing blow that seemed to have no effect. Ivan squeezed George's arms, just until it hurt, and then he…well, he didn't quite *throw* George, but George definitely didn't hurtle across the room of his own volition.

He struck a table, knocking it over and sending a couple of beers flying. He grabbed for a chair to stop his fall, but it toppled along with him and he crashed to the floor, a leg of the chair bashing into his kidney, hard.

The pain was unbelievable. He'd be pissing blood for sure.

He blinked away the wave of dizziness, and took a half-second to survey his surroundings. People were screaming and running for the exit in a mad panic, with at least two of them on the floor being trampled.

The twenty-one year-old knelt on the floor, wailing and cradling her older dance partner in her lap. Blood gushed from a laceration in his forehead and his neck was bent at a hideous angle.

A man behind the bar cocked a shotgun.

Lou, dazed and confused, was trying to get back up.

George wanted to get up as well, but he needed just a few seconds for the worst of the agony to fade before he'd be of any use to anybody. Just a few. Not long.

The man behind the bar pointed the shotgun at Ivan, but Ivan was at the counter before he could shoot. Ivan knocked the barrel of the gun upward just as the man squeezed the trigger, firing into the ceiling, creating a cloud of plaster, and eliciting a scream of pain from above.

Holy shit. Had he actually *shot somebody upstairs*?

Ivan wrenched the shotgun out of the man's hands and shoved the barrel in his face. The man held up his hands in surrender. "Don't shoot!"

The werewolf seemed to consider that. Ivan moved the shotgun barrel away from the man's face, fumbled a bit with his claws on the trigger, then fired into one of the man's upraised hands, blowing it completely off. The man's shriek was silenced a moment later as Ivan tossed the gun aside and swiped off his entire lower jaw.

Before the impact of that could even sink in, Ivan pulled the man forward by the front of his shirt, opened his mouth wide, and then bit down on what remained of the man's face. Ivan spit the bloody chunk onto the counter, let the man's corpse fall, and then turned toward George.

Ivan held up his index finger and wiggled the talon.

The message was clear: *That's one…*

Chapter Sixteen: Massacre at the Cotton Mouse Tavern

George and Lou both got up. Despite the agony, George was able to find his voice, if not his wit. "I'll fuckin' kill you!"

Ivan beckoned. *Bring it on.*

But instead of waiting for George, Ivan ran over to the formerly dancing couple, pouncing on them with his claws and fangs bared. The girl died first, unless the old man was already dead when the werewolf got there, which was entirely possible. Ivan didn't try to be inventive—he just ripped their bodies apart in a matter of seconds, tearing off flesh with such speed and intensity that George couldn't be certain which piece came from which victim.

Lou patted his pocket, then frantically looked around on the floor, presumably for his switchblade. Had he lost it in the fall? Lou quickly gave up the search and went for the cross.

About half of the patrons had made it out of the bar already, but there was a bottleneck at the doorway. Panicked drunk people shoving each other was not conducive to an efficient exit.

An overweight bearded man pushed a skinny girl out of the way, his hand cupping one of her small breasts in the process. She bashed a beer bottle against the side of his head, spraying glass and Bud Light everywhere. The bearded man fell, taking the two people in front of him down with him.

Another man, clean-shaven, his eyes wide with terror, had apparently retained his sense of chivalry and pulled a blonde woman out of the way before she could get trampled.

It didn't surprise George that Ivan went after the nice guy.

Ivan leapt off the two mangled dancer corpses, knocked another man out of the way, and grabbed the nice guy's arm. As the guy cried out and tried to pull away, Ivan gave it a brutal yank. It wasn't enough to rip off the limb, but it was clearly enough to pop his arm out of its socket.

With the second yank, the skin split. The arm remained attached. A third yank, and the arm came most of the way off. Ivan quickly finished the job with his teeth.

Lou crawled around on the floor, searching unsuccessfully for the cross.

George slammed his foot down on the wooden chair, breaking off the leg that had bashed his kidney and creating a makeshift wooden stake. Even if it didn't kill Ivan, they might be able to injure him enough to finally subdue the creature.

Ivan shoved the one-armed nice guy toward George. The guy, spurting blood and almost completely drained of color, dropped to the floor before he could get in George's way. George leapt over him, tried to fake a swing to the left, but took a werewolf fist to the face and stumbled backwards, almost but not quite losing his footing.

Ivan snarled and tossed the severed arm aside. There was so much gore in his fur that it was hard to say for certain, but his gunshot wounds no longer seemed to be bleeding.

Most of the bar patrons had finally made their way out of the place. Aside from the bearded guy and the two people on the floor with him, only a man and woman who looked to be in their early twenties remained at the doorway. They were presumably a romantic couple, since they were dressed in matching cutesy light green shirts.

One of the people who'd been trampled had apparently made it outside to safety. The other, a middle-aged lady with pigtails, lay dead on the floor, her body broken and bloody.

Ivan ran to the doorway, bashed the cutesy man out of the way with his right hand, then grabbed the cutesy woman with his left. Instead of killing her, he tossed her over with her lover, then pulled the door closed.

The bearded guy scrambled away, his ass dragging along the floor as he did a clumsy version of a crab-walk. George ran at Ivan again, focusing all of his attention on Ivan's heart, but the werewolf knocked him aside once more. George's landing was not gentle.

As he got up, he noticed two other people in the bar, hiding underneath the table of a booth. Assuming the nice guy with one arm hadn't bled to death yet, that left eight potential victims in there, not counting George and Lou. Ivan might very well make his body count goal.

George caught a glimpse of silver as Lou found the cross and quickly palmed it. Lou got up and wobbled a bit on shaky legs, but didn't fall.

"Hey, Ivan!" George shouted. "You hit like a ferret!"

Ivan let out what was clearly meant to be a derisive laugh. George tried to think of an animal comparison more rage inducing than "ferret" but nothing immediately came to mind.

George had hoped that Ivan might change back just to offer up a snappy retort, but he didn't. Instead, he looked around the bar, still smiling, as if joining George in tallying up his potential victims.

Ivan's ear perked up a bit as he noticed the people under the table in the booth.

The man and woman who were dressed alike grabbed each other's hand and sprinted away from Ivan, running toward a plate-glass window covered by neon signs. Ivan followed, taking down the man before they made it halfway across the bar. The woman bellowed and desperately pulled on her boyfriend or husband's arm, refusing to let go of him even as Ivan slashed at his legs and back.

"Just leave me!" the man shouted, gurgling the words. George winced as Ivan ripped out a particularly meaty strip of his leg, exposing bone.

George picked up another chair.

Lou moved cautiously toward the werewolf, not revealing the cross. His breathing was as heavy as if he'd run a marathon and George hoped that he wouldn't have a massive heart attack before he made it to Ivan.

Ivan extended all ten of his fingers, then slammed his claws deep into the man's neck all at once. The woman finally let go of her lover and ran for the window again.

The two people who'd been knocked down by the bearded guy—another man and woman, also in their twenties, but hopefully not a couple considering their complete lack of interest in assisting each other in a moment of crisis—got the door open again. It slammed into the man's shin and he let out a grunt of pain as the woman opened it, but they both rushed through the doorway and out of the bar.

Two more survivors. If this upset Ivan, he didn't show it. The woman who'd just lost her boyfriend or husband ran straight at the window, arms extended.

Lou took another hesitant step toward Ivan. The werewolf's attention was directed toward the running woman, but it was pretty hard for a guy the size of Lou to sneak up on somebody in a wide-open bar.

George threw the chair as hard as he possibly could, so hard that he thought he might have injured his shoulder. His intent was for the chair to smash directly into Ivan's head, distracting him from the woman long enough for her to escape, during which time George would figure out how to deal with a murderous werewolf whose attention was now on him. The chair didn't hit Ivan's head, but it smashed into his side with enough force to stop him in his tracks.

The woman struck the window. The glass did not shatter. She bounced off, careened to the side, and doubled over in pain.

Taking advantage of Ivan's distraction, Lou picked up his pace and held the cross like a dagger. George hurriedly grabbed another chair to keep Ivan's attention focused on him.

"Did that hurt, you hairy bitch? Did you get a boo-boo?"

Lou was only a couple of steps away from being able to slam the cross into his back. They were, of course, assuming that the silver cross would do a lot more damage than just stabbing him with a regular old sharpened object, and if that turned out not to be the case, Lou was in a lot of danger.

"C'mon, Ivan, you feeble little fuck! We kicked your butt back in the other house, and we'll kick it here!"

Without taking his eyes off George, Ivan suddenly reached out his arm, grabbing Lou by the throat.

Shit...

George was about to rush him, but Ivan held up a hand, palm-out. *Don't move.* George decided not to move.

Ivan's head transformed back into its human form. Though it should have looked ridiculous to have a big strong wolfman with a human head, George found nothing even remotely comical about his appearance. The bloody bullet holes in his face helped with the lack of amusement value.

"Hey, George, remember when I had my claws on *your* throat?"

Just had to talk, didn't you? Couldn't resist a little mockery.

"I remember."

"I let you live. Lou's fucked."

Lou slammed the cross into Ivan's arm, burying it about an inch deep. Ivan screamed and released his grip on Lou's neck. His face began to switch between human and wolf features the way it had after George kicked him in the nuts.

Now!

George moved forward. No other chairs were immediately available, so he'd just use his goddamn fists.

Ivan ripped the cross out of his arm, which sizzled at the wound. He flung the cross at the bearded guy, who had almost made it to the open doorway. It struck the back of his head with skull-shattering velocity, and the bearded guy slumped forward, clutching at the immense gash.

The woman kicked the window. This time, her foot broke through.

George threw a punch, aiming for Ivan's kidneys. Let him find out how it felt. The punch connected and Ivan howled.

Ivan spun around and grabbed George. Using both hands, he threw George into Lou, and the two of them stumbled across the bar and hit the floor for the umpteenth time that evening.

The woman kicked at the glass twice more, opening up a hole big enough to escape through. She ducked through the new exit, then lost her balance as Ivan grabbed her by the ankle, digging his claws in deep. She fell onto the glass, breaking through it most of the way to the floor. Ivan dragged her back inside over the jagged remains. Her screaming and flailing around made things much worse for her.

George cringed. Where the hell were the cops?

The cross wound had stopped sizzling and bleeding. Ivan stepped on the woman's legs, grabbed a handful of her long black hair, and jerked her head back, snapping her neck.

The one-armed man lay on the floor and groaned.

The bearded guy wasn't moving. He was either unconscious or dead. Probably dead. Six for Ivan, if you didn't count the trampled woman or the person who'd been shot upstairs.

That only left the couple underneath the table, George, and Lou.

Ivan held up five clawed fingers on one hand and his index finger on the other hand. Then he pointed to the man and woman under the table and held up two more.

They screamed as the werewolf strode over to them. Ivan picked up the table, exposing them completely, then threw it at the bearded guy. Direct hit. Even if he wasn't dead now, he'd never walk, speak, or eat solid food again.

The man and woman cowered against the wall, hands in front of their faces as if that would stave off Ivan's attack.

Ivan transformed his head back again, then beckoned to the man. "Come here."

"No!"

"Here's my offer," Ivan said, speaking calmly although he was breathing heavily. "You get up, walk over here, and let me gouge your eyes out, and I'll let your woman live. Otherwise I'm going to jump over there and rip you both to shreds."

George picked up another chair.

Ivan looked back at him. "Are you fucking kidding me? *Enough* with the chairs, George! I'm tired of punching you around."

"Really? I'm sure not tired of hitting you with chairs."

"Hilarious. You're a funny guy, George. But I'm not talking to you right now." Ivan looked back at the couple. "It's a straightforward deal, sir. Walk over here, let me poke out your eyes, and she goes free. I swear. How about it?"

The man stood up. Without hesitation and ignoring the woman's horrified wail, he walked right up to Ivan, fists clenched and head held high.

"Holy shit! You actually did it!" Ivan looked around the bar as if to confirm that everybody had seen the same thing. "I can't believe it! I am absolutely flabbergasted! You must love the absolute shit out of her, huh?"

The man nodded. "Yes, I do."

"Well, I—I honestly don't know how to react to this. I kind of figured that I'd just be ripping you two apart." Ivan gestured to the woman. "Go. Get out through the broken window."

"Please don't hurt him," she said, getting to her feet. Sobbing, she ducked underneath the broken pane of glass and left the bar.

"I'm stunned," said Ivan. "Just stunned. Wow. I don't know if you're brave or a complete idiot. You know what? I don't even feel like gouging your eyes out after that. You deserve to keep them. Go follow your woman and get some mega-pussy tonight."

The man turned and hurried out through the broken window. Ivan let him go.

"Can you believe that?" Ivan asked George. "He was going to let me do it. Would you do that for your girlfriend?"

"I don't have one."

"And it's probably because you wouldn't give up your eyes for her. So what's my count? Six…" Ivan walked over to the nice guy with one arm, and slammed his foot down on his head, several times. "Seven. I could cheat and count the poor bitch who got crunched at the door, but I like to play fair."

"So you're one short," George said.

"Yeah. What a disappointment. Do you think anybody else will be dumb enough to come inside?"

"The cops."

"Cops count. I could definitely make it to eight if the cops show up. But that would involve more waiting around, and I can't help but feel that there's another way to achieve my goal. Hmmmm. Let me think…"

George looked at Lou. They exchanged a knowing glance, and then both rushed Ivan at the same time. The "bash him with a chair" tactic hadn't been entirely successful thus far, but if they *both* got in good hits simultaneously…

Ivan leapt at George, jumping into the air like a wolf going for the kill. George didn't even get to swing the chair before Ivan landed on him, knocking him to the floor yet another time. He had an instant to think that counting the number of times he hit the floor would make a good drinking game, and then his head struck the floor and nothing mattered anymore.

CHAPTER SEVENTEEN: A Bad Time To Be Lou

Considering the circumstances, Lou thought he'd done a pretty good job of keeping himself together. He wanted to yell and cry and run around in circles and let the dark specter of madness completely engulf his ass. He could use a little bit of insanity right now to keep him from focusing so much on the current reality.

Unfortunately, either he was locked away in a padded cell having hallucinations about a bloody werewolf massacre at the Cotton Mouse Tavern, or he was entirely sane. If this was a hallucination, he could just sit back, relax, and enjoy his tranquilizers and lobotomy, but for now he had to assume that this was all real, and so he had to act.

Lou was not a man who liked to lose. If he wasted fifty bucks at the slots, he'd be pissed about it for hours. The big difference between himself and George was that Lou would ultimately decide that losing fifty dollars was punishment enough and walk away, whereas George would keep pumping coins into the machine hoping to win enough to make up his losses. And, usually, George would leave with enough cash to pay for the hotel, meals, and a topless show, whereas Lou would be out his fifty bucks and fuming.

But there was no "win" this time. Maybe they'd recapture Ivan, and maybe they'd kill him, but there was no happy ending in store for anybody here.

As George hit his head on the floor, with that werewolf bastard on top of him, Lou saw a sudden flash of his partner's funeral. Closed-casket, of course. Maybe a separate coffin for each piece.

You know, George, Lou had said once, *when I die, I don't want a funeral. I don't want people sitting in a church crying over my dead body. I just want a few of my close friends to get together and drink to my memory. Maybe share some stories.*

Fuck that, George had replied. *When I die, I want people to be depressed. I want them to wear black and I want a thunderstorm and I want people to throw themselves on the casket. Why should people be happy I'm dead?*

I don't want them to be necessarily happy that I'm dead. They just don't have to be all bummed out about it. They should remember the good times.

Well, Lou, I hate to break it to you, but when you die, I'm going to be sad.

Lou figured that the best way to save his partner's life was to jam the cross right into the back of Ivan's neck, deep enough that it popped out the other side, and watch him claw at it desperately as his throat dissolved.

Lou would probably fail at that. Especially since he didn't have the cross anymore, and the cross wasn't long enough to go all the way through Ivan's neck anyway. He'd also somehow lost his sterling silver switchblade when Ivan threw him across the bar.

So he had to resort to the second best way to save George's life: lure the werewolf away from him.

He ran past Ivan, shouting "Ferret! Ferret! Ferret!" The insult was just as lame when he shouted it as when George used it, but hopefully the sheer inanity of it would piss Ivan off enough to make him follow.

Ivan did.

Lou ran behind the bar counter. There was a swinging door that he assumed led to a kitchen, but first he grabbed the nearest object, a bottle of white wine, spun around, and flung it at Ivan. It shattered against Ivan's chest, sending glass spraying back at Lou. He grabbed a second bottle and threw it, hitting Ivan in his now-wolfman face. The bottle bounced off and broke in half against the counter. The third bottle also hit Ivan in the face and smashed against his teeth.

Lou pushed through the swinging door, which did indeed lead to a small filthy kitchen. He kicked the door back as hard as he could, and it bashed into the werewolf, knocking him against the counter. Lou heard the crash of a few more bottles falling to the floor.

The door flew open with enough force to knock it halfway off its hinges.

Lou decided to attack before Ivan could leap at him. He rushed forward just as Ivan made the jump, colliding with the werewolf's stomach. The werewolf was stronger. Lou let out a loud grunt as Ivan knocked him back against the metal sink.

Lou thrust his hand into the warm soapy water, grabbed the handle of a frying pan, and smacked it into Ivan's face with a loud clang. Ivan growled and spit out a bloody fang.

Lou took another swing. This time Ivan ducked out of the way. Ivan grabbed Lou's wrist, squeezed hard, and then bashed the frying pan against Lou's face using Lou's own hand. Lou released his grip and the pan clattered to the floor.

Some blood trickled from Lou's nostrils.

Ivan grabbed the back of Lou's neck and shoved his head into the sink. Lou's forehead struck a pot or some other large metal object as he plunged into the water.

He braced his hands against the edge of the sink and tried to push himself up again, but Ivan was too strong. Holding his breath and closing his eyes against the sting of the soapy water, Lou pushed as hard as he could.

His head popped out of the water for an instant, not long enough to gasp for air. Ivan shoved him back down, and Lou hit the same fucking pot. At least he knew his head was durable.

He stomped his feet several times, trying to crunch one of Ivan's paws underneath his shoe, but didn't even hit a toe.

Lou put his hand back in the water and fished around for a moment. He found a fork. He grabbed it by the handle, then slammed it over his shoulder, hoping to strike lycanthrope.

He hit something.

Ivan's grip on his neck loosened. Lou pulled his head out of the water and gasped for breath.

He spun around. The tines of the fork were buried halfway into Ivan's upper right arm. Ivan yanked out the fork and tossed it aside. Too bad it wasn't silver. Then, in a motion like flicking a bug off a table, Ivan slashed his talon across Lou's cheek. He immediately repeated the gesture with his other talon, giving Lou matching cuts.

Ivan grabbed the front of Lou's shirt, then threw him away from the sink. He almost collided with the grill, which was still on. A pair of burnt hamburgers sizzled on it. Clearly the cook had been smart and gotten the hell out of there.

The werewolf pounced. Lou tried to move out of the way but was unsuccessful, and a quick contortion later he found himself in the same predicament as before, except that instead of his face being shoved into warm dishwater, it was being shoved toward a hot grill.

He tried to elbow Ivan in the gut but couldn't get sufficient leverage. His foot slipped out from under him, and his chin came down on the surface of the grill with a thump and a hiss.

He yelped and lifted his head. The searing pain gave him an extra burst of adrenaline, and he wriggled his way out of Ivan's grip, just in time for Ivan to give him another pair of matching cheek slashes.

Now the son of a bitch was just trying to humiliate him.

Lou punched him in the face—a solid uppercut that connected with Ivan's jaw. His teeth snapped shut on his tongue. The werewolf howled.

Ivan swiped at Lou's chest, a ferocious swing that was obviously *not* meant to humiliate Lou but rather disembowel him. It missed. Not by much. The second swipe missed by even less.

A thick rope of bloody drool dangled from Ivan's lower jaw. He snarled, then attacked.

Lou screamed. It wasn't something he would've ever expected to do. He shouted a lot, but he'd never screamed in his life.

He bashed into the grill again as Ivan struck him. Rational thought disappeared. Lou thrashed wildly, trying to use his own fingers as claws to lash out at Ivan's eyes. He slid to the floor, screaming some more as Ivan slashed at his arms and legs and chest.

He hit Ivan, several times, but the pain kept coming. He punched and clawed and kicked in blind panic, thinking that this might be the end because suddenly time seemed to be creeping along as if in a weird dream and he could see a few droplets of his own blood flying into the air in slow motion, almost a beautiful thing, yet his life wasn't flashing before his eyes, and wasn't that supposed to happen when you were moments away from death?

Time sped up with a jolt.

Ivan howled and clutched at his eye. Lou had gotten the son of a bitch. Incredible.

Lou scooted away, forcing himself not to completely lose it over the sight of so much of his own blood. Ivan removed his hand from his eye. Instead of the gooey orb dripping jelly that Lou hoped for, his eye was just dark red. Not punctured. Not a fight-ending injury by any stretch of the imagination.

Lou got up, elated that he wasn't hurt badly enough to simply lie bleeding to death on the kitchen floor, and rushed for the food preparation counter. He saw a flash of metal. A meat cleaver.

He grabbed the meat cleaver and slammed it into Ivan's chest. The blade sunk in deep. He wrenched it out and slammed it in again. Got him in the heart.

A wave of pain shot through his arm as he pulled the blade out again. Holding the handle of the meat cleaver with both hands and swinging it like a baseball bat, Lou smacked the blade across Ivan's throat, trying to chop his fucking head right off.

Ivan threw his head back and howled as a geyser of blood spewed forth. The cut was so deep that he shouldn't even be *able* to howl, not with severed vocal chords.

Lou swung again but missed as Ivan pushed past him and raced for the swinging door. Lou flung the meat cleaver at him. It sailed through the air, rotating end over end, and hit Ivan in the back—unfortunately, handle-first. The kitchen implement dropped to the floor as Ivan threw open the door, now ripping it completely off its hinges, and rushed back into the main part of the bar.

Lou heard a cry of "Shit!" that obviously came from George.

He glanced down at himself and wished he hadn't. Ivan had gotten him *good* in a couple of places, and there were several other small gouges that would have, at another time, ruined his entire day. But he'd worry about that later.

He ran out into the main tavern area just as George tossed the silver ring-lined blanket over Ivan. George struggled to get the blanket completely over him, but could only get it over his head, and as Ivan violently thrashed, even that bit of progress looked extremely temporary.

"Lou, get over here, you lazy fuck!" George shouted.

Moving as quickly as he could, which wasn't all that fast anymore, Lou ran over to help his partner. George now had Ivan in a bear hug from behind and clutched the blanket tightly in his fists, and though he wasn't coming close to holding Ivan in place, he did seem to be successfully steering the werewolf in an awkward stumble toward the exit.

The blanket was already soaked red.

Lou reached them just as the werewolf changed direction, claws slashing through the air as he struggled to get free. Lou stuck out his foot. Ivan lost his balance and fell to the floor, with George landing on top of him.

He'd actually tripped a werewolf. Holy shit. Something new to add to his resume.

"He's getting loose!" George shouted. "Don't let him get away!"

Lou kicked Ivan in the head, as hard as he possibly could.

"Do it again! Do it again!"

Lou did it again. He wasn't sure if it was the slit throat or the silver rings or both, but Ivan did seem to be legitimately weakened. A few stomps on his head and they might be able to drag him back out to the van and—

"Get away from it!"

Two cops stood at the broken window, guns raised. Young guys, one black, one white, and both quite visibly horrified by the grisly and absurd scene in front of them. Mutilated corpses, two blood-covered thugs, and a thrashing werewolf with a blanket over its head.

"Everything's okay!" George insisted.

"Get away from it!" the white cop repeated.

Are the cops seriously trying to save Ivan? Lou wondered, incredulous. Then he realized that, no, they were trying to save him and George from the homicidal beast.

"We can't do that! But you could help us hold him down!"

The cops exchanged an uncertain glance. Lou didn't blame them. He sure as hell wouldn't come through that window if he were them.

"Get away!" said the black cop. "We'll shoot it!"

"Bullets don't hurt it!"

"Of course bullets hurt it!"

Lou vigorously shook his head. "No, they don't!"

Ivan pushed himself up and almost got out from underneath George, but they managed to keep him on the floor. The blanket was dripping. George punched him in the back of the head. "Shouldn't he be out of goddamn blood by now?"

The cops remained at the window. The white one put a walkie-talkie to his mouth. "Dispatch, where the hell is that backup?"

Lou felt the werewolf slipping away. *Oh, crap, we're losing him...we're losing him...*

"Get over here and help us!" Lou shouted to the cops. At this point, getting arrested was a minor concern. If the cops dragged Ivan away, Lou and George might be able to take advantage of the distraction to get away and live out the rest of their years as hermits.

The cops, apparently not being complete idiots, remained where they were.

Ivan shook his head from side to side, shaking off most of the blanket. Lou felt himself start to panic. They definitely weren't going to be able to hold him. "Throw me some handcuffs!" Did cops use handcuffs anymore, or was it just those plastic things?

George angrily reached into his pocket, pulled out his keys, and slammed one deep into the back of Ivan's neck. "Stop moving, damn it!"

Ivan stood up part of the way. George remained clamped onto his back for about a second, as if going for a piggyback ride, and then Ivan bucked him off. Lou grabbed for him again and got the werewolf's arm, but it popped out of his grasp.

The cops opened fire as the werewolf, George's keys still dangling from the back of his neck, rushed at them. Ivan flinched with each shot but didn't fall. He broke more glass as he went through the window and pushed through the cops, swiping with both hands simultaneously. Both cops went down, screaming.

They really should have believed Lou about the whole bullets thing.

Instead of finishing them off, though, Ivan left their fallen bodies and ran away.

Chapter Eighteen: Bloodbath Aftermath

Michele was having difficulty reconciling her previous beliefs about tornado chasers with her current plan not to run away.

Tornado chasers were idiots. Why would you ever go *toward* the storm? Why would you stand outside in a hurricane doing a weather report? Why would you take pictures in a war zone while mortar shells exploded all around you? She'd spent many hours vocally criticizing this kind of stupidity while she watched the news on television, even if nobody else was around to hear. Stay out of the shark tank if you don't want to disappear in a cloud of blood. Don't wrestle the alligator and be surprised when you lose a hand.

So when George and Lou set her free, she should have just run as far away from this whole mess as she could. Let her role in this little drama come to an anticlimactic conclusion. Find a hospital, get better bandages for her shoulder, finish off a bottle of wine to celebrate her survival, finish off a second bottle of wine to celebrate the fact that she wasn't pregnant, and happily pass out.

Instead, she stood at the edge of the parking lot and watched George and Lou walk into the bar.

Was Ivan already inside? Probably not. He had to suspect that George and Lou might burst in there with a dozen cops, so he'd want them to get settled first, give himself a chance to scope things out.

A few minutes later, her theory was proven correct (or Ivan was just running late) as she hid behind a pickup truck and watched him pull into the parking lot. Where had he gotten a car? She prayed there wasn't a fresh corpse in the trunk.

Ivan drove around the building a couple of times, slowly, then parked at the closest space to the front entrance.

She crept a little closer to the building as Ivan walked inside.

This was still her story, her cash cow, and she needed to know how it all turned out. *"Oh, yeah, I was terrified,"* she'd tell the person who was hired to ghostwrite her book. *"I'd never been so scared in my life. Every bit of common sense I had, every piece of knowledge I'd acquired in my entire life was screaming at me to get out of there, but I just couldn't."*

The ghostwriter would nod as if she understood completely. Her expression would say *You were so very brave* without having to speak the words, which would be ass-kissing. *"And is that when you called the police?"*

"Yes. I mean, there was a dangerous werewolf in the building, so I had to let the authorities know. I couldn't let more innocent people get hurt."

"And you'd have a better story if the cops actually caught him or shot him down, right?"

"You said that, not me."

"Do you want to say it in the book?"

"No. That sounds kind of bad."

Michele didn't have her cell phone or any change, but there was a pay phone next to the entrance, and she was pretty sure you didn't need the fifty cents to make an emergency call. She hurried over to the phone, picked up the receiver, and cursed. The entire mouthpiece was gone, exposing a few broken wires.

She placed it to her ear anyway. They'd still trace a 911 call even if nobody said anything.

No dial tone.

Okay, this was a pretty big problem.

Now what? She certainly wasn't going to go inside the Cotton Mouse Tavern and ask if she could use their phone.

A large, burly man walked out of the bar, looking annoyed and angry, as if he'd just had a heated argument. "Sir?" she said, gently touching his arm.

His eyes lit up, but then he frowned as he noticed her bandaged-up shoulder and bloody clothes. "Yes?"

"Can I borrow your cell phone? It's an emergency."

"What kind of emergency?"

"I need to call the police. A man just went in there with a gun and I think he's going to start shooting."

"Is this a scam?"

"No, I swear."

"I can't give you my phone."

"Then could you call the police for me?"

"Sure, sure." He took out a cell phone and punched in three digits. "You say a guy with a gun?"

"Yes."

"Should we be standing here?"

"Probably not."

They began to quickly walk away from the building. The man touched a button on his phone, and the speaker came on. "911, what is your emergency?" The man kept the phone in his hand, but held it toward Michele so she could talk.

"Hi," she said. "I think there's going to be some trouble…"

《《《—》》》

Ivan didn't look back at the cops after he savaged them. They were both probably still alive, but they'd be needing some serious skin grafts. Fuckers. He hoped they spent the rest of their lives being shunned as disfigured freaks.

The pain was almost unbearable. Yeah, he was a fast healer, but he'd been shot, sliced, punched, stabbed, and kicked. Bullets didn't just pop out of his body when he healed—he had to dig them out, and that was not a pleasant process. He didn't mind getting mangled every once in a while, but Jesus Christ, this was insane.

He reached back and tugged the car keys out of his neck. Slit throat, stabbed neck—he was lucky he hadn't been decapitated. When he'd fully recovered he'd hunt George and Lou down and make them die ever so slowly, but for now, he just needed to get away. Revenge could wait. A dish best served cold and all that shit.

Or…not.

He saw their black van. If he couldn't kill them, he could at least steal their van using the keys they'd stabbed him with. *That* would keep them nicely frustrated until he came back into their lives.

He transformed back into his human form as he reached the driver's side door and hurriedly unlocked it, blood gushing down onto his hands as he did so. He got inside, slammed the door shut, and started the engine.

Shit. He was really bleeding bad. He didn't think he could die from this, but he'd never sustained these kinds of injuries. He'd gotten cocky again. Time for that to stop.

He sped off, but then managed a smile. It didn't matter how badly he was hurt, the sight of George and Lou running after their stolen van was fucking hilarious.

«««—»»»

"He stole our van!" Lou shouted, as they ran after Ivan in a rather pathetic half-run, half-limp.

"I know!"

"A werewolf just stole our van!"

"I know, Lou!"

"With the keys you stabbed him with!"

"I can see! I still have my eyes!"

"So now what do we do?"

"We get the hell out of here before more cops show up!"

"We should have just waited for the reinforcements."

"Well, freakin' duh! How'd you figure that out? The slaughtered corpses? Your eight thousand werewolf wounds? The fact that he just drove away in our goddamn van?"

"It's not even our van."

"I realize that! Believe it or not, I'm not a complete ignoramus and I *am* aware of the severity of the situation!"

Lou stopped running. "I bet you're not."

"What do you mean?"

"We left the briefcase of cash in the bar."

"Fuck!"

"Yeah."

"Oh, that is *bullshit!*"

"What do we do?"

"So, what, you're back to being cool with me making decisions again?"

"George, we don't have time for this!"

"I know, I know. You keep running. Find us a car that we can hotwire. I'll run back in and get it. It'll only take a minute."

"All right. Don't get killed."

"I'll try." George turned and ran back to the bar. He couldn't believe how badly things were working out for him today. Next there'd probably be some kind of earthquake that split open the earth and swallowed him up, dropping him right into Hell, which might be preferable to dealing with Ivan.

Oh, how he hated that werewolf. Despised him. Loathed him. Abhorred him. He could take every synonym in the thesaurus, plus all of their foreign language equivalents, including dead languages that only a couple of scholars in the world still knew how to translate, and it wouldn't come close to expressing just how deeply he hated that man-beast.

From now on, every old man whose thumbs he broke would have Ivan's face superimposed over his own. And George expected to start doing some mad cackling in the near future.

The black cop lay on the ground, walkie-talkie to his lips. "Officer down..." he said, voice weak. The white cop looked at George with pleading eyes, which was one of the only facial features that was still recognizable. George was not a cop-hater—he had no problem with them or their duties as long as they weren't specifically coming after him—and he felt horrible. What if the guy had kids? Still, there was no time to offer a moment of comfort. He hurried past the cops and went back into the bar.

He could hear somebody sobbing upstairs. He wondered how badly the woman up there had been hurt when she got shot.

George ran to the booth where they'd sat in slightly happier times. He stepped on some viscera but, thankfully, did not slip on it.

He picked up the suitcase, the side of which was stained with werewolf blood. He quickly glanced around for the guns they'd dropped, or the sharpened cross, or Lou's switchblade, but didn't immediately see them and he could hear sirens in the distance, so he ran back out of the bar. Not stepping in blood was a challenge.

Now they needed a vehicle. George and Lou both knew how to hotwire a car, but it wasn't as easy of a task as it looked in the movies. They couldn't do it here. Hopefully they'd find another car relatively nearby where they could break in without arousing suspicion.

«««—»»»

Ivan was getting blood all over the seat. Good. Another reason for Bateman to hunt down his unfortunate, incompetent thugs. Ivan rubbed his palm on the dashboard, smearing blood everywhere.

No, wait. He didn't want George and Lou to get exterminated by their employer. That would be too painless, even if Bateman used a red-hot poker and a cheese grater. And besides, Ivan wouldn't get to watch.

He stuck his tongue in the gap from his missing tooth. He'd never lost a fang before. He didn't think it would grow back.

He could turn the van around and—

No.

Let them go. Even if their ghastly fate didn't come at his hands, he had to let this drop. He was too badly injured right now. Werewolves who didn't learn from the past ten minutes were condemned to repeat them.

It was also disappointing that Michele hadn't come with them. He still wanted to sink his teeth into her. He wondered where she'd gone.

Then he laughed out loud. He knew exactly where a person in her position would go. The GPS was still mounted on the dashboard, so he bloodied up the screen and found the nearest hospital. Six miles away. He floored the accelerator and sped off.

«««—»»»

Right after she'd gotten into his car, Michele suddenly decided that the burly guy was a serial killer, and that her arms and legs would turn up in four different counties. Then she decided that he was just kind of weird.

When the chaos inside the tavern began, she'd rolled down the window, leaned out, and vomited onto the pavement. She should've called the police sooner, but she didn't want them to scare Ivan away.

The man had insisted that they drive off. She'd protested. The man had explained that it was his car and that she was welcome to get out. She'd decided that it was time to revert back to her stance on tornado chasers and leave with him.

"Could you take me to the hospital?" she'd asked.

"Of course."

There hadn't been much in the way of conversation during the drive. He kept asking her if she was okay. He kept insisting that she'd be fine. She kept thanking him for going out of his way to help her. He kept saying that it was absolutely no problem.

He pulled right up in front of the emergency room entrance. "Do you want me to come in with you?" he asked.

Michele shook her head. "No, I'll be fine. You've done enough."

She got out of the car, waved goodbye, and shut the door. She caught a flash of movement in the glass door, turned around, and the werewolf pounced upon her. The punch to her stomach knocked the wind out of her.

Michele tried to scream as Ivan tossed her over his shoulder but couldn't find her voice. He ran off, claws digging into her back, and then within a few seconds they were behind George and Lou's black van. The back doors were open.

Ivan tossed her into the cage. She landed on her elbow, crying out in pain. Ivan slammed the cage door shut and transformed back into a human predator.

The man who'd given her a ride was running towards the van, but he'd never make it in time. Michele tried not to cry as Ivan shut the van doors, got back into the driver's seat, and peeled out of the hospital parking lot.

Chapter Nineteen: Grand Theft Auto

There was a small restaurant two buildings away from the Cotton Mouse Tavern with parking in the back. George and Lou walked back there and glanced at the selection of about four cars.

"That one?" George asked, pointing at a rusty orange Chevrolet. It looked like the oldest one, the least likely to have an alarm, and the least likely to give them problems with the hotwiring process. Hopefully it belonged to an employee and not a diner. Less chance of them being discovered, unless somebody took a smoke break.

"Yeah, that works."

They walked over to the car. With the proper tools, either one of them could break into a car with no noise or damage to the vehicle, but at the moment they didn't have tools or time. Lou picked up a rock and smashed the driver's side window. Though the noise seemed like a nuclear blast, there was loud music coming from inside the restaurant and hopefully nobody overheard them.

George got in the car, reached over, and unlocked the passenger side door for Lou. As Lou got in, George immediately looked around the car for a screwdriver or something that could be used like one.

There was plenty of litter in the front seat, but fast food containers and soda cans weren't going to help them. Lou popped open the glove compartment and quickly rifled through the contents. "Nothing here."

George twisted around and searched the back seat. More fast food containers, a few magazines, a Justin Timberlake CD with a cracked jewel case...and a hammer. Good enough. George picked it up off the back seat.

"I can't believe he stole our van," said Lou.

"He'll suffer for it."

"He might not. Karma seems to be on his side."

George pushed his seat back and adjusted his position so he could use the claw end of the hammer to break open the access panel beneath the steering wheel. The seat was a tight fit already, so this would be a lot easier if he could crouch outside the vehicle and lean inside, but that might attract unwanted attention.

"Karma? Why would he have karma?"

"I don't know. I mean, maybe we're being punished for what we've done. You know, hurting people and stuff."

"Give me a break, Lou. A sociopathic werewolf is not going to have better karma than us. You're just having brain problems from all the blood you've lost."

Lou looked horrible. Ivan had really done a number on him. The entire bottom half of his face was stained red from the four cuts on his cheek, and the rest of his body looked like he'd been in a losing battle with a Weedwhacker. Good thing Lou was one tough son of a bitch.

Lou scratched at his chin, which had several blisters on it. "Maybe."

"Is that a burn?"

"Yeah. My face went on a grill."

"How the hell did your face go on a grill?"

"He pushed me on it."

"That's crazy." George strained to pry off the access panel, but it wasn't budging. "Are you going to bleed to death?"

"I'm not sure."

"Let me know if you get close."

"I will."

"I'm glad he didn't kill you."

"Aw, that's sweet," said Lou. "I'm glad he didn't kill you, too."

"Of course, before too much longer, we might be wishing that he killed us both."

"Nah, I think we'll be okay."

"Why would you think something stupid like that?"

"Well, we aren't dead *yet*, are we? We're luckier than a bunch of other people tonight."

George sighed. "Don't remind me. Do you think that was all our fault?"

"Do you think there's any way it *couldn't* be?"

"I was hoping for a guilt loophole."

Lou shook his head. "Nah. I hate to say this, but it's our fault those people got murdered. Ivan did it, but it's still our fault."

"Shit."

"Yeah."

"Why didn't you stab him eight thousand times with the cross on your bracelet?"

"Didn't get the chance."

"I'd suggest that you sharpen it, but then there wouldn't be anything left."

"Bite me. Like I said before, how do we know the 'cross stops vampires' idea didn't come from werewolves? Did you see the way his flesh sizzled? Maybe the cross had as much to do with it as the silver."

"You could be right."

"I bet I am."

"This goddamn access panel won't come off."

"Can I help?"

"How are you going to help? I can barely get in here by myself."

"I was just offering. Don't be rude to somebody who might be bleeding to death."

"I think you'd be talking less if you were really bleeding to death." The corner of the access panel came loose…and then snapped off. "Damn it!"

"Do you want to switch spots?"

"No, just let me do this." George wedged the claw end of the hammer in the crack and began to pull.

"Where do you think Michele went?"

"Straight to the cops."

"You're probably right. At least we didn't get her killed."

"Yeah. I'd be so much more bothered by this situation if we were responsible for eight deaths at the bar instead of seven. At least he didn't make his prediction."

"I'm just going to stop talking to you until you're done with the car."

The access panel broke in half. "Damn it!"

"We should place a bet on how this night ends. Jail, death, or escape?"

"How much are we betting?"

"How much do you want to bet?"

"Twenty bucks."

"Let's do twenty-five."

"Fine," said George, breaking off the rest of the panel. "You pick first."

"I'll pick 'escape.' That way I can enjoy my twenty-five bucks."

"I'll pick jail."

"Good choice. I'm glad to hear that you're not completely cynical."

George leaned forward and tried to duck his head underneath the steering wheel. Not a chance. There simply wasn't room.

"If you pop the trunk, I'll see if I can find a flashlight," said Lou.

"It's not the light." He opened the door. "Keep watch. Let me know if somebody's coming.

"Will do."

George got out of the car and crouched down. There were several wires beneath where the panel had been. The shadow of the steering wheel made it hard to see their colors, but he didn't want to admit to Lou that he really could use a flashlight.

His cell phone rang. "Aw, crap."

"Is it Ricky?"

George pulled the cell phone out of his pocket. The shell was cracked, but it still seemed to be working. He flipped it open. "Yeah, it's him."

"Want me to talk to him?"

"Nah, I've got it." He punched the "talk" button. "Hello?"

"George! Who do you love?"

"Right now I pretty much hate everybody."

Ricky chuckled. "Aw, don't talk like that. I'm about to become your very best friend. Even though you're heterosexual, you're going to want to make sweet love to me. I'll turn down your advances, but you'll be insistent, and finally—"

"Will you get to the point?"

"If you're going to act that way, maybe I won't."

George found the two red wires he needed. If he had a pair of wire strippers, this next part would take a couple of seconds, but he'd have to use the claw hammer, which was going to be a bitch.

"Ricky, just tell me the good news," George said.

"He has good news?" Lou asked.

"Salvation is near. Werewolf Hunters Incorporated—that's not their real name, that's just what I'm calling them—is in the area. I don't think they have an actual name, or if they do nobody told me, but they are armed to the frickin' teeth and that werewolf is *toast*, baby!"

George scraped the claw of the hammer against the first red wire. "They're going to kill it?"

"No. I guess I didn't mean 'toast' like *toast*, y'know, dead. I just meant that they're gonna catch it. Then we'll throw it back in the cage, get it to Dewey, and everybody can kiss and make up."

"Ah."

"You should be a lot happier than you sound. What's wrong? Did you kill the werewolf? Please tell me you didn't kill the werewolf."

"No. But there was a…uh, slaughter."

"What?"

"He murdered a bunch of people."

"How many is a bunch? Fifty?"

"No. Nine or ten."

"Nine or ten? He killed nine or ten people? Aw, shit, the cops are going to be crawling all over this!"

"And he mauled two cops."

"Mother fuck!"

"I'm sorry."

"Y'know, I actually had two minutes of happiness where I thought everything was going to be okay. That's what I was thinking: 'Wow, this was a bad scene for a while, but help is almost there and everything will be fine. I'm sure my good buddies George and Lou won't screw things up any worse than they already have, right? Oh, no, they're professionals, they won't cause me to have to chug down any more Peptol Bismol! It's all wonderful! Life is ducky!'"

The claw hammer was sort of working, but not efficiently, and George was scraping carefully to avoid accidentally cutting the wire in half. "I'm really kind of busy right now," said George.

"Busy? *Busy*? Are you seriously trying to tell me that you're too busy to talk to me?"

"Will you please get to the point?"

"I need you to punch this address into your GPS. Are you ready?"

"We don't have the GPS."

"Why the fuck don't you have the GPS?"

George saw no reason to confess *everything* that had gone wrong. "It broke."

"Well then somehow you need to find 7151 Pegg Avenue. Two G's. It's just a parking lot. The Werewolf Hunters Incorporated are on their way over there, and they need all of the information you've got. Everything you can tell them about his powers so that they don't get screwed like you did."

"All right." The hammer slipped and George cursed.

"They'll move the cage to their own van, and you can ride along while they recapture him."

"Ah."

"What?"

"We lost the cage."

"Explain."

"He stole the van."

"Please tell me I didn't hear you right. Because otherwise I'm going to have a nervous breakdown."

"The werewolf stole the van, okay? What do you want me to say?"

"I want you to say any goddamn thing but 'The werewolf stole the van!' Are you in league with him? Is that what's going on? Have you formed some kind of werewolf alliance?"

"No, we just lost control of the situation."

"You owe me one punch, George. When you come back here, I get to punch you in the stomach, as hard as I can, and you can't hit back. Same thing with Lou. One punch for each of you."

"Fine." George had finally stripped the first wire, and started on the second.

"Somebody's coming," Lou whispered.

George immediately dropped the hammer, got in the car, and shut the door, trying to behave in a casual and completely non-suspicious manner.

"I just can't believe this," said Ricky. "I thought I was going to deliver good news, and we'd laugh, and there'd be some homoerotic banter, and I'd get to go home. You realize that you're basically unemployable at this point, right? Who's going to hire thugs who messed up like this? You'd better get a real social security number, because you're going to be flipping burgers for the rest of your life."

"I understand that." George discretely looked over his shoulder. A well-dressed couple stood by their car, talking.

"And I don't mean that you're going to be flipping burgers at a classy place. You're going to be flipping shit burgers at a rat-infested restaurant where everybody in there is a fat redneck and you have to wear some kind of dumbfuck uniform and a zit-faced teenager barks orders at you all day. That's your future, George!"

"Can we do this later?"

"And you'll probably get food poisoning just from the fumes of the crap you have to cook! You'll have your stomach pumped, and the doctor will say 'Oh, shit, it's cancerous!' But it won't be the good kind of cancer that you can get rid of with chemotherapy, George, it'll be the kind where your whole body decays inside, where your guts turn into this big goopy blob of rot!"

"I think I should hang up now."

"Yeah? Well, I think you should *not*. Are you on your way to 7151 Pegg Avenue yet, you jerk-off?"

"I'm hotwiring a car."

"Oh. Need me to talk you through it?"

"No."

"Did I tell you about when I hotwired this guy's car and drove it into a lake?"

George hung up on him. The couple finally got into their car, started the engine, and backed out of their parking space. As they did so, their car scraped against the one next to it. They stopped.

"You have got to be kidding me," George muttered.

The man got out of the car to inspect the damage. He ran his finger along the spot where the two vehicles had scraped against each other, looked nervously at George and Lou, did a double-take at their grotesque appearance, then hurriedly got back in his car, backed the rest of the way out of the space, and sped away from the restaurant.

George opened the door, returned to his previous position, and began to strip the second red wire. His phone kept ringing, but he ignored it.

"Are they going to exterminate us?" Lou asked.

"It doesn't sound like it."

"Well, that's good."

"Yeah. They want us to tell the reinforcements everything we know about Ivan."

"Should we do it?"

"Tell them about him?"

"No, meet up with them."

"I don't know. Ricky was having a meltdown yelling at me, so I doubt that he was trying to be sneaky about anything. I think we'll get our asses chewed out—and for what it's worth, I'll make sure I take the heat on that—but I don't think there's any reason for them to kill us."

"What about pure anger?"

"What I mean is, we won't give them a reason to kill us. We'll just make sure we don't give up all of our information right away. Keep ourselves needed."

"Are you sure that'll work?"

"Do you want to spend the rest of our lives as fugitives from the law *and* from other criminals?"

"I guess not."

George finished stripping the second wire. He wrapped the two stripped wires together. "I'm going to let you make the final decision on this one. My choices today haven't worked out so well."

"I don't know. We should at least return the case of money, so they'll stop looking for us *eventually*."

The phone had gone to voice mail three times, but Ricky kept calling. George pressed "talk." "Give it a rest, will you, Ricky?"

"What happened to the girl?"

"What girl?"

"Don't be coy with me. The girl you had with you. Did you create a Wikipedia page for our whole operation and drop her off at the CNN studio?"

"The werewolf killed her." George assumed that the lie would be exposed before too long, but for now he just wanted Ricky off his back.

"Well, that's one good thing to come out of this. Didn't I tell you not to hang up on me?"

George stripped a brown wire. Now that he'd gotten some practice with the claw hammer, the process was going more smoothly. "We got disconnected."

"The hell we did. Did you finish the car yet?"

George touched the brown wire to the red wires. The engine roared to life. "Just got it."

"I could've done it in half that time."

"Can I hang up now?"

"Are you going to 7151 Pegg Avenue?"

"Yes."

"Are you going to create any more disasters on your way there?"

"No."

"Then you can hang up. Jerk."

Chapter Twenty: An Unpleasant Conversation

And, just like that, Michele was screwed again.

Honestly, it wasn't all that surprising that Ivan had snatched her, but she would have expected it to be when she was being stupid and hanging around the tavern, not when she was being smart and going to the hospital.

They'd been driving for a few minutes. Ivan hadn't said anything, though she caught him glancing at her in the rear-view mirror several times, and she made no effort to start a conversation. Thus far she'd successfully forced herself not to cry. He could carve the entire Bible into her skin before she'd give him the satisfaction of watching her cry.

She wouldn't beg, either.

There was nothing she could do about the trembling, though.

God, she was scared. She didn't want to die. She considered lying and telling him that she was pregnant, to see if she could appeal to some tiny shred of goodness, but she didn't think he had any. He'd probably *love* it if he thought she was pregnant. She could just hear him: "Oooooh, then I'd better save your belly for last!"

She adjusted her position. Her only solace was that he'd have to open the cage to kill her, at least if he wanted to do it with his teeth and claws, and she'd have an opportunity to escape.

"How are you holding up?" he finally asked.

"I'll be honest with you: not so well."

"Oh, I don't know about that. You can still talk, can't you? A lot of my prey gets so scared they can't even do that."

"Then I'm honored."

"You should be. Mute people just aren't much fun."

"Are you going to kill me?"

"Do you think I should?"

"No."

"Why not? Appeal to my sense of reason."

"I never did anything to you. I tried to help you."

"I don't recall that."

"I guess I was being too subtle, then. We were both victims."

"Correction. I was no victim. I had George and Lou exactly where I wanted them the entire time. There's evidence of this back at the tavern we just left. How many people do you think I killed? Guess."

"Six."

"Higher."

"Twelve."

"Lower."

"Ten."

"Lower."

"Nine."

"This is going to take all night," said Ivan. "I killed seven people. Murdered two people earlier today, for a twenty-four hour total of nine so far. Messed Lou up in a big way. Shredded two cops. Got a lady shot. Let two people go on purpose, and believe me, that's the only reason they're not dead."

"What about George?"

"I didn't kill him yet."

"Why not?"

"He comes later. Got to save the good stuff. Are you impressed by the seven people I killed at the tavern?"

"Sure."

"I think you're just humoring me. I'll bet *you've* never killed nine human beings in a day. I bet you haven't even killed two. Am I right?"

"You're right."

"You know what sucks about the number nine? It's not a monumental number. Nobody celebrates the ninth anniversary of something. It's all about those nice round numbers. That's what people like. If I went around telling everybody that my body count for today was nine, they'd be amazed by my awesomeness, of course, but they'd feel that something was missing. It just wasn't quite at the next level. You can't really have a party for nine. Do you see what I'm saying? Can you think of any possible way for me to fix my little quandary with the whole number thing?"

"Just lie and say you killed ten."

"Hmmmm. I never thought about that. I hate to be deceptive, though. There has to be a better way. Thinking…thinking…thinking…"

"Do you really want people to know about your feat?"

"I like that you called it a feat. I figured you'd feel a little more revulsion than that."

Michele ignored him and tried to steer the conversation back toward reasons he shouldn't kill her. "I could have run away. They let me go."

"You did run away. I found you at the hospital."

"I had a chance before that. I stuck around because I want to tell this story."

"Is that so?"

"Yeah."

"So, what, you want to write *The Dastardly Deeds of Ivan the Werewolf*?"

"Something like that."

"Or maybe *Interview With a Werewolf*. Let Anne Rice sue."

"If you let me go, I'll make you famous."

"If I wanted to be famous, I'd walk onto Oprah's set and transform in front of her cameras. Then I'd rip out her throat. I appreciate your efforts, Michele, but there's really not much you can offer me."

"I disagree."

Ivan smiled. "Well, I mean, there's *that*. You like it wolfy style?"

Michele felt the blood drain from her face, but tried to keep her voice steady. "Why are your aspirations so low?"

"What do you mean?"

"You have this incredible power, something that's so amazing that nobody who hadn't seen it for themselves would ever believe it could be true, and yet you just use it to kill people."

"Killing people is fun. It's better than *not* killing people, I'll tell you that."

"There's so much more you could do."

"Like what? Bring canned food to homeless people? Teach our children about the wonders of volcanoes?"

"You could be a superstar celebrity. How much earning potential do you think a werewolf in the public eye could have?"

"A lot, until somebody put a silver bullet in his heart."

"There are plenty of rich celebrities who a lot of people want to assassinate and they do just fine. With that much money, you could keep yourself safe."

"I've got it! Maybe I could be a superhero!"

"Maybe you could."

"I could be Werewolf Man, and I'd go around biting evildoers. I could wear a furry cape with a big W on it. Oh, man, I never even dreamed I had so much untapped potential. You've opened up a whole new world for me. How can I ever repay you?"

"I'm serious, Ivan."

"Are you trying to become my manager or something?"

"Maybe."

"I think you're talking just to keep yourself alive. I think you're too adorable and innocent to actually want to go into business with a big bad werewolf, who would probably ruin all of his promo ops by going on bloody rampages."

"That's not true."

"You're certainly an opportunist. I admire that. But, again, let's say for the sake of argument that I was interested in your idea. Maybe I looked in the mirror one day and said 'Golly, I've devoted my whole life to evil. How shameful. Woe is me for my poor decisions. I must balance out all of the death and destruction by doing good deeds.'"

"I didn't say they had to be good deeds."

"You mean I should become a supervillain? Now that might be cool."

"You're not taking me seriously."

"What's a good name for a werewolf supervillain?"

"Ivan…"

"What about Wolf Killer? No, wait, that sounds like I'm killing wolves. Death Wolf. Blood Wolf. Ghost Wolf. I'm not really a ghost, but that sounds kind of scary, doesn't it? Beware the evil done by the Ghost Wolf. Oh, hell yeah."

"I'm trying to help you."

"No, but thanks. You really aren't very good at trying to negotiate yourself out of death. The only thing I might need you for is a sweet piece of ass."

"If you try it, I'll rip your dick off."

"There's no need to be crude. You could have just said 'penis.'"

"I'm serious."

"Are you? Do you really think that I'm afraid of you? With all the people I've slaughtered today, you expect me to be worried about you injuring my wee-wee?"

"If it gets anywhere near me, you'll lose it. I promise you that."

"See, now, you almost had me convinced to go along with your idea about cashing in on my werewolf fame, but then you had to go and threaten my genitalia. Rude, rude, rude. And yet, strangely arousing."

"Try it and see what happens."

Ivan laughed. "Relax, sweetheart. There'll be no sexual violence tonight. I'm not the kind of guy who needs to take it by force, if you know what I mean and I think you do. I am going to murder you, though."

Michele clenched her fists. *Don't cry, don't cry, don't cry...*

"Nothing to say to that? Surprising. Do you want to know how it's going to happen?"

"Okay."

"I love how you tried to sound brave when you said that. Here's the plan: I'm going to pull this van over to someplace nice and secluded. I'm going to search through the radio stations until I find some appropriate mood music—hopefully they've got a jazz station around here, but if not, we might go for some classic rock. Then I'm going to walk back there, open the van doors, and then I'm going to stand there and stare at you. You know that creepy feeling you get when somebody is just staring at you, where your skin crawls and you can't concentrate on anything else? You'll have that, except you'll know that as soon as I'm done staring at you, I'm going to kill you. I might stare at you for a minute, I might stare for an hour, but when it's over, I'm going to very slowly unlock the cage."

"You're making a big mistake."

"No, I think I'm making a wise decision. Don't interrupt my scenario. After I open the cage, I'm going to—"

"I don't want to hear it."

"I don't care what you want to hear, little lady. You're going to hear what I want you to hear, and I want you to hear about your upcoming horrible death. If you want to put your hands over your ears and go 'la la la la la' there's not much I can do, but it would be kind of childish."

"There's no reason to kill me."

"I want to. That's a pretty good reason. I mean, if you really think about it, there's no reason to eat a great big chocolate chip cookie dunked in a glass of cold milk, but it's something you'd want to be doing right now, isn't it? You're my cookie. That's what I'll call you from now on. How's it going, Cookie?"

"Fuck you."

"Oh, see, now you're just resorting to expletives. Not cool, Cookie. I guess that means you're done trying to have an intelligent conversation, which in turn means that it's time for you to die. Oh well."

They drove in silence for a few more minutes. At one point Michele had to choke down some vomit, but she still didn't cry. She refused to cry.

Ivan stopped the van and shut off the engine. "Here we are. Looks like you'll be dying in…actually, I don't know the name of this place. It'll be in the obituary, though. Your family will know."

"You don't have to do this."

"That's already been well established. You're not bringing anything new to the table. Offer me something better than the lame observation that I have a choice in the matter. Come on, offer something now. You've got ten seconds. Nine…eight…seven…"

"I can bring you George and Lou."

"No, you can't."

"Yes, I can."

"Did you bond with them? Got some of that Stockholm syndrome going on, huh? Sorry, Michele—I mean, Cookie—but I feel like I have no other choice but to messily kill you."

Michele's mind raced as she tried to think of something to offer him. But she just couldn't concentrate. She was going to die. Oh, God, she was going to die.

Ivan got out of the van. A moment later he opened the back doors. "Miss me?"

Michele scooted to the back of the cage.

"Don't do that. I'll think you don't trust me." Ivan grinned. He ran a hand through his blood-slicked hair. "How does it feel to know that you only have minutes to live? Wait, don't answer that, let me guess…it feels…wait, I can get this…it feels *bad*! Am I right? Do I win?"

Michele didn't respond. If he opened the cage, she'd attack him like a wild animal. She'd probably lose the fight, but she'd go for his eyes with her fingernails and put up a hell of a struggle.

Ivan's grin faded. "You know, I like to joke around a lot, but when it comes right down to it, I'm a pretty serious guy. So let me present you with your options, and I'd like you to truly focus on which one you prefer. The first option is to let me come into that cage after you, at which point I will transform into a wolfman, pin you down, and *ruin* you." He paused, presumably to let that sink in. "In the second option, I won't kill you at all."

"What do I have to do?"

"Just give me your hand."

"No."

"No? I just offered you the chance to stay alive. Don't dismiss it so quickly."

"What are you going to do?"

"It's a surprise. Give me your hand."

Michele shook her head.

"When I said that I was going to ruin you, I didn't mean that in a 'put you out of your misery' way. You will die worse than anybody you've ever read about. You'll be wishing that all I was doing was ripping out your fingernails with my teeth. We are talking about a level of agony that people base religions on. Is that your choice? Because it seems like a bad one."

Don't cry, don't cry, don't cry...

"You really should give me your hand."

"Come in here and get it."

"So let me get this straight. You are choosing a horrible, bloody death where your body parts will be scattered for miles over the option where you live?"

"I'm not giving you my hand."

"I'm not going to *keep* it! Jeez. Okay, I'm going to do something that I never do. I solemnly swear that if you give me your hand, I will not kill you. Not tonight, not ever. That's a promise."

Visions of being chained in his basement as a torture slave for the rest of her life flashed through Michele's mind. "I don't believe you."

"Do you believe me about the horrible bloody death part?"

Michele hesitated. "Yes."

"The 'let you live' part is just as true. I think you should trust me on this one. I'm not sure I can emphasize enough how much better of a deal option two would be for you. Give me your hand."

Michele really did not want to do this...but for some freaky, messed-up reason, she believed Ivan when he said that he wouldn't kill her. Whatever he did to her would be awful, there was no question about that, but she could either trust him or hope that she could beat him when he crawled into the cage.

Better to trust him.

She scooted to the front of the cage.

"You're making a good choice."

Michele took a moment to work up her courage, then slid her right hand through the bars.

Ivan took it.

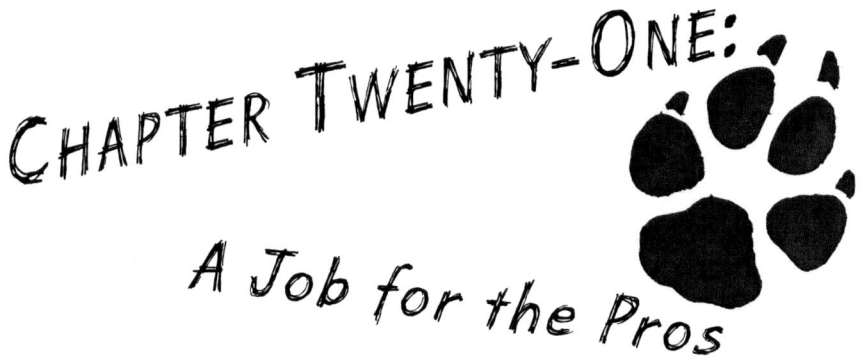

CHAPTER TWENTY-ONE:
A Job for the Pros

"Are you sure you're not going to bleed to death?"

Lou nodded. "I'm getting blood all over this poor guy's car, though."

"It's probably insured."

"This piece of crap? No way. I guarantee you he's only got liability. It would probably cost more to insure it than the trade-in value of the car."

George considered that. "What do you think it'll cost him to get the bloodstains out?"

"A shitload."

"Poor bastard."

"Yeah."

"I guess in the grand scheme of what happened tonight, the guy with a bloody car isn't getting such a bad deal, but I'd still be pissed if I were him."

"Plus, we're not done with the car yet," said Lou. "We could end up wrecking it."

"Yeah, the way things are going a blown-up car is a definite possibility. Although I think the worst is over."

"Well, so did I, until you just now went and jinxed it."

George smiled, but there was no humor in it. "Hey, Lou, is it okay if I get all deep on you?"

"Aw, crap."

"Bear with me. It's my fault that all those people died today."

"No, it's the werewolf's fault. Don't beat yourself up."

"I *should* be beating myself up. This is a really appropriate time for that kind of thing. Look, I know we're basically scumbags. We hurt a lot of people, but it's usually people who deserve it."

165

"Not always."

"That's why I said 'usually.' When we do bad things, we're shaking people for money, breaking a couple of bones, maybe cutting somebody if they need it. We never orphaned kids. We never murdered people just for kicks."

"We didn't, but we still suck."

"I don't want to do this anymore. I want to be a good person."

"May I speak freely?" Lou asked.

"Of course."

"Fuck you, George."

"That's how you respond to me wanting to be a good person?"

"Yep. You don't want to better yourself. You're just a selfish prick. This is about making *you* feel better, not about helping anybody else. If you wanted to become Mother Theresa, you should have done it when that poor old guy begged you not to break his thumbs, not while we're driving away from a bloodbath. I don't want to hear about any recanting of your previous ways in the middle of a really bad situation. You want to be a better person? Make that decision when we're sipping Margaritas on a luxury cruise."

"Margaritas are chick drinks."

"No they're not. Jimmy Buffett sings about them."

"Yeah, I guess you're right. But I'm going to make it up to the victims for what happened."

"How? By bringing them back as zombies?"

"I don't know yet. Those kids who lost their mother, maybe I'll pay for their college education."

"*What*? Are you brain damaged?"

"What's wrong with doing that?"

"I know I said the term was offensive earlier, but George, that's completely retarded. You're not going to send those kids through college. What are you going to do, go around offering financial support to everybody we've wronged?"

"Not everybody. Just the worst ones."

"Give me a frickin' break. You want to help somebody you've wronged? Help me. Buy me a new shirt and pants. Get me some goddamn Band-Aids."

"I will."

"Thank you."

"I'm being completely serious. I'm going to start helping people. Sure, maybe I'll wake up in the morning and decide that the college education idea is kind of stupid—"

"You will, I promise."

"—but I'm going to do whatever it takes to clear my conscience. Maybe it won't be big things. Maybe it'll be a bunch of little things. Maybe I'll…I don't know, entertain kids or something. Dress up as a clown."

"Kids don't like clowns. Kids are scared of them. You're going to terrorize the children you're trying to entertain."

"You know what I mean."

"No, I don't. I've never been more lost in a conversation in my life."

"I just want to be a better person."

"We've established that. We've also established that it's stupid."

"Becoming a better person is stupid?"

"Maybe the concept isn't, but the ideas you're throwing out there are."

"Well, my brain isn't working at full capacity right now, okay? Give me a break. You should be encouraging me."

"Fine. Be a scary clown."

"I don't mean the clown thing. But if I have a major life epiphany, a positive one, you shouldn't sit there and make fun of it. I wouldn't do that to you."

"You make fun of me for ordering a diet soda! Don't pretend that you're some self-improvement cheerleader. Our relationship is based on blunt honesty, and my bluntly honest opinion is that you're being an idiot. I'm not saying you shouldn't be affected by what happened, but do I believe that you're going to become Santa Claus? Hell no."

"I think you could stand to be more affected by all of this."

"I'm compartmentalizing."

"Fine. We'll let the whole thing drop."

"Good idea."

"Are you sure you're not bleeding to death?"

"As far as I know."

"How much further?"

They'd found a mustard-stained road map underneath the back seat. Lou ran his finger along it. "A few more blocks."

"I hope these guys know what they're doing. What I really hope is that they let me pull the trigger when they've got Ivan in their sights. That'd be sweet."

"Right. We've performed so well up to this point, I'm sure they'll be more than happy to turn the responsibility right back over to us, just to keep our high self-esteem intact."

"I can fantasize, at least. God, I hate Ivan."

George still wasn't one hundred percent certain that they should be driving to the rendezvous point. The idea that one of the professionals would say "Lost the werewolf, huh? Time for you to die," and put a bullet in each of their brains seemed like a legitimate concern. But ultimately, much like the rhetorical question of pigeons crapping on your car versus alligators eating your limbs, it came down to the certainty of a life spent hiding from vengeful criminals versus the potential of being executed for incompetence. If the reinforcements successfully recaptured Ivan, it would be much better to be hanging out with them at the time than to get the news from Ricky.

And, to be safe, they'd make sure the reinforcements knew that George and Lou hadn't shared all of their werewolf wisdom.

"I think it's this next one," said Lou, pointing with a bloody finger.

Like Ricky had said, the address was just a small parking lot. As soon as they turned in, a white van with "Ray's Air Conditioning" on the side pulled out of one of the spaces and drove forward. A man in a tan jumpsuit got out of the passenger side and beckoned to them. George looked at Lou, shrugged, and then pulled into the newly vacated space.

George shut off the engine. "Well, if we get shot, I just want you to know that it's been a pleasure working with you."

"If we get shot, I won't be able to say the same."

They got out of the car. The man, who looked about fifty and sported a brown handlebar mustache, whistled in amazement. "The wolf did that to you?"

"Most of it, yeah," said George. "Some of mine came from dogs."

"You should've been more cautious."

"Yeah, we figured that out once we started bleeding all over the place. I'm George, and this is Lou."

"I've got a question for you, George."

"Sure."

"Do you think it's better use of our time to get in the van and get moving, or to stand out here introducing ourselves?"

What a dick. "Fair enough. Let's go."

The man slid open the side door, revealing a woman in a similar tan jumpsuit. She was in her thirties, had her blonde hair pulled back in a ponytail, and would have been extremely attractive if she didn't have such a sour expression. She held a crossbow on her lap.

George nodded at her politely and they got in the van. The man slid the door closed behind them, almost slamming it shut on Lou's foot.

There were two rows of seats. Out of consideration for Lou's more extensive injuries, George climbed into the back seat. Lou sat down next to the woman, eyeing her crossbow nervously. There was no room in this van for the cage even if Ivan hadn't stole it; Ricky could just suck it.

The driver, who looked like a college kid, turned around and gave them a salute that seemed more than a little condescending. *Just stay polite,* George told himself. *You need these people. It'll all be okay.*

The handlebar mustache guy got into the front passenger seat. "Let's go."

"Yes, sir."

The van sped out of the parking lot fast enough to make George momentarily lose his balance. He fastened the seatbelt.

"*Now* is the appropriate time for introductions," said the handlebar mustache guy. "I'm Prescott."

"Angie," said the woman.

"Sam."

"Nice to meet you," said George. "Is it okay that we're getting blood all over your van?"

Prescott shrugged. "It's had worse."

"So you're the mighty werewolf hunters?"

"We hunt what needs to be hunted."

"But have you specifically hunted a werewolf before?"

"What do you think?"

"I have no idea. That's why I asked."

Prescott gave him a look of pure contempt, as if George were the stupidest human being ever to reside on the planet. "Of course we haven't."

George snickered. "Ah. I get it. You don't quite believe in what you're hunting yet. That's where we were not too long ago. You'll learn."

"I'm sure we will. Why don't you start the education process by answering some questions?"

"What do you want to know?"

"What are its capabilities?"

"Well, first of all, he's a human being who can instantly change into a wolf-creature. That's a pretty big capability."

"Please don't editorialize. Just the facts."

Dick. "Fact: my partner and I shot him several times, close range, in the frickin' head, and it didn't kill him."

"Did it injure him?"

"Not a lot."

"But it did injure him?"

"He bled and reacted with pain, yes."

"What kind of bullets did you use?"

"Regular old lead bullets. I don't suppose you guys have silver ones, do you?"

"No. They're not something you can get quickly, even with our connections. Not a lot of call for silver bullets in the real world. We'd have to make them ourselves. We've got somebody on that, but it won't happen today."

"Well, that sucks."

"Are there any other weaknesses we should know about?"

"Possibly."

Angie, who had been glaring at him the entire time, tightened her grip on the crossbow. "I'd hate to think that you were trying to withhold information to make yourselves indispensable." Her voice sounded like she'd been a chain smoker her entire life. No, worse than that, it sounded like she extinguished cigarettes on the back of her throat.

"Would I do something like that?"

"For your sake, I hope not."

"Relax," said Prescott. "We wouldn't take you out even if we wanted to."

"Good to know."

"After all, we may need bait."

Serving as bait didn't sound like much fun, but George would take it over an execution any day. Prescott looked as if he really wanted to watch George cringe at that idea, so George made sure to maintain a casual front. "Sounds fine. Happy to help."

"What are his other weaknesses?"

"Pretty much just silver, as far as we can see. And he's an arrogant son of a bitch. Now can I ask you a question?"

"Shoot."

"How exactly are you going to catch him? Because all I can think of is to follow a trail of corpses."

"We're quite a bit more sophisticated than that." Prescott pulled what George had thought was a GPS from its mounting on the dashboard. "Ivan Spinner had a chip implanted into his arm while he was in custody. We know exactly where he is."

"Holy crap! Really?"

"Really."

"That's fantastic! That's the best news I've heard all day. I mean, sure, pretty much all of the news I've heard today has sucked shit, but still, that's great news! Did you hear that, Lou?"

"Where is he?" Lou asked.

"You're on a need-to-know basis."

"Why?"

"Because I don't like you very much and don't feel like sharing."

"Can we at least have some weapons?" George asked.

"Bait doesn't need weapons."

"So are you catching him or killing him?"

"As of right now, the plan is still to capture him. If that changes, you'll know by the dead werewolf at your feet."

"Will he be tortured after we get him?"

"That's not for us to decide."

"If I get a vote, I hope he is. One last question: if you guys are so fantastic, why didn't they have you do this job in the first place? Why hire us?"

"Because we're expensive as hell."

"Are you worth it?"

"We'll find out, won't we?"

Chapter Twenty-Two: Trackers

"He hasn't moved for the past few minutes," said Prescott. "He's probably resting, licking his wounds."

Or he's dead, thought George. Now that they had the professionals on their side, the thought of Ivan's death wasn't as appealing. Much better to get him tranquilized, back in custody, and over to Dewey where he belonged.

"He heals quick," said George.

"Did he expel the bullets?"

George shook his head. "Nah, not that I saw. As far as I know, he still has a bunch of bullets rattling around in his skull and ribcage. How do you think he gets them out?"

"Hopefully through an extremely painful process of manual extraction. But his body may just reject them and squeeze them out like a splinter."

George had an amusing mental image of bullets popping out of Ivan's head like zits. Then he had an even more amusing image of Ivan's entire head popping like a zit. Actually, any mental image that involved harm coming to the werewolf provided George with at least a small level of entertainment.

"How's it going?" he asked Lou.

Lou held up another one of the bloody antiseptic wipes for George's inspection. He'd made a pile of about a dozen of them now. Lou was clearly doing his best not to wince and show weakness while he disinfected his wounds, but his jaw was clenched tight and it was definitely not a pleasant process.

"You'll need to get bandaged up quickly," Angie told him. "Looks like we're almost there." She didn't offer to help.

Lou ripped open the front of the left leg of his pants. He unwrapped a large bandage and pressed it against a six-inch-long cut that ran lengthwise above his knee.

"So what's the big elaborate plan?" George asked as Sam took an exit off the highway that promised gas, food, and camping.

"It's not elaborate," said Prescott. "We will park a safe distance from where he's resting, and either you or your partner will walk out there and make your presence known. The way your partner looks right now, I think it should be you."

"Agreed," George said.

"When the target shows himself, we'll get the net on him. Problem solved."

"How exactly does that work?" George asked. "Are you setting the net up beforehand?"

"No, George," said Prescott, once again making no effort to conceal his disgust. "We have a net gun. An expensive one. Believe it or not, it's much more effective than tossing a blanket over an animal's head."

"How'd you know about that?"

"You're famous."

"Just so you know, the blanket did have a few silver rings sewn into it."

"And you thought something like that would slow him down?"

"It might have. We were dealing with a supernatural creature. For all we knew, those rings could've sucked out his energy or something."

"Did it work?"

"Maybe. A little. Or it might have been all the times we shot him, hit him, and kicked him that slowed him down. Either way, it didn't hurt to try."

"I suppose it didn't."

"Do you disagree?"

"I can't honestly say that I would have tried it myself. There's a fine line between innovation and just being silly."

"There's also a fine line between being honest and being an asshole."

Prescott actually smiled in a non-asshole manner at that. "You're right. I apologize."

"And I accept your apology. Are you guys good shots with the net gun?"

"Absolutely."

"Will he be able to get free?"

"Not easily. And by the time he does, we'll have pumped a few darts into him. You'll be safe." Prescott looked at Sam. "One mile away."

Sam turned onto a dirt road that reminded George of the one where Ivan had escaped. At least the first time.

"You're going to walk straight," Prescott told George. "Angie and I will be on either side of you. If he runs away, we'll give chase, but try to keep him from running away."

"If he runs, you won't be able to catch him."

"We'll catch him. We can always track him with the chip. He's not going to escape."

"Where is the chip?"

"Need-to-know basis. This is far enough, Sam."

Sam stopped the van. Angie got out of her seat and slid open the side door. George patted Lou on the shoulder as he followed Angie out of the vehicle. He, Angie, and Prescott went to the back of the van.

"I'd feel a lot better about this if you gave me something to defend myself," said George.

Angie opened the rear doors, revealing an impressive stockpile of weapons. "We'd give you a tranquilizer gun," she said, "but they're too big for you to hide, and we don't want him to know that we've got one. Best we can do is this." She took a small pistol down from a shelf and handed it to him. "If what you've said is true, it won't stop him, but it might give you a couple of extra seconds to live."

George tucked the pistol into the holster under his bloodstained shirt. "I'll take it."

"And I'll go you one better," said Prescott, giving George a tiny plastic baggie. "That's a cyanide capsule. If you find yourself about to suffer a fate worse than death, swallow that."

"I think I'll pass."

"Trust me, we've got ours." He touched his earpiece. "Sam, how's our connection? Good."

Angie quickly strapped the crossbow to her back. Prescott handed her a long rifle, then took one for himself. George tossed the baggie back into the van.

"Just walk along the path," Prescott told George. "Stay calm. Don't do anything suspicious. If you can get him out into the open, that'll be extremely helpful. Don't let him know we're here—we will decide the appropriate moment to strike."

"All right," said George. "I'm trusting you guys to have good aim."

"We're almost perfect."

George extended his hand to Prescott. "Best of luck. If we all survive this, I'm buying the beer. As much as you can drink."

"I'll take you up on that."

George walked past the van, giving Lou a thumbs-up sign that Lou returned, though neither of them seemed sincere.

He walked down the path, moving at a brisk pace. Prescott and Angie disappeared into the trees next to him. George at least had to appreciate that he wasn't joining them in wandering through a swamp, though Sam was getting a pretty sweet deal if he was that well-paid just for hanging out in the van.

He focused on taking deep breaths to keep himself calm. He wasn't quite on the verge of freaking out, but he couldn't imagine that Prescott and Angie had his personal safety as a top priority, or even *any* kind of priority. If Ivan suddenly charged him, he expected that they'd be perfectly happy to fire the net, entangle both of them, and let the werewolf shred him. George very much doubted that there'd be any kind of penalty for letting the hired thugs perish.

Still, he had to cooperate. They weren't going to go out of their way to protect him, but it also didn't seem as if they were going to go out of their way to kill him, so his best bet for long-term happiness was to be their bait, try to keep himself alive, and hope that the plan to recapture Ivan was a great big rousing success.

And then, assuming they could ever get hired again, George and Lou would vow never to take any kind of job that involved cages or man-beasts. That's how he'd start every conversation with Ricky: "Does this job involve a cage or a man-beast? Because if it does, tell them to shove it." And they'd never come back to Florida. Fuck Florida and its sweltering heat and ugly alligators and evil serial killer werewolves. Fuck it right in the face.

He kept walking. There was no sign of Angie and Prescott. They were good at staying hidden, he had to give them that, unless they'd lagged behind for a cigarette or a quickie or something.

Maybe Ivan would be lying on the ground, barely alive, huge ring-shaped burns in his flesh from being underneath the blanket. Oh, George would love that. It would almost be worth all of this happening, just for that moment of victory.

Ivan grins, sliding the blade across Diane's neck, as blood spills down the front of her shirt…

George tried to force the memory out of his mind. He couldn't let himself get distracted.

He could hear the little boy wailing "*Mommy!*"

For all George knew, the cops had never actually been to the house. The little boy could still be in the kitchen, sobbing while he held his mother's blood-soaked body. Or the boy could be staring off into space, never to really see anything again.

Stop it.

George hadn't been just talking bullshit with Lou. He really did plan to make things right. He wasn't naïve enough to think that he'd become some kind of saint, strolling from town to town doing good deeds, but he'd find a way to make up for this. Though he'd never be able to completely clear his conscience, maybe he'd at least be able to soothe it a bit, silence the voice inside that was screaming at him and telling him he was a monster.

But, again, it was not something to worry about now. For now, he needed to worry about that goddamn werewolf.

George thought he heard the crack of a branch to his right. Apparently Prescott wasn't a total ninja.

His stomach really hurt. He just wanted this over with.

If you die, that's a pretty crappy legacy you're leaving behind. Lots of people's lives are worse because you were born. Even if you died this morning, before you met Ivan, there'd be no good reason for anybody to mourn, except maybe Lou since he'd have the hassle of finding a new partner. If an angel seeking his wings went It's a Wonderful Life *on you and showed you a world where you'd never been born, it would probably be a festival of smiles and balloons and merry children.*

His stomach really, really hurt. Throwing up might actually make him feel better, but he didn't want Prescott or Angie to see it.

He wiped some sweat from his forehead. He looked at his hand, which seemed to have more blood than perspiration on it.

Focus on the positive, he told himself. *When this is over, you and Lou will check yourselves into a luxury hotel—separate rooms—and spend the next seven days soaking in a hot tub. You'll catch up on all of those books you've never quite found time to read. Drink fine wine and eat grapes. Watch porn.*

He came around a slight corner and, about a hundred feet ahead, he could see Bateman's van.

Son of a bitch. Ivan really was here.

George forced himself not to run. *Stay calm. Don't get too excited.*

The back doors of the van hung open, and George could see the cage inside. Somebody was in there. Had Ivan actually gotten back into the cage? Why the hell would he—?

No. It was Michele, huddled into the back corner.

Shit.

This had to be a trap. But how could Ivan have known they were coming? He couldn't, unless the reinforcements were actually working for the werewolf, and that idea was really dumb.

The situation was making George uncomfortable and paranoid, but he had to stick with the plan. The absolute last thing he needed was for Ivan to rush off and find another well-populated area for a killing spree. George's official role was "werewolf bait," and he was going to play it out.

He walked over to the van. Michele was seated, head down, arms wrapped tightly around her legs, her whole body quivering as she silently wept.

"Michele...?"

She looked up. Her eyes were red and puffy and her whole face was blotchy from crying.

"I'm here to get you out of there," said George. "Where's Ivan?"

"I don't know."

"Which way did he go?"

"I didn't see."

"Michele, I need you to focus. Everything's going to be all right. I promise, I'm not going to let him hurt you."

"You can't promise anything," Michele said. She sniffled, then held up her right hand, revealing a curved row of deep puncture wounds.

Chapter Twenty-Three: The Wolf's Bite

"It'll be okay," George assured her. "That's an ugly bite but it's not too bad. Lou got clawed up a lot worse and he's still kicking around."

"Don't pretend to be dense. You know what this means."

"No, he doesn't play by the werewolf rules. This doesn't mean anything."

"He said it did."

"Well, Ivan's a liar. He just said that to scare you. Don't listen to anything he says. I swear to you that you'll be fine."

Michele shook her head sadly. "No. I can feel it."

"You're just stressed out. It could be anything."

"I've been stressed all day. This is something *horrible*. As soon as his teeth went into me I knew what he'd done."

George hurriedly glanced around the area for any sign of Ivan. There was none. "Okay, okay, for the sake of argument let's say that he did make you into a werewolf. Is that really such a bad thing? He seems pretty happy."

"He can control it."

"Maybe they all can. Maybe that's why we never hear about werewolves—they all have total control over their powers, so only the lunatic idiots like Ivan let out the secret."

"You shouldn't be here." She began to sob uncontrollably.

"Just calm down. I know you don't believe me, but it's all going to be fine. I need to know, did Ivan set a trap?"

"*Me*, maybe."

"Why did he leave you? Was I supposed to find you?"

Michele shook her head. "He looked nervous all of a sudden and just left."

"Good, good. So he's either running or watching us."

Ivan spoke. "What the hell do you want, George?"

George spun around. He couldn't see Ivan's face, but he was at the edge of the trees, mostly obscured by some tall bushes.

"I want the girl back."

"Bullshit. You wouldn't put yourself at risk for her. Why are you here?"

"I just want her back. That's the truth."

"You weren't even around when I nabbed her."

"It was on the news."

"Then where did I catch her?"

Crap. "A gas station."

"Wrong. How did you find me?"

"There were several reports of the van coming this way. You should be more careful."

"Uh-huh. Then why aren't the cops here?"

"How should I know? Maybe they've got the area surrounded. Do you really think I work with the police?"

"George, I've had a good time ruining your life today, but I'm tired. I know you're tired, too."

"Exhausted."

"Why don't we just go our separate ways and work this out some other time, huh?"

"See, I'd love to, and if you give me the girl, I will."

"What's stopping you from taking her? I'm all the way over here."

"Not a goddamn thing."

Ivan stepped to the side, revealing his smiling face, which was now missing a tooth. His wounds were no longer bleeding, though his entire face was so caked with blood that he was almost unrecognizable. "I should warn you, though, that she's damaged goods in a big way. My recommendation is that you just discard her."

"Why would you do that to her?" George asked. When the hell was Prescott or Angie going to put a tranquilizer dart into that prick?

"I guess there are a lot of possibilities," said Ivan. "Maybe she's the first inductee into my werewolf army. Or, this should have you quaking in your booties; maybe she's the *thousandth* one. Maybe my whole purpose is to enslave humanity, and you just got caught in the middle. You could be humanity's last chance, George. Hell of a bad deal for the human race."

"I don't buy that one. What's the next possibility?"

"Oh, gosh, I don't know. Let me think. Maybe I've been looking to get it on in my werewolf form, but I can't find any chicks who are into the whole bestiality scene, so I decided that my only option was to make a she-wolf who can handle me."

"That sounds more reasonable."

"But, no, that can't be it, because it's way more fun when the coin is bigger than the slot, if you know what I mean. You probably do. Despite our differences, you seem like you might be pretty well-endowed."

"So how does this end, Ivan? I know you don't want to just stand around and gab all day."

"You're right. I've actually been pretty bored with this conversation for the past thirty seconds or so but I didn't want to say anything. The plan was actually to just hide out for a moment, wait to see who was coming, and then give them the ol' Cotton Mouse Tavern treatment. I had no idea it would be you. Where's Lou?"

"He's in police custody."

"Aw, man, that's too bad. You must be pretty bummed. Well, my original plan was to murder whoever came down the path, and I can't think of any good reason to change that, so I think it's all over for you, Mr. George."

Ivan stepped onto the path.

George took out the pistol and pointed it at him. Ivan stopped walking and stared at him for a moment.

"And...?"

"This is loaded with silver bullets."

"Really? And where exactly does one acquire silver bullets these days?"

"It was a shop for Goth kids. A novelty item."

"You are a *good* liar," said Ivan. "You don't blink, you don't break eye contact, you don't put your hand over your mouth—I'm impressed. The only problem with your lie is that you're standing there talking instead of shooting me with the legendary silver bullet."

Ivan stepped completely out of the bushes. His hands transformed into claws as he strode toward George.

A dart struck him in the side of the neck.

Ivan looked confused for a moment, then positively furious. He plucked the dart out of his neck, tossed it to the ground, then transformed into a full wolfman and leapt back into the bushes.

George resisted the urge to raise his clenched fist into the air and let out a victory shout. They got him!

Still no sign of either Prescott or Angie, but George heard the rustling as Ivan ran off. Hopefully the tranquilizer wouldn't take too long to take him down.

He stood there, listening carefully.

"What happened?" Michele asked.

"The cavalry's here," George said. "He'll be snoozing any second now."

"What'll they do with me?"

"Nothing. I mean, they won't hurt you. I won't let them. We'll get you help."

"You'll deliver me just like you were going to deliver Ivan."

"No. That's not part of any bargain." He thought he heard something, and gestured for Michele to stop talking. "Shhhh."

He stood as still as possible. The only sound was Michele's rapid panicked breathing.

And then a scream.

Not from Ivan.

Prescott's scream was a mixture of agony and terror. George couldn't hear any attempt at bravery—this was the sound of a man who knew that screaming would be the last thing he ever did.

The scream did not cut off. It did not fade.

What the hell was George supposed to do? He couldn't just go running off after them. He'd get himself killed, too. Ivan had been hit with the dart, so maybe he'd succumb to the drug's influence before he could finish off Prescott. If not, thanks to the noise, Angie had to know exactly where they were.

George thought about running back to the other van, but if Ivan came back for him, he didn't want to be on the unprotected path. Instead, he slammed the back doors of the van shut, then hurried around to the front and climbed into the driver's seat.

He really wished the windshield weren't missing. And there definitely wasn't time to hotwire this one.

The screams continued.

"Damn you," he whispered.

Finally the scream began to fade. Not quickly. It was obvious that Prescott never got to use his cyanide capsule. George wondered if Lou and Sam could hear it, too.

After what felt like several minutes but couldn't possibly have been that long (could it?), the screaming stopped.

"I think the cavalry is dead," said Michele.

"I saw the dart go in his neck." What if the tranquilizer didn't work on supernatural monsters? Or did a werewolf just require a second dose? Or had Prescott stopped screaming because Ivan fell asleep on top of him?

Rustling in the bushes.

"I think he's coming back," George said.

A dark shape, like a basketball, flew into the air from amidst the trees. George realized that it was Prescott's severed head about two seconds before it splattered against the hood of the van. It rolled off and fell to the ground.

Damn it. That wasn't the action of a sufficiently tranquilized werewolf.

Something else flew into the air. Half of an arm. It sailed right through the broken windshield and landed on the seat next to George. He recoiled in horror.

A leg followed. This one came up a few feet short and landed on the dirt path in front of the van.

The second leg struck the front hood, only a couple of inches from where the head landed. It remained there.

"Stop it, you son of a bitch!" George shouted. *Oh, nice one, dumb-ass.* As if Ivan would cease his grotesque attack based on George's request.

The rest of the first arm missed the van. The second arm, thrown in its entirety, hit the roof. Michele screamed.

Where in the world was Angie? Ivan was out there throwing body parts at them. How could she not find him?

The next wave was a volley of internal organs, flung quickly, one after the other. And, finally, Prescott's bloody and shredded jumpsuit.

George just stared at the carnage in a state of disbelief. Even having seen Ivan's malicious thrill-killing ways up close, it was still hard to imagine that he'd tear somebody into pieces and pelt a frickin' van with them!

He wondered what happened to the ribcage and spinal column.

Ivan stepped onto the path, still fully transformed as a wolfman. He wasn't holding Prescott's ribcage—that was presumably a mystery never to be solved.

Ivan rushed at the van.

Something swished through the air toward him.

The net struck Ivan, knocking him to the ground. He immediately began to roll around in panic and fury, getting himself more tangled.

Angie ran onto the path on the opposite side from which Ivan had emerged.

I never stopped being bait…

Though he was more inclined to stick with the phony perceived safety of the van, George threw open the door and got out to help her. Angie pointed the rifle at Ivan's thrashing body from about ten feet away and fired a tranquilizer dart into him.

He didn't stop moving.

Angie pulled her crossbow off her back and notched a bolt. It appeared to be a makeshift silver bolt—a silver tip duct-taped to a regular one.

"Shoot him!" George said.

"I don't want to kill him!"

"Look what he did to your partner! Shoot him!"

Angie kept the crossbow pointed at Ivan, yet didn't fire. George understood that it would be her ass on the fire if she killed the werewolf, but Prescott was in chunks all over the ground!

His claws slashed through the net, cutting through the webbing like scissors. George's stomach plummeted.

Ivan sat up, the net no longer covering the top half of his body. He snarled.

Angie fired the silver bolt at him. It went through his upper arm, bursting all the way through and popping halfway out the other side.

Ivan's werewolf howl changed to a human scream as his face began to transform back.

George had attacked Ivan and been knocked aside so many times that day that he didn't see the reason to give it yet another try. He settled for offering unnecessary advice: "Shoot him again!"

Angie snapped another bolt into the crossbow.

Ivan leapt completely free of the netting before she could fire. The tranquilizer dart dropped out where it had been lodged in his chest.

Angie still got off the shot before he reached her, but it sailed harmlessly over Ivan's right shoulder and struck a tree. Ivan knocked her to the ground.

George went for the bolt.

Angie didn't scream, and as George ran for the silver he thought she might be dead already. But when he yanked the bolt out of the tree and turned back around, he saw that she was very much alive. Ivan, his face still shifting between wolf and man as he stood, clutched the back of her jumpsuit with his good hand and dragged her toward the van.

Ivan slammed her into the front grille of the van, headfirst, with enough force to visibly crack her skull. He smashed her a second time with just as much impact before George reached him.

George thrust the silver-tipped bolt at him and missed. Ivan swung Angie's corpse in front of him as a shield, and George's second thrust plunged into her chest. For an instant he thought he was going to lose his weapon, but he pulled it out just before Ivan tossed her body aside.

Ivan took a swing at him, his claws slicing across the tip of George's nose. The werewolf had a longer reach than George, so his own swing with the bolt missed completely.

Sizzling, foamy blood ran down Ivan's injured arm.

Get him in the heart, George thought. *One good jab to the heart and he's finished.*

He didn't want to let go of his weapon, but there was no way he could get past Ivan's claws. So he flung the bolt as hard as he possibly could, praying that he'd get lucky.

Chapter Twenty-Four: Swapping Roles

He did not get lucky.

Ivan knocked the bolt away. "*Now, Sam!*" George shouted, looking over Ivan's shoulder.

Taking advantage of Ivan's momentary distraction, George ran for the van. Wow. He couldn't believe that lame-ass trick worked.

It would've been nicer if it were some planned-out moment where Sam really was standing there with a crossbow, ready to put a silver-tipped bolt deep into Ivan's heart, but for now George would happily accept the extra two seconds of life he'd been given.

He scrambled into the driver's seat with the werewolf right behind him. He scooted onto the passenger side, opened the door, and got back out of the vehicle. It was even more difficult for Ivan to maneuver in here than for the oversized thug, so George got out with just enough time to slam the door in Ivan's face. Hopefully he'd flattened his goddamn snout.

What now?

Where *was* Sam? The team had to have a backup plan prepared in case Prescott and Angie got murdered, right?

George ran around to the rear of the van. Actually, that cage looked nice and safe right about now. If it had been unlocked, he might have been inclined to jump in there with Michele.

There was just enough room for him to get in the back of the van. Since there was no way he could outrun the werewolf, his best bet was to keep hitting him with doors until Sam and Lou figured out that he needed some frickin' assistance. He got in, pressed himself against the cage, and pulled the doors shut.

Ivan was at the doors in a few seconds. George heard his claws very slowly scrape against the outside steel—even now, the prick was still trying to be spooky. George took the pistol with its mostly useless lead bullets out of the holster.

Ivan pulled the doors open. He'd changed his hands back to human for the task.

George squeezed the trigger over and over, pumping several bullets into Ivan's chest. Every few extra seconds helped, and if Sam had somehow missed hearing Prescott's screams, he had to hear gunshots, right?

Ivan looked down at the bleeding holes in his chest, his expression incredulous even with his face in werewolf form. It changed back to human. "Bullets. Don't. Work."

George shot him in the face.

Ivan ran his tongue over the new hole in his upper lip. "Did you fucking hear me?" he asked, his words kind of slurred.

"You want one in the eye?" George asked. He'd actually been aiming for Ivan's eye with the lip shot, but didn't tell him that.

Ivan grabbed George's left arm, not sinking his claws in. He gave it a sharp *yank* and George cried out in pain. The gun fell out of his hand as George's arm, his shoulder now dislocated, flopped uselessly next to him. Ivan grabbed George's ankle and dragged him out of the van. He hit the ground with a painful jolt, fortunately not crushing his twisted arm underneath him.

Ivan picked up the pistol and pointed it at George's face. "So who else is out there? Is Sam real?"

"Nah."

"Liar." Ivan looked around uncomfortably. "I don't hear him. I hear pretty well when I'm paying attention. He must've run away when he heard me tear your buddy apart limb from limb."

"Must have."

"You know that with a couple more tugs I could rip your arm right off. You saw me do it back at the bar."

"I know."

"Why do you keep messing with me, George? You got away. Why not just leave well enough alone?" Ivan wasn't nearly as articulate anymore, but George could still understand him.

"I wasn't going to let you kill anybody else." God, his arm hurt. He'd dislocated his shoulder once in high school, and twenty-seven years later still remembered how bad it felt.

"Really? So, thanks to your plan to—*fuck*!" He wiped some blood from his lip and then continued. "Thanks to your plan to stop me from killing anybody else, I killed two more people. That's a very poor plan, George."

"So am I next?"

"Maybe. Wouldn't that just *suck* to get shot by a werewolf? I mean, how unglamorous is that?"

"Pretty unglamorous."

"What I should do is rip your arms and legs off and leave you as a human torso. But you'd probably just die of blood loss, and that's no fun. I guess you're coming with me."

Ivan tried to reach into his pocket, but his free arm didn't seem to be working quite right. He cursed. "Screw it, I don't need this." He threw the pistol off into the swamp, then snapped off the end of the bolt. He pulled each half out of his arm and threw them aside, then got the set of keys out of his pocket and tossed them at George. They bounced off George's chest and onto the dirt. "Unlock the cage."

George shook his head. "No."

"Five…four…three…"

"Okay, okay." George picked up the keys and stood up. He couldn't even feel the fingers on his left hand anymore.

"Do it quickly. You have ten seconds to get in that cage before I kill you."

Ivan sounded completely serious. Despite his earlier thoughts, George really didn't want to get into that cage with Michele, and not just because Ivan's future plans for George probably involved something even worse than what had happened to Prescott.

Still, he'd rather risk a much worse death later than let Ivan kill him now, so he unlocked the cage door.

This would be a good time for a surprise bolt to pop through his chest…

No surprise bolt popped through Ivan's chest. George climbed into the back of the van—an awkward process with only one good arm—and then crawled into the cage.

He slammed the door shut and scooted to the back, next to Michele.

"What the hell are you doing?" Ivan asked. "Give me the keys."

"You want them? Bend the bars."

Ivan let out an incredulous laugh. "Oh, that's hilarious. Do you honestly think you're safe in there?"

"Well, saf*er*."

"So you're going to make me count again? Do you really want to make me even madder than I already am?"

"Why not? Will that make you kill me even more slowly?"

"Oh, you little shit. Good one. You're really going to make me run over and get the gun, huh?"

"Yeah, I think I am."

"All right. Point for you."

Ivan ran off to where he'd thrown the pistol. George took a very brief moment to bask in the joy of pissing him off, and then prodded Michele. "Hey, you okay?"

"Leave me alone," she said, speaking so quietly that he could barely hear her.

"C'mon, sit up. We need to work together." He pulled her to a sitting position.

She looked awful. Her skin was pale except for dark circles under her eyes, she was sweating profusely, and her breathing was a soft rasp.

"I just…I just want to die…"

"No, you don't. There's help on the way. If we can keep Ivan from doing anything to us until they get here, we'll be fine."

"I'm sick, George. I'm just…I'm sick."

"No, you're fine. Just stay with me. I need you."

She closed her eyes.

"No, no! Michele, stay awake. Think about how good it's going to feel when we kill that son of a bitch. Imagine his face crunching underneath your feet."

"I don't wanna."

George's cell phone rang. He dug it out of his pocket. Lou.

He answered, watching for Ivan to return. "Lou, get over here! Now!"

"We're—"

George hung up and pocketed the phone as he saw the bushes rustle. Not good for Ivan to know he was in contact with anybody. He wanted the werewolf to take his time as much as possible.

"Come on, Michele," he whispered. "I really need you."

To be honest, George wasn't completely sure what he needed her for, but two people trying to distract a werewolf while they waited for help to arrive was better than one person working alone, right?

Michele responded by throwing up. Though she didn't turn her head, the majority of the spew missed George's pants. Michele let a large chunk roll down her chin, not seeming to care.

Ivan ran back to the van, holding the pistol. He pointed it at George. "Three...two...one..."

George tossed the keys out of the cage. Ivan caught them.

"Thanks." He grimaced. "Ooooh, your girlfriend isn't looking so good. I hope she doesn't change into something that might hurt you."

Ivan slammed the van doors shut.

CHAPTER TWENTY-FIVE: Last of the Useless Saviors

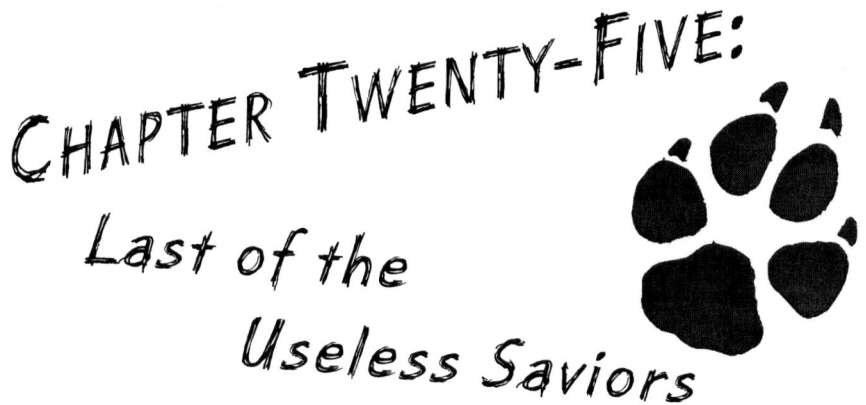

"Holy shit," Sam whispered as Prescott screamed in the distance. "Holy shit."

Lou leaned forward in his seat. "Shouldn't we go help him?"

"Are you kidding me? Do you hear that?"

"Yeah, I hear it! That's why I asked!"

Sam violently shook his head. "No way, dude. I've seen Prescott get branded before, I mean with an actual red-hot cattle brand, and not make a sound. This is bad."

"Are you an idiot? I know it's bad! My partner is out there and so are yours, so let's go help them!"

"*Listen* to that!" Sam tapped the window as Prescott's screams continued. "I'm just the driver, dude."

"You're going to let a lady die and not do anything to help her?"

"Like I care that Angie is a lady! Hey, if you want to go out there, be my guest. But I'm telling you that if this guy took down Prescott, he's not somebody I want to be around!"

"This is not new information! He's been killing people left and right! Look at me—do you think I accidentally fell down a flight of stairs or something?"

"I'm just the driver."

"I'm not saying you have to even get out of the van, but let's drive closer, see if there's something we can do to help."

"No way. They make the big bucks. If they can't handle it, I'm sure not going out there for what I get paid."

"You goddamn coward."

"Coward?" With admittedly impressive speed, Sam took out a gun and pointed it at Lou. "What do you think now? Is this gun cowardly?"

"Well, yeah, it kind of is."

"I don't have to take any lip from you. Do you know what your status is on this mission? 'Highly expendable.' We're here to recapture the cargo that you lost, and none of us, not Prescott, not Angie, not the bosses, and definitely not me, care what happens to you."

"Well, that's not something I wanted to hear, what with my fragile self-esteem and all. Nice job taking me out of my bubble of comfort. Even if you don't care about your partners, shouldn't you at least be concerned that the werewolf sounds like he's getting away?"

"Angie will take care of him."

"How do you know that?"

"Because she's good, that's how! We're not bumbling incompetent thugs like you. We actually have a plan of action. We worked this whole thing out a little better than to just run in there and start shooting."

"I think—"

"Enough! You can shut up, get out, or take a bullet to the head. I don't care which one you pick."

Lou glared at him. Sam returned to peering out the window, looking scared as hell.

The screams finally faded.

"Shit." Sam reached for the keys in the ignition, hesitated, then lowered his hands again. "Shit, shit, shit."

"He's finally stopped screaming," Lou noted. "That must mean that everything's just fine now."

"Are you trying to get shot?"

"I'm trying to get you to take some action!"

"One more word, dude. One more word and I'll shoot you right where you sit."

"No, you won't, because for all you know everybody else is dead and you need more bait. Today I faced off a werewolf in frickin' hand-to-hand combat—twice—so I apologize if having a little kid point a cap gun at me doesn't make me shiver and shake."

Sam's walkie-talkie crackled. He pressed a button on the side. "Angie?"

"He got Prescott. I mean...I mean he really got him."

"Aw, shit."

"I don't know exactly what it is we're hunting—I guess I have to go with 'werewolf' even though I don't believe it. But he's messing with George. Throwing body parts at him."

"Jesus Christ. That's horrible."

"No, it's not. If he's toying with his prey instead of running away, that's a good thing for us. At some point he's going to go directly after George. When he does, I'll have a clear shot with the net."

"Perfect!"

"Contact Bateman. Let him know that Prescott is down. Wait for my signal, and then drive over here as fast as you can."

"Yes, ma'am." Sam set down the walkie-talkie, then took out his cell phone.

"Mind if I call George to see how he's doing?" Lou asked.

"Yeah, I mind! As far as Ivan knows, he's killed the only reinforcement that's out there. Use your brain."

Sam punched in a number on his cell phone. "Mr. Bateman? Status report. Prescott is down. Yes, sir. Deceased, sir. I'm not certain. She used the term 'body parts.' Yes, sir. Lou is right here, so I can confirm his status. I believe George is still alive, too. Yes, sir, I will. Thank you, sir." Sam hung up.

"What'd he say?" Lou asked.

"Nothing of any importance to you. He did *not* say to speed over there and start firing like a maniac, just so you're aware."

"I figured."

"You can wipe that judgmental expression right off your face, dude. I've already told you that you're more than welcome to jog over there and help your friend. Won't bother me one bit."

Lou liked to think that if he weren't so badly injured, that he *would* run over there, guns blazing. He certainly couldn't do it in his current condition. Of course, early on, when his only physical ailment was some extra belly fat, he'd sat in the van with Michele and patiently waited for George to retrieve Ivan from inside the doomed mother's home. Quite honestly, he was probably giving this poor kid a bunch of crap for something that Lou himself might not do.

No. George hadn't been screaming at all when he was in the house, and certainly not in tones that indicated he was meeting a ghastly demise. This was much different. And if the little brat would drive Lou close enough to the action, there was no question that he'd get out of the van and do what he could to help.

Absolutely.

"How good is Angie with that net?" Lou asked.

"Flawless."

"Does she get a lot of opportunities to use it?"

"Yeah, she spends every Wednesday out on the street netting pedestrians. Don't ask stupid questions. Trust me, she's good. And she's good with the tranquilizer darts. If he comes out in the open, the werewolf will be caught."

"What kind of darts is she using?"

"Like that would mean anything to you. She's using a Pneu-dart rifle with Zoletil. It'll take down a lion, so it'll sure as hell take down a wolf."

"What about a werewolf?"

"Same difference."

"No. You haven't seen this bastard change. It's not like a…you know, I don't even have a point of reference. He can change instantly. Any part of his body he wants. It's like frickin' CGI effects in a movie."

"Maybe Hollywood has taken it to the next level. The 3-D craze got out of hand and he jumped out of some computer animator's computer."

"What I'm trying to say is that I think there's something more going on than just some guy who can change his body like a chameleon…no, not even a chameleon, that just changes its color…what animal am I thinking of…?"

"A butterfly?"

"No…yeah, we'll go with that. He's like a butterfly that can change back and forth from maggot to butterfly in seconds. Less than seconds. You can't do that shit in nature."

"We heard all of this on the drive over. What's your point?"

"My point is, don't assume that just because it can take down a bear, that your dart can take down a werewolf."

"He'll be in a net."

"He has sharp claws."

"So do lions."

"A lion doesn't have the rational thought to cut through a net."

"Gloomy, aren't you?"

"When it's appropriate."

"Well, you're not exactly helping plead your case that we should go after him, are you?"

"What I'm trying to say is that your partner, the one that isn't dead already, doesn't necessarily have things under control. And since we have a nice big van full of weapons, we should be over there helping out."

"I think we should be right here, staying alive. Fortunately for me, I've got the gun."

Lou took out his cell phone. "I'm going to check on George."

"Whatever. You know what, I don't even care anymore."

George picked up on the first ring. "Lou, get over here! Now!"

"We're on our way," Lou assured him. The line went dead. "George? You still there?"

"He hang up on you?" asked Sam.

"They need help," Lou said. "Let's go."

"Uh-uh. What did he say?"

"He said to get over here! What else does he need to say?"

"Your partner isn't the one giving the orders."

"Fine." Lou slid open the side door.

"What do you think you're doing?"

"I'm going to help him."

"No. You're staying here. I may still need you."

"You said I could leave!"

"Yeah, because I didn't think you'd actually try to go out there." Sam kept his gun pointed at Lou, but adjusted the aim a bit, as if trying to center the target between Lou's eyes. "Close the door."

"Just let me go."

"Close the door."

"You already said I was very expendable. What difference does it make?"

"If you die, it's going to be as bait, not as a wannabe hero."

Having a gun pointed at him was always a scary thing, despite his earlier attempt to convince Sam otherwise, but realistically, Lou knew that if Sam was unwilling to risk the ire of his boss by letting him run out and get killed by Ivan, he probably wasn't going to just shoot him in the head. That would be more difficult to explain.

Lou jumped out of the van. After a moment of hesitation, Sam fired.

Damn. He wasn't quite as reluctant to use the gun as Lou had expected.

Lou's leg buckled beneath him as he stepped onto the ground but he maintained his footing and did a fast limp to the back of the van. He winced as he did so—if he'd actually had any stitches in, they definitely would have torn at that. Hopefully Sam would waste a few precious seconds trying to work up the courage to get out of the van and come after him.

He threw open the back doors and grabbed the first thing he saw. He pulled the pin out of the grenade and tossed it over the van. He'd used a couple of fragmentation grenades before, but strictly for recreational purposes out in the New Mexico desert and never in a moment of extreme urgency. He couldn't remember how much time he had between pulling the pin and the explosion—not that it mattered, since it wasn't as if he could leisurely stand there waiting for the optimum moment to throw.

He slammed his hands over his ears and ran.

The grenade went off. Over the explosion, Lou heard Sam's cry.

The questionable wisdom of throwing a grenade near a van containing a wide variety of explosives was not lost on Lou, but what else was he supposed to do?

Sam lay on the ground, half of his face black and charred. Though his limbs all remained intact, the bone was visible in several places on his body. The sight was grisly and sickening enough that Lou didn't immediately notice that Sam still held the gun.

The bullet grazed Lou's left thigh. He clutched at the wound and dropped to his knees.

Sam shouted something incoherent that might have been "I'll get you" and fired another shot. Thank God he'd been so badly injured—the shot missed by almost nothing, and Lou was confident that it would have been an easy kill shot otherwise.

He forced himself to get back up. At least three of his bandages turned red all at once. He quickly stepped over to the right back corner of the van, which put him out of Sam's sight unless Sam dragged himself across the ground a couple of feet. That seemed unlikely.

Lou hastily looked over his weapon selection. He didn't want to kill Sam if he didn't have to, but he couldn't have the guy shooting at the van as he drove off. There had to be another tranquilizer rifle.

There were a couple of normal-looking rifles, and a few handguns, but nothing that seemed to be a tranquilizer.

There were several more grenades. A box labeled "Dynamite." Another crossbow.

Sam fired another shot. It didn't come anywhere close, and he couldn't possibly see Lou, so he was just firing wildly. Lou didn't blame him for losing his mind.

Screw it. There was no time to make a careful selection of weaponry or mentally debate the moral elements of the situation. He had to take Sam out of the equation, get in the van, and drive off to help George.

He picked up one of the handguns, then limped the long way around the van, focusing on not passing out. He peeked around the corner, saw that Sam was still looking toward the rear, and shot him in the head.

Lou immediately dropped the gun, leaned against the van, and let out a violent dry heave.

Fuck.

He'd seen a lot of awful things today, but that didn't change the fact that he'd never murdered a human being. Even a cowardly little shit like Sam.

Focus.

Since he'd been forced to take a life, it was very important that he not waste it. If he used this opportunity to save George's life, things would balance out, sort of. If he let George die because he was too busy wallowing in his guilt, well, that was a pretty lousy reason to guarantee himself eternal damnation.

The grenade had really done a number on the side of the van, but the tires looked okay. He offered a silent apology to the dead kid, got in the driver's seat, and started up the engine.

He couldn't wait to see how well Ivan did against *this* arsenal.

Chapter Twenty-Six: Caged Madness

"Do you know what I'm going to do to you, George?" Ivan inquired.

"Something antisocial?" George asked, trying not to give away that he was in incredible pain and was scared out of his mind. Being Ivan's prisoner like this was bad enough, but Michele was most assuredly *not* doing well. Her skin color had gone from pale to looking almost jaundiced, and he thought her eyes had become a much darker shade of brown. She reminded him of a druggie having a massive overdose, except that instead of heroin coursing through her veins, she had werewolf spit.

"You cannot even imagine what I'm going to do to you," said Ivan. "Not even in your worst nightmares can you conceive of what's going to happen."

"That's pretty vague," George noted. "I'd expect more from you. When a guy like you is reduced to threatening me in generalities, I can't help but feel less frightened than I was before you started running your mouth."

"Is that so?"

"Yeah."

"Then let's just drive in silence, so you can think about what I might do to you instead."

"That completely works for me."

George needed full concentration for this next part, anyway. It was really going to suck. He pressed his dislocated shoulder against one of the cage bars, trying to line the ball up with the joint socket. Of course, he couldn't see the bones inside his shoulder, so he wouldn't know if this was correct until the unpleasant moment of truth.

Thank God Ivan couldn't see what he was doing in the rear-view mirror. He'd purposely swerve or hit a bump.

"So what are you thinking about?" Ivan asked.

"You know, when you keep talking like this, it makes you seem insecure," George said. "Why are you insecure, Ivan? It seems to me like you've got the upper hand. Is there something you're not telling me?"

"Just keep talking. You're only making it worse for yourself."

"You're not even listening. My point is that *you're* talking too much. It indicates a lack of confidence. I'm supposed to be sitting here thinking 'I'm gonna die! I'm gonna die!' but when I hear all of that jabber from you I can't help but believe that you're worried about something."

"Let's say for the sake of argument that I *was* talking because I was worried. How does pointing that out work to your advantage? I'm curious."

"You might get so mad that you make a mistake."

"Like you did right before I escaped from the cage?"

"Exactly."

"Well, Georgie, I hate to break this to you, but not only am I not going to stop the van so I can go back there and try to scare you, but you're unlikely to do a surprise transformation into a wolfman. You're at quite a bit more of a disadvantage than I was."

"I understand that."

"But if you find my chatter reassuring, hey, that's your decision."

"It's not really a decision. More of a mood."

"Fuck you."

"Now, when I said 'fuck you' before, you made a big deal out of it, like it was a sign of weakness. I don't want to be a jerk about this, Ivan, but my theory about your lack of confidence is still holding up."

Ivan was silent for a moment. "I'm taking your eyelids first."

"I beg your pardon?"

"You wanted specifics? The first thing I'm going to do is very carefully slice off your eyelids. Then we're going to play a fun little game where we each get one of the eyelids, and we flick them against the wall, and we see whose falls off first. It's really kind of a fun game. You'd be surprised how long an eyelid will stick to the wall if it hits with the wet side."

"What if it doesn't?"

"Then it drops to the floor, and it's not a very fun game at all. You have to flick it just right."

George had nothing else to say to that. He took a deep breath, worked up his courage, and then slammed his shoulder against the metal bar as hard as he could.

He bellowed in pain. Michele looked at him with mild curiosity.

"Whoa! What're you doing back there, George?" Ivan asked. "That sounds like it hurt."

George flexed his fingers. His shoulder was throbbing but his arm hurt much less now. One dislocated shoulder fixed.

"You got any aspirin?" George asked.

"Sorry."

"No problem. So where are we going?"

"It's a surprise."

"It's a surprise because you have no idea."

"Hey, George, what was that chick's name I killed? Diane, right? Do you think her kids are home from school yet? I bet the older one got a hundred percent on his spelling test—no, let's say a ninety-five—and he ran all the way home because he was so excited. And he rushed inside, thinking he was going to get a big hug and a kiss and maybe a new video game, and instead he just found a dead mommy."

George clenched his fists and didn't respond.

"What's the matter, George? Decided to stop playing along with our clever repartee? I saw the way you looked when I cut her throat. That was a life-changing moment for poor little Georgie. If you were going to live long enough to experience nightmares again, you'd have a doozy of a bad dream over that."

A trickle of what might have been pus was leaking from one of Michele's eyes. She looked totally out of it.

"Still nothing to say?" Ivan asked. "You know, George, all that stuff you've been saying about how me talking is a sign of insecurity? That's how I see your *lack* of talking. What's the matter? Is the big bad thug all sad because of the dead mommy's kids?"

"I'm sad about everybody you killed. It doesn't make me weak."

"I say it does. I think you own a vagina now."

"Funny."

"There's nothing funny about vaginas. Some of them have teeth—did you know that? Whenever you've slipped yourself inside one and you're thinking about how nice it feels, there's been about a one-in-ten chance that sharp teeth will close on you."

"What the hell are you even babbling about, Ivan?"

"Just making conversation with the dead man."

"Well, Jesus Christ on a crutch, now you sound stoned. How did vaginas with teeth ever become part of this discussion? Those bullets in your head are starting to mess with you."

"Aw, *shit*!"

The way he said those words, George knew that they were not Ivan's response to a sudden realization that the bullets in his brain were indeed impeding his thought processes. George couldn't get a good view out of the front of the van from his cage, but it was enough to see that the path had dead-ended in front of a small wooden house.

Now this was a development that George could get behind…unless it was a house full of innocent victims.

Ivan slammed his fist against the steering wheel. He uttered a string of profanity that made even George's own liberal use of expletives sound like baby talk, and then put the van into reverse.

Ivan couldn't possibly know that there was another van on the path. If Lou and Sam were following them, there'd be nowhere for the werewolf to go.

Fantastic.

The front door opened. A large greyhound bolted outside and ran at the van.

"Aw, for God's sake," Ivan muttered.

The dog jumped against the front of the vehicle, barking furiously. But it wasn't a psycho-rabid dog bark; just the regular old bark of a dog that was way too excited to see strangers.

A thin man in filthy overalls came out of the house. "Roxie!" he shouted. "Get back in here!"

Ivan picked up the pistol, pointed it through the broken windshield, and shot the man in the face. His body dropped right to the ground.

Ivan turned around to look at George. "Did you see what you made me do? I had to kill somebody with a goddamn *gun*! Do you know how that makes me feel?"

The loud barking from the greyhound continued. Ivan held up his hand, transformed it into a wolf claw, then got out of the van. A few seconds later, there was an equally loud yip. Ivan got back inside, his claw dripping with fresh blood. The thumping had stopped.

"That's another one on you," Ivan told George.

If anything, this man's death was less George's fault than any of the other murders today, but he certainly didn't feel any better about it.

Ivan resumed driving the van, backing it up through the path the way they'd come. "If anybody is following us, they're dead," Ivan said.

"Understood." George looked back at Michele, and gasped. Her face had transformed. The change was subtle, but her jaw now protruded a bit and her fingers had grown in length.

"Michele...?"

She shifted position, and there was a loud cracking sound from her legs and back.

"Ahhhhh, shit." George pressed himself against the other side of the cage. Though the hairs on her arms didn't seem to be growing, they definitely seemed to be swaying in a non-existent breeze.

In terms of self-preservation, the best thing to do was reach over there, grab her head, and give it a sharp, violent twist. Break her neck.

But he just...couldn't.

He couldn't kill an innocent girl.

She cried out in sudden pain, revealing wolf-like fangs.

Okay, if she was about to change into a goddamn werewolf while he was locked in a cage with her, he really needed to break her neck. Morality...stupidity...it was a fine line.

He made a move for her, and she growled. Actually *growled*.

"Hey!" Ivan snapped. "Don't touch him! He's mine!"

Michele growled again, but then cowered in the corner of the cage. George found it very disconcerting that Ivan had felt the need to warn her and not him.

The hair on her arms continued to move, and it seemed to be getting thicker.

He lunged at her. She hissed and bit at him. George pulled his arm away and decided to scoot back to his side of the cage. He sure as hell didn't want a werewolf bite that might turn him into something like that.

"George, you need to keep your hands to yourself," Ivan warned. "I don't want her to have all the fun, but I'm not going to save you from her. If I only get to watch you die, that's fine, I'll deal with it." Ivan sounded a lot more stressed than he'd been before they realized that the path didn't have any other exits.

Michele began to cry again. He couldn't be certain with her cowering in the corner like that, but her arm seemed to be bent at a weird angle.

He desperately hoped that by the time this was over, he wouldn't be jealous of Prescott and his peaceful demise.

"All you had to do was stay away," Ivan said. "You were *free*! Do you really think I would have stuck around Florida, or even the United States? I would have fled. I would have been somebody else's problem. How stupid are you?"

"You kidnapped the girl. That's not exactly fleeing."

"Fine. So I would have left the country with a girl that you'd kidnapped yourself, and who may very well murder you any minute now. You should have left it alone. There was no reason for you to stay involved."

At the moment, George was more than inclined to agree with this logic. But let Ivan be the one to dwell on the past—George just needed to stay calm and hope that this she-wolf continued to listen to her master's instructions.

Michele's body shook and tears trickled down her cheeks but she resumed the growling.

"Michele, fight it!" George said. Yeah, it was a stupid thing to say—he wanted to think she *was* fighting it, but the encouragement couldn't hurt.

The hair on her arms was definitely growing thicker and darker.

"Fight it! Don't let him win!"

"You're wasting your time," said Ivan. "You might as well be saying that to a cancer patient."

George's father had beaten cancer a decade ago, and he credited it to his optimistic outlook on life, so George continued with renewed enthusiasm. "Michele, listen to me! I promise you that you can beat this!"

Michele shook her head and let out a miserable sob.

"You saw what he can do! He can change whenever he wants! That means that you can, too!"

"Fight it!" Ivan urged. "Use the power of love in your heart!"

"Michele! Stay with me!" George watched in horror as her index finger grew by at least half an inch, and the fingernail changed shape, becoming more like a talon.

"Michele, pray to Zeus!" Ivan said. "Accept Buddha as your one and only savior! Fight it! Fight it! Go team go!"

George wanted to punch him in the face, but had to satisfy himself with an earlier memory of punching Ivan in the face. He scooted a little closer to

Michele, though he kept himself a cautious arm-length away. "You have to listen to me. Ivan retains full consciousness when he changes. He doesn't become an animal. He's had more practice, but you're a lot stronger than that little shit! There's nothing he can do that you can't do better!"

"Leave me alone, both of you!" Michele screamed. Her low, distorted voice sounded like she'd been possessed by a demon. It was almost more unnerving than the way her fangs now protruded from her mouth.

"You heard her, George. Obey the lady's wishes." He chuckled. "I am so very glad you're in that cage and not me."

"Michele—"

"*Enough!*" She let out a long, piercing scream and began to rip at her hair. As her scream went on and on and on, George realized that Ivan was right; she was most definitely not going to be able to fight this.

Chapter Twenty-Seven: Desire to Feed

Michele's entire body was on fire.

Her vision was red.

She thought her flesh was going to blister and split open, sending bursts of hellfire throughout the world.

She wanted to die.

She wanted to *live*.

What was happening to her? Was that George? Why was she in a cage? Why was he with her? Were they lovers?

The pain was blinding.

She could feel the blood rushing through her head.

Her bones were breaking inside of her body.

"Michele…?"

She couldn't tell who said that. Dad?

Why did her arms look like that? Were they hers? Whose were they?

Why did her teeth hurt so much?

Who was Michele?

She wanted to die.

She wanted to live.

She wanted to kill.

《《《—》》》

Ivan bit the inside of his cheek and tasted the coppery blood. He hated this. Hated losing control. Oh, he still had every intention of taking George somewhere nice and private, and destroying his body one square inch at a time. But he'd completely lost control of the situation. And if he had to abandon the van, he'd have to postpone his revenge, and possibly lose George to Michele's newfound ravenous hunger.

That was bullshit.

He wondered why there weren't any choppers in the air. If the news was reporting the path he'd taken, why wasn't there a police helicopter overhead searching for him?

He wasn't going to be able to easily back the van around this upcoming corner. He'd either have to take it really slow, or risk going off the path and getting the van stuck. Damn it.

Ivan slammed on the brakes as a white van came into view. As he saw that Lou was driving, he transformed his hand into a claw and raked his talons across the passenger seat, howling in fury even though the rest of his body remained human.

Now he had no choice. He had to cut his losses.

«««—»»»

Lou stopped his van just a few feet away from the other one. Though he couldn't see who was inside, he assumed it was Ivan driving.

Prescott and Angie had taken all of the silver-tipped bolts with them, but Lou had placed several grenades on the seat, ready to go. Even if it didn't kill him, a blown-off leg would certainly slow down the werewolf.

Ivan got out of the van, transformed into a full wolfman, and darted off into the trees.

Lou got out as well, a grenade in each hand. He pulled the pin from the first one, and heaved it toward where Ivan had run. It was a good throw. Unfortunately, the blast was not accompanied by a lycanthrope scream.

He'd save the other one.

Lou hurried to the front of the van, as quickly as he was able, and peeked inside. The passenger seat was empty. George was in the cage with Michele, who was flailing around and tearing at her hair.

"Get me out of here!" George shouted. "Hurry!"

"Jesus." Lou limped to the rear of the van and threw open the back doors. What was wrong with her?

From this angle, it was obvious: she was half wolf.

"Unlock the cage! Unlock the cage!"

Michele ripped out a huge chunk of her hair, exposing bloody scalp underneath.

Lou tugged on the cage door. "Does Ivan have the key?"

"I don't know! Go find it!"

Michele pounced upon George. He cried out and tried to fend her off. She mounted him like a lover, slicing at him with her new claws.

"Push her over here!" Lou said. "I'll get her!"

"Find the keys!"

Lou went back to the driver's seat, praying that the keys were dangling from the ignition. They weren't. Ivan had them.

He fought off a momentary dizzy spell. The loss of blood was really starting to get to him.

«««—»»»

"Fight it!" George shouted as Michele raked her claws across his chest. He didn't expect this to work anymore, but it was certainly better than shouting something like "Get off of me!" He punched her in the chin. Her head flew back, almost dipping back far enough that it looked like she had no neck, and then it snapped back into place.

George could see the fur sprouting all over her arms and legs. The bandage fell off her shoulder, revealing no trace of a wound underneath.

"Ivan has the keys!" Lou shouted. "Get her over on this side! I'll take care of her!"

George threw another punch but she blocked it. Though she was a werewolf now, she was still smaller than him, and he shoved her off of him. She hit the bottom of the cage, snarled, and bit at his arm. He pulled away.

Oh, God, don't let her bite me. I don't want to become something like that.

What a horrible fate. Better to die at Ivan's claws, with some degree of honor, than to become a drooling, snarling beast and have to be put down like an animal.

He screamed as she bit him.

«««—»»»

Lou couldn't believe how much he was being forced to move around with injuries like his. He went back to the van, climbed inside, and slammed his foot through an opening in the bars, kicking Michele in the head as she bit George on the arm.

Her mouth popped free. George had a red mark but it didn't look like she'd broken the skin.

Now she was out of Lou's range. He turned his attention away from the cage and opened the glove compartment. He grabbed a handful of the contents and tossed them onto the floor, flipping through random papers until he found several of them fastened together by a paper clip.

He pulled off the paper clip and began to unbend it as he returned to the back of the van.

«««—»»»

She was almost fully transformed now—or at least appeared to be, since George had no idea how far this was going to go. She seemed to be more of a traditional wolf form than Ivan was in his changed state.

He didn't bother asking her to fight it anymore.

Her claws sunk into his shoulder, deep, the same shoulder he'd dislocated. He grabbed her chin and slammed her head against the roof of the cage. That didn't seem to rattle her.

«««—»»»

Lou jammed the paper clip into the lock and jiggled it. He wasn't very good with locks. When necessary, that was usually George's job.

He had the grenades, but they were fragmentation grenades. They wouldn't blow the door off a thick steel cage like this. If the paper clip didn't work, he'd try to shoot it.

He jammed the paper clip in deeper, as George and Michele struggled, her jaws snapping shut over his face. He slammed her head against the top of the cage again, then a third time, and though it seemed to be helping she still had a hell of a lot of fight left in her.

Lou's spirits soared as he thought he heard a click, but he tugged on the cage door and it didn't budge. False alarm. He continued to wiggle the paper clip around in the lock, having no idea what he was doing but hoping that he'd luck out. He prayed to every god that he could think of that he'd get this right.

"Open the cage!" George shouted, unhelpfully.

This wasn't going to work. Lou had no idea if this was even the kind of lock you *could* pick with a paper clip. If it was, Ivan would have no doubt figured out a way to make his escape sooner than he did. Hell, if nothing else, he could have used his talons.

Shit.

«««—»»»

Michele was wild-eyed and scary and George had thoroughly gotten over his qualms about fighting with a woman. There was nothing left of the real Michele, as far as he could tell.

Why was Lou still screwing around with the lock? Popping that thing should have been no problem. Couldn't he see that the she-wolf was winning?

She hadn't bitten him yet, at least not hard enough to pierce his flesh, but not for lack of trying. In fact, her jaws never stopped snapping open and closed, almost like a slower version of a pair of chattery teeth. His hand was clamped over her throat, and he pushed up as hard as he could, trying to keep her teeth away from his face, but he wasn't going to be able to sustain this for much longer.

"I can't do this!" said Lou. "Get her away from you! I'll get a gun and shoot her!"

"What? No!"

"What else do you want me to do?"

"Get the cage open!"

"I can't get the cage open!"

"Fuck!"

"I know!"

George's hand slipped off of Michele's throat, but he elbowed her in the face before she could bite him. He slammed her into the side of the cage.

Her growl deepened. She seemed absolutely furious.

«««—»»»

Rage.
Pure unrestrained fury.
Nothing else mattered.
Kill the prey.
Eat him.

«««—»»»

Lou pulled the paper clip out of the lock and tossed it aside. He was wasting time. He took out the gun and fired two bullets into the lock, turning his head and squeezing his eyes shut in case there was a ricochet.

"Be careful!" George shouted.

Lou opened his eyes. "I am being careful!" No impact. Bullets weren't going to do it, either. He could try to shoot Michele and see if bullets worked better on her than Ivan, but there was no way he could guarantee that he wouldn't put a bullet in George instead.

Once again he ran to the front of the van and climbed inside.

He shoved his foot into the cage again, but this time Michele avoided his kick. She grabbed his foot and he had a momentary flash of terror as she pulled him toward her.

George slammed his fist against her arm, breaking her hold. Lou withdrew his foot from within the bars, but then braced both feet against the side of the cage, tightly held the seats of the van, and shoved as hard as he could.

He was already shot and mauled. Why not add a hernia?

The pain was intense but not quite unbearable as the cage began to slowly slide along the floor of the van. It had good traction. After everything he'd been through today, he deserved to have *something* work out.

Michele slashed George's chest. It looked like a savage wound, although George had suffered so many injuries that Lou wasn't sure if that was a brand new one or an old one being reopened.

The edge of the cage slid over the back of the van.

«««—»»»

George cried out as Michele's claws ripped into his chest. He'd been hit in that same goddamn spot at least two other times today. If it were on the other side, his heart would practically be exposed.

He grabbed her arm, squeezing hard enough that it might have broken a bone if she were in her human form, and tossed her to the other side of the cage. She struck the door, twisted around, and came back at George.

Lou continued to shove the cage forward. George wasn't entirely certain that this was a good idea.

George began to frantically kick at Michele as she lunged at him. Her jaws closed over his shoe and it took three tugs to get it loose.

The cage began to tilt.

«««—»»»

Ivan watched the struggle with a combination of disbelief and amusement. Yeah, he should've just run away, but he *had* to know what was going on. It was absolutely crazy. Lou should be sobbing over his buddy's corpse while Michele feasted on George's remains. He should most definitely not be pushing the cage out of the van.

Insane.

He planned to remain hidden unless it was absolutely necessary to join in the chaos, but there was no way he could turn away from the show.

«««—»»»

There was definitely a hernia in Lou's future.

His legs were now extended all the way. The cage wasn't quite ready to topple over the edge, but it was getting close.

«««—»»»

George kicked Michele for what felt like the hundredth time since she transformed. His muscles were so sore that the agony almost threatened to overpower his flesh wounds.

Michele struck the cage door again, and her weight started the point of no return. The cage did a sharp downward tilt and then slid off the edge of the van, crashing to the ground corner-first with a teeth-rattling clatter. George bashed against Michele, nearly knocking the wind out of him but hopefully hurting her just as bad.

The floor of the cage slammed down, stirring up a cloud of dirt.

Michele dove at him. Nope, the impact of the fall definitely hadn't hurt her as much as it did him.

She pinned him down. George was having difficulty focusing his vision. A trio of she-wolf faces loomed above him.

Then she slid away as Lou grabbed her leg.

"I've got her!" Lou announced.

George scooted to the back of the cage. "What good does that do me? Are you gonna hold her forever?"

Lou pulled until her leg was entirely out of the cage, and then grabbed the back of her shirt, holding her tight.

"Get some silver!" George shouted.

"We don't have any!"

"What do you mean, we don't have any?"

"Prescott and Angie took it all!"

"Why'd they do that?"

"They didn't think they'd get killed!"

"Well, do *something*!"

Lou glanced to the side. George thought he might be looking for an item that might prove to be useful in this situation, but realized he was wrong as Ivan's werewolf form knocked Lou away from the cage.

Chapter Twenty-Eight: Lou's Decision

Lou lost his grip on Michele, who instantly pounced back upon George. Lou fell to the ground and raised his gun, but Ivan was already back in the swamp.

What was that all about?

He doesn't know what kind of weapons we have, Lou realized. *He has to play it safe.*

At this point, Lou didn't give half a crap about capturing the werewolf. Let Bateman and Dewey seek them out to the ends of the earth. If Lou had the opportunity to stuff a grenade down Ivan's throat, he'd take it without hesitation.

He did not, however, want to spend the rest of his life in prison, and they'd made a lot of noise. *Somebody* had to be coming to investigate.

Lou reached his hand into the cage, nearly got bit, and quickly withdrew it. "Throw her over here," he told George. "I'll shoot her!"

Lou watched carefully for Ivan as George struggled some more with the she-wolf. After a few violent moments, he managed to push her to the edge of the cage.

"Hold her still!"

"I can't hold her still!"

Lou shot her in the head. Some blood sprayed on George.

Michele howled and bled. But she didn't flop over and die.

George scooted away as she came at him again. He kicked repeatedly, desperately trying to keep her on her own side of the cage.

Now what?

Leave George to fend for himself?

No. Absolutely not.

He wasn't going to leave George here to be torn apart by Michele, although if they ended up in police custody, Lou thought he'd be more than justified in trying to cut a deal and let his partner take most of the fall. He wasn't entirely certain what crimes they'd be charged with, beyond the obvious investigation into their criminal past, but being responsible for a werewolf who killed about a dozen people had to be a pretty serious offense.

Hell, even if he did kill Michele, it wasn't as if Lou could simply load the cage onto the other van and drive away. George would be a nice little present for the cops. Or, much worse, Ivan.

He had to get George out of that cage, no matter what. Even if it meant putting his life at risk.

Concentrate. Get through this. If you pass out now, it'll be a really humiliating and unsatisfying end to this whole thing. Think of how good a warm shower is going to feel tonight. Oh, yeah.

He went back to the other van, hesitated for a moment as he tried to figure out if he really wanted to do this, then opened up the box of dynamite. It had about ten sticks inside. He probably only needed one, but he took the whole box.

There were no lighters inside the box, which made sense for safety precautions, but a quick search of a shelf of random supplies turned up a butane lighter with a long shaft, just like the one he had for his grill at home.

George screamed.

Lou grabbed a couple more grenades and tossed them into the box, just in case Ivan came back, and then returned to the cage.

"Did she bite you?" Lou asked, taking out a stick of dynamite. It already had a short fuse attached. Perfect.

"Not hard! Hurry!"

"I've got this, George. Don't worry." Okay, if he put the dynamite right next to the cage door, George would be caught in the blast. That was no good. Three feet away, maybe? He was far from a demolition expert.

"What the hell are you doing?" George demanded.

"I'm getting you out of there!"

"Not with goddamn dynamite, you're not!"

"It's the only way!"

"No, no, no, no! There are millions of other ways!" George had his hands around Michele's neck again, and his arms quivered as he tried to keep her fangs away from him.

Lou lit the fuse. "Stay at the back of the cage!"

"No! No, Lou! Fuck this!"

"Hands over your ears!" Lou grabbed the box and ran. He caught a glimpse of movement from the swamp. Ivan?

Michele snarled.

Lou grabbed a grenade out of the box, and then let the entire box drop to the ground. He pulled the pin and hurled it in what he hoped was Ivan's direction.

The grenade went off first.

Then the dynamite went off in a nearly eardrum-bursting explosion. The entire cage lifted several inches off the ground, and toppled onto its side. Lou's ears rang as he watched the smoke clear.

The cage door hung slightly ajar.

Victory! Lou hurried over to the cage. George lay on what was now the bottom of the cage, clearly stunned but also clearly still alive.

Michele's legs had taken the worst of the blast. There wasn't much left of one of them.

Lou kicked the cage door all the way open. "C'mon, George!"

George pushed Michele off of him and then scrambled out of the cage. "What the hell was that?"

"I saved your life!"

"You could have killed me!"

"So could she!"

"Don't *do* things like that!"

"You're out of the cage, aren't you?"

"My legs are all burnt up!"

"They're not that bad. They're singed."

"Look what she did to me! I look as bad as you do!"

"That's why I tried to get you out!"

"Why didn't you just pick the lock?"

"It didn't work!"

"Why didn't you just get the keys from Ivan?"

"How the hell was I supposed to do that?"

"I don't know!"

"Stop yelling at me!"

"I have to yell! I'm deaf now!"

"Just thank me, okay?"

"Okay. Thank you!"

They both looked down at Michele. She was back to human form, bleeding badly.

Lou crouched down next to the cage. "Aw, shit, I'm so sorry, Michele."

She gave him a weak smile, revealing red teeth. "How bad is it?"

"Pretty bad," said George.

"I don't think I'll die though," she said. She turned her head and coughed up some blood. When she looked back at them, her eyes glistened. "Don't leave me like this."

"We won't. I promise."

"I mean...don't leave me like *this*. Put me out of my misery. I don't want to be this way. I don't want to hurt people."

George nodded. He felt absolutely terrible, but if he were in her situation, he'd feel the exact same way. "Lou, are you sure there aren't any silver-tipped arrows left?"

"I didn't tear the whole van apart, but I didn't see any. George, I don't want to be cold-hearted or anything, but we really need to get out of here."

"Use the dynamite," Michele said.

"What?"

"It'll hurt less than silver, I think."

Lou took another stick of dynamite out of the box. "Are you sure this is what you want? Maybe we can get you help."

"There's no help for me. I'm sorry, George. I didn't mean to hurt you."

George almost looked like his eyes were tearing up. "I'm sorry, too. I thought I was helping you by rescuing you from those dogs. Bad call, huh?"

"Yeah." Suddenly Michele cried out in pain. The hairs on her arm began to sway as they did before the first transformation. "Oh, God..."

Lou lit the fuse and dropped the stick of dynamite into the cage.

Michele picked it up and hugged it to her chest.

The thugs walked away from the cage.

The explosion sounded even louder than the first one.

They looked back. There was nothing left of Michele but some burnt pieces, scattered around the area.

"Shit," said George.

"At least she didn't suffer."

"What do you mean? She suffered a lot."

"Not from the dynamite, though."

"Well, that's lovely. If you count only that last second when she got blown to bits, she died a peaceful death. Wonderful. I guess coming into our lives was the best thing that ever happened to that young girl."

"I just won't say anything else." Lou took another stick of dynamite out of the box while watching carefully for any sign of Ivan.

"Hey, Ivan!" George shouted. "Did you see that? Sorry you didn't get to make yourself a girlfriend! She was a good choice!" George walked over to the white van and opened the passenger side door.

"Is he still around?" Lou asked. It seemed unlikely that Ivan would stay in the area having witnessed what happened to the other werewolf, but anything was possible with that cocky bastard.

George picked up the tracking device. "Yeah. He's still close." George pointed at the swamp in the same direction where Lou had thrown the grenade. "Do it."

Lou lit the fuse and tossed the dynamite.

The explosion sent up a cloud of smoke and burning leaves. Lou felt too sick over what they'd done to Michele to enjoy the sensation of hurling explosives.

"Did we get him?"

"No," said George. "Crap. He's on the move."

"Should we go after him?"

George stared at the tracking device for a moment. "No, he's running. I don't blame him. We won't be able to catch him on foot. Let's get in the van. When he comes out of the swamp, we'll be ready."

They got in the van, with George driving. Lou figured that this was around the time when several police cars would come into view, red and blue lights flashing, with a few dozen officers pointing rifles at them, but the path remained empty.

"Once again, we could just let him go," said Lou.

"Are you kidding me? With a van full of great stuff? That furry son of a bitch is *dead*."

Lou sighed. "All right."

"You're with me, right?"

Lou thought about that for a moment. "You know what? I actually think I am. I will be really, really relieved when he's dead."

"Me too."

"So…Mexico or Canada when we flee from our former lives?"

"People are polite in Canada."

"But it's cold there."

"I don't speak much Spanish."

"But again, it's cold."

"So what?" George asked. "You've spent the entire day complaining that it's too hot."

"And it is. I don't like Florida heat or Canadian cold."

"Which is worse?"

"I'm not sure. Florida heat, I guess."

"Well, Mexico heat is worse than Florida heat, so I guess that settles it. Time to relearn how to say 'about.'"

"About," said Lou, pronouncing it *a-boot*. "I can't believe Michele is dead."

"Let's not talk about it."

"What if her pieces are still alive?"

"*What?*"

"I'm just saying."

"You jackass. Why the hell would you say something like that? I mean, even if you thought it, why would you say it? Her pieces are not still alive, got it?"

"Yeah, yeah, you're right. I'm just freaked out by it all."

"So am I, but that doesn't mean I'm sharing 'living hell' scenarios. She's dead. If we blow Ivan into a billion pieces, he'll be dead, too. Did you see any of those pieces moving?"

"No, they were…they were pretty much just lying there, burning."

"Right. Stop coming up with macabre shit like that."

"Sorry."

George looked over at the tracking device. "He's still running. We put a nice scare into him. Let's appreciate that instead of dwelling on horrific stuff."

"When we catch up to him, I'm using all of the remaining dynamite."

"That's the spirit!"

Chapter Twenty-Nine: Distress

Ivan ran through the swamp, so enraged that he thought his head might explode like the dynamite.

He didn't mind losing Michele. She was only intended to be a temporary plaything, and he probably shouldn't have bitten her in the first place. No big deal. It was like having a child—a responsibility he didn't want.

Losing George hurt worse. He'd really been looking forward to making the thug weep. Ivan had probably exercised bad judgment in staying around as long as he did. As soon as he saw that they had grenades, he should have gotten out of there. He was a fast healer, but not immortal, and even if there was no jagged silver involved he wouldn't survive having his head blown off.

Still, that wasn't the reason for his misery.

They were *tracking* him. George had been holding some kind of device that could follow his movements. It had to be a chip or something, like what people used for their beloved pets. That's how those fuckers with the net and crossbow found him.

Ivan was almost in tears.

He'd stopped for about a minute to check his ears, even though he would've noticed a chip in there long before now. The way he healed up, they could have stuck it in him at Bateman's place while he was unconscious and he never would have known.

Where was it?

This was awful. This was the worst possible thing. Sure, he was a werewolf, but he still had to sleep. What was he going to do, find some kind of impenetrable bunker to hide out in? Even if the chip only had a limited range, that didn't do him any good unless he was able to jump on a plane. He couldn't help but feel that he was going to have difficulty using air travel for the foreseeable future.

Damn them!

He could turn back, try to kill George and Lou, and steal their tracker, but that couldn't be the only device. Ivan wasn't good with technology and didn't know how these things worked, but they probably even had a fucking website where they could track him.

He stopped running. He had to think. He couldn't just let them hunt him down. Better to get blown up than to be Dewey's little experiment, but he wanted to avoid both of those possibilities.

Where would they stick the chip?

If he were tagging a werewolf, where would he put it?

He changed back into his human form and searched his arms for scars. All of this blood wasn't helping. A tiny incision wouldn't leave any trace, but if they got overzealous, there might be a mark.

He had lots of marks, but they were all from today, as far as he could tell. He feverishly rubbed his arms, trying to get off as much of the dried blood as he could.

He could feel himself losing it. This wasn't good.

If they beat him, it wasn't going to be because of some chip. No way.

He stripped off what little remained of his pants and stood there, naked, searching his body for any scars he couldn't identify. There had to be one. Just a faint trace.

Still too much blood.

Fine. This was the Florida Everglades. There was water all over the place. He ran for less than a minute before he found a pool of water. It looked stagnant and thousands of mosquitoes seemed to be swarming around it, but it would do.

He lay on his back in the water, splashing around, washing off the blood. He didn't care about the bugs. Let them take his blood. They could have as much as they wanted.

Losing it...

Ivan sat up. He inspected his stomach, his legs, his feet. Nothing.

It wasn't fair.

Where would they put it? Where the hell would they put it?

For all he knew, there was a big crooked scar across his back. He twisted himself around, trying to glimpse his reflection in the water, but the water wasn't still enough and he couldn't see anything.

Chill the hell out. You're going from "losing it" to "batshit crazy."

So they had a chip in him. So what? He'd massacred a whole bunch of people in the Cotton Mouse Tavern who'd known exactly where he was, and it sure didn't save their lives. George and Lou had been following him, and they hadn't fared very well. Neither had the reinforcements.

Following Ivan Spinner with a tracing device meant that you got your arms, legs, and head torn off and thrown into the air like confetti. That's what your precious chip did for you.

If Bateman showed up, Ivan would rip his heart out.

If Dewey showed up, Ivan would make him measure his own intestines by the yard.

If George and Lou found him, Ivan would hold them in this foul water and laugh while the mosquitoes drained them.

Watch the skeeters drink until they burst. Pop, pop, pop.

Where would they put it? It had to be something relatively easy—it's not like they would saw open his cranium and glue it to his brain. They'd want to keep it someplace simple, like his arm.

His arm. That had to be it.

Which arm?

He was right-handed, so they'd probably go for his left. That would be the best way to keep it undetected.

Where on the left arm?

They'd go for a fleshy part. Somewhere he'd be less likely to feel it. So…the bottom of his upper arm. Absolutely. That's exactly where a sneaky bastard like Bateman would hide the chip.

Ivan transformed his right index finger into a claw. The problem with Bateman's oh-so-brilliant plan was that he didn't think Ivan would cut open his own flesh to dig out the chip. How wrong he was.

Ivan held up his arm, bent it at the elbow, and poked the talon through his skin. He was spilling new blood to replace what he'd washed away. Let the mosquitoes drink their fill.

He dragged the talon across his arm, cutting deep into his flesh.

He didn't scream. He wanted to, but he didn't. He'd felt much worse pain than this, and here he was in total control. He could stop whenever he wanted.

Ivan cut all the way to his elbow, then withdrew the talon. There was no chip on the end.

He took a deep breath to steel himself, and then slipped his middle finger into the gash, running along its length, searching for the chip. This hurt far worse than the initial cut. Worse than the bullets he'd taken today. Even worse than the process of having bullets extracted, which was something he'd been through several times before, and something else he'd have to endure in the near future. Drugs didn't work on him anymore, so he was forced to remain totally conscious and alert as the non-licensed physician dug out the slugs with a scalpel and tweezers.

Now he screamed.

What difference did it make? Until he got rid of the chip, it didn't do any good for him to remain quiet.

No chip.

He dug around in the wound some more.

"You can't beat me," he whispered. "Not a chance."

He'd have to try the other arm.

He slapped at the mosquitoes.

Other arm. Same spot. That's where they'd hide the chip.

He transformed his left index finger, then slit his other arm, wishing that he could just shut off all sensation. Scrape his arms down to the bone.

He probably wouldn't heal from that.

He wasn't entirely sure where the limits of his healing power ended. He'd certainly tested that over the years, but never to the point of skeletonizing a limb to find a hidden tracking chip.

He worked his finger through the wound, blinking back tears.

What was that?

He'd definitely felt something odd.

He poked around in there, arm twitching, the pain more intense than anything he'd ever experienced in a lifetime of pain. He could do this. He was strong.

I think the word is "insane."

Was he touching bone?

He couldn't take it anymore. He pulled his finger out, then kneeled back down in the water and washed off his hands.

What was he going to do?

Maybe the chip wasn't in his arms. Maybe they'd implanted it in his heart. Or maybe it was microscopic, and it was right there on the tip of his nose but he couldn't see it.

Pull it together...

What a horrible way to end this conflict. Sitting here in a bug-filled pool practicing self-mutilation. Oh, George and Lou would get a great big laugh at that. They'd point and take pictures. Look at the formerly amazing werewolf, reduced to a filthy animal hurting himself.

He picked up his pants—well, the pants formerly belonging to the guy who he'd killed—and slipped them back on. He needed to do that. The pain brought clarity.

He'd get the chip out before too long. He knew a "doctor" in Atlanta who could X-ray him, find exactly where it was, and cut it out. No problem.

No reason to panic. And no shame in panicking. Everybody did it.

They could follow him, but they couldn't catch him.

Not a chance.

Ivan transformed back into a wolfman, let out a howl, and then resumed racing across the swamp.

«««—»»»

When he emerged onto a two-lane paved road, he kept running.

A couple of minutes later, he saw a car.

There was no time for jokes. No time to mentally torment his prey before he ripped them apart. No time for fun. He needed that car, and he needed it now.

He leapt onto the front hood, opening his jaws as wide as he could. The woman shrieked and drove off the road.

He opened the door, dragged her out of the vehicle, and snapped her neck.

He checked her pockets for money, found none, and tossed her body off to the side. Somebody would find it quickly, unless an alligator dragged it away for an evening meal, but that didn't matter. Ivan would be long gone.

He got in the car and sped off.

Chapter Thirty: Hot Pursuit

"Are you absolutely positive you're not going to bleed to death?" George asked.

"Look, I promise that if I get ready to bleed to death, I'll give you a five minute warning, okay? How are your legs?"

"They hurt."

"Sorry."

"It's okay. I apologize for yelling at you after you blew open the cage with dynamite. You have to understand why I'd be stressed out at that particular moment."

"I do."

George's phone rang again. "I'd better get that or he's never going to stop calling." He pressed the "talk" button and placed the phone to his ear. "Yeah, Ricky?"

"Where have you been? What's going on?"

"Rescue team's dead. Werewolf's still loose."

"We know. We're tracing him."

"So are we."

"I hear Bateman and Dewey are both trying to put together a new team. I mean, like, every dogcatcher from here to New Orleans. From a friend to a friend, George, I'm suggesting that you get out of the country as soon as you possibly can and don't look back."

"Sorry, Ricky. We're killing the werewolf."

"Don't do that! Just stay out of this now."

"Not going to happen. There'll be bits of fur for a six-mile stretch of I-75."

"Then we never had this conversation."

"Fair enough. And you're not my friend. I pissed in your coffee cup twice a week."

"You did what?"

"Okay, that's not true. I never did that. Take care of yourself, Ricky." George hung up the phone. "He's a rotten little prick," he said to Lou, "but he deserves to enjoy his cup of coffee in the morning. How far ahead is Ivan?"

"Looks like about two miles."

"Good." Ivan seemed to be sticking to the speed limit. George was doing about ten miles faster and cruising along at eighty miles per hour. Neither of them could afford to get pulled over by the cops, but George was apparently more willing to take the risk.

The plan, which was straightforward and inelegant, was to catch up to whatever car Ivan was driving, and fling a stick of dynamite at him. Watching that bastard go up in an explosion would be better than every Fourth of July celebration George had witnessed in his entire life combined.

If he had a hostage in the car with him, they'd use guns instead of explosives. Either way, unless he was in a bus filled with nuns, orphans, and kittens, that werewolf was only a few minutes away from death.

They'd discussed the idea of just following behind him, out of sight, until Ivan was forced to stop somewhere to get gas. The problem with that plan was that their van was already getting low on fuel, and they had to assume that he'd outlast them in that regard. They couldn't afford to lose ten minutes to get off and refuel. Twenty if there was another frickin' dog attack.

"Are you sure we shouldn't be more subtle?" Lou asked. "There are a lot of cars around."

"If we get the opportunity to be subtle, we'll take it. Otherwise, dynamite out the window."

"All right. I can't say I won't enjoy it."

George pressed harder on the accelerator, bringing their speed up to eighty-five. Plenty of other cars were going that fast. As far as he knew, the cops weren't looking for a white van that said "Ray's Air Conditioning" on the side, so they'd be okay until they started flinging explosives.

"He's a mile ahead."

"Cool. Maybe if we're lucky, there'll be a semi we can hide behind or something."

George pressed down on the accelerator a bit more, letting their speed creep up to eighty-seven.

"Slow down," Lou said, glancing at the speedometer. "You're getting too impatient."

"I want him gone."

"So do I. Slow down."

George relented and dropped their speed back down to eighty-five.

"Do you think he knows we're coming?" Lou asked.

"I hope so. I don't like the idea of an ambush, but I do like the idea of him being scared out of his mind."

"Well, let's not get overconfident. I don't think we're going to be able to narrow this down to a single car unless the traffic really clears up, and he knows what we're driving."

"Believe me, after the way things have gone, the last thing I am is over-confident."

Lou rolled down his window. Several sticks of dynamite and a few grenades rested in his lap. Yesterday, that was a sight that would have made George extremely uncomfortable. Now it made him happy.

"Shit," he said, as red-and-blue flashing lights became visible in the rear-view mirror. "Cop."

"I'm not throwing a grenade at him."

George slowed down to seventy and moved into the far right lane, desperately hoping that the cop was pulling over somebody else.

The police car drove ahead of the van and came up behind a brown truck. The truck slowed down and moved into the right lane. The cop followed him. As the truck pulled off to the side, George breathed a sigh of relief.

Lou picked up a stick of dynamite. "This would've been difficult to explain."

"No kidding."

They drove in silence for a couple of minutes. "Okay, start watching for him."

There were no big trucks or other vans to hide behind. Since Ivan would've had no way of knowing where they were, they just had to hope that he wasn't keeping a close watch on every single vehicle on the road.

"Up there," said Lou, pointing at a small blue Volkswagen. "Does that look like the back of his head?"

George leaned forward and squinted. "I...I think so. No, wait, the hair is wrong. It's not him."

George and Lou both surveyed the cars ahead of them. "He's got to be in one of these. Maybe in the—*there*! That's him!" Lou pointed to another small car in the left-hand lane that was a darker shade of blue than the first.

Yep. Definitely him. "He's on the wrong side."

"There aren't any windows in the back. You're gonna have to throw them."

"Aw, shit."

"Get at least a car-length ahead of him so that when you throw it, it hits the front of his car."

George nodded. The van began to shake, clearly not having been designed to go this fast.

They passed Ivan's car. Ivan looked over at George and scowled. George would've expected a grin. Things were looking up.

"Don't let him see what you're doing," said George, as Lou pulled the trigger to start the lighter. There were no cars behind Ivan. No innocent victims.

Keeping the stick of dynamite below window-level, Lou lit the fuse. George's heart felt like it leapt into his throat, which managed to be simultaneously a good feeling and a bad one. Lou passed him the burning stick and grabbed the steering wheel.

George flung the stick of dynamite out the window.

It struck Ivan's windshield dead center.

Then bounced off.

The dynamite sailed harmlessly over Ivan's car then exploded against the pavement behind him. Tires squealed as a convertible swerved into the other lane.

"Grenade!"

Keeping one hand on the wheel, Lou pulled the pin out of a grenade and handed it to George. He immediately tossed it out the window.

It struck the front hood of Ivan's car, bounced up onto the roof, off the rear, and then exploded in mid-air.

"Damn it!" George shouted.

Ivan swerved, moving directly behind the van.

George tilted the side-view mirror. "I can't see him! Try to throw something out the back!"

"The shelf with all the weapons is in the way!"

"I know that! Knock it over!"

"It's bolted in place!"

"Fuck!"

George slammed on the brakes. That little car would fare much worse in a collision than the van.

Ivan swerved to the right, coming up on Lou's side.

A sign announced that the next exit was half a mile away.

"Blast the bastard!" George shouted.

Lou flicked on the lighter again, but hesitated. There was a minivan up ahead in the right lane, blocking Ivan's potential escape. "Try to match his speed," Lou said. "He won't be able to pass us."

The traffic had cleared out behind them. Apparently the other motorists wished to give some space between themselves and the explosive-hurling psychos in the white van.

«««—»»»

Ivan couldn't believe this. He'd taken plenty of risks in his quest for sadistic pleasure, but he'd never expected George and Lou to reach this level of fanaticism.

He was almost impressed.

«««—»»»

Lou lit the next stick of dynamite. He held onto it, watching the flame devour the fuse.

"Throw it!"

"Not yet!"

With alarmingly little left of the fuse, Lou flung the stick of dynamite out the window. It twirled end-over-end toward Ivan's driver's side window, leaving a trail of smoke.

It struck the window exactly where Lou wanted it to hit. Right next to Ivan's goddamn face.

Then it bounced off, hit the road, and rolled away.

Lou leaned out the window and watched it.

Nothing.

"It was a dud! Son of a bitch!"

"Does he look like he's going to take the exit?" George asked.

"I can't tell!"

"We're coming right up on it! Make a call!"

"I think he is! Get behind him!"

George braked. At the last instant, Ivan swerved into the exit lane, going so fast that George thought he might careen right off the curve. George followed him.

"Slow down!" Lou shouted.

George braked some more as they drove onto the highway exit. Ivan's car shot up ahead of them, but that was better than having the van fly right off the road.

"A dud," Lou muttered. "I can't believe it. He's one lucky bastard."

"Oh, no. He most certainly is not. It's just going to be worse for him when we finally catch him."

Having made it around the curve, George accelerated to catch up with Ivan. They couldn't let him out of their sight, in case he decided to bring innocent people into this again. Nobody else was going to die.

"I'm just going to ram him," said George. "Knock him right off the road."

Before Lou could protest, George floored the accelerator again. The van rocketed forward as they pulled onto the four-lane street. There was a traffic light just ahead, showing amber.

"Cop!" Lou said.

George instinctively braked. Ivan sped through the light just before it turned red.

"Don't run it!" Lou warned. "If we have to waste time with a cop he'll get away completely."

They waited at the light, hoping this particular police officer was not looking for a white van matching their description.

It was a long, agonizing red light.

"I can't believe we're doing this," said George.

"We've got the tracer. We can still find him."

George impatiently drummed his fingers on the dashboard.

"Calm down," said Lou. "We're still good."

"I'm not letting him get away."

"I know. That's not new information."

"I just need to say it."

"That's fine. Talk it out."

The light turned green. George drove through it, careful not to exceed the speed limit. But how were they supposed to catch Ivan if they had to obey traffic laws?

"He's not that far ahead," said Lou. "Keep going straight."

"How are we supposed to throw dynamite around a place like this?" George asked. "On the highway during a high-speed chase, we can sort of get away with it, but we can't do it here. We'll get nabbed for sure."

"He won't want to get out of his car, either. He's not going to stop around here."

"I hope you're right."

"I am," Lou said. Then he frowned. "Oh, shit, no, I'm not. He's over there. He's going into that bowling alley."

Chapter Thirty-One: Unleashing the Beast

George was not, in concept, a fan of bowling. It was pretty much just the same thing over and over, and the best you could hope for in terms of variety was that somebody in the other lane might slip and fall on their ass. Still, he actually found the "sport" kind of fun, and bowling might have been on his future list of ways to detox from the whole miserable Ivan experience.

He had a feeling that bowling was going to be forever tainted for him.

Ivan ran through the front doors of the bowling alley. He was in human form, but though he'd gotten rid of most of the blood, it was a human form covered with cuts and holes, not to mention the fact that he only wore shredded jeans. He clearly wasn't going inside in an attempt to blend with Uncle Frank's bowling league.

"What should we take?" Lou asked.

George wasn't certain. They couldn't just run in there and start lobbing dynamite. "Okay, give me two of the grenades," George said. "I'm going in there after him, but you take the van and drive behind the building. My job will be to chase him out one of the back entrances. When you see him, let him have it."

"Sounds good."

"Make sure it's him before you start throwing dynamite."

"I can handle that."

"If he kills me, avenge me." George pulled the van right up in front of the bowling alley. There were no screaming people rushing out of the exit yet, so things still had the potential not to completely lose control. George took two of the grenades from Lou, slipped one into each pocket, then got out of the van and ran inside the building.

237

He glanced around. Surprisingly decent music played over some speakers. He could die to Guns n' Roses if he had to. Only about five of the twenty or so lanes looked like they were being used. Obviously it wasn't League Night. Some guy dropped to his knees and raised his hands, apparently cursing the heavens as he got a gutter ball.

Where was Ivan?

The main desk where you paid for your game and got your shoes was to the right, so Ivan probably would've gone in the other direction. George turned to the left and walked, bracing himself for a werewolf attack at any moment.

There he was. In the game room. Seated in a stool in front of *Ms. Pac-Man*. Facing George and not the video game.

Ivan held up his hands to show that they were empty. His voice sounded tired, resigned. "Why are you still following me, George?"

"We've already been over this. You're a killer."

"And I'm going to continue to be a killer as long as you follow me. How many people do you think are in this bowling alley?"

"It doesn't matter. What you did before—it's never going to happen again."

"Look, George, we both have the potential to be reasonable men. This is stupid. You don't want me to kill any more innocent people, and I don't want you following me trying to blow up my car. Remember when you wanted to cut a deal? I'm ready to cut a deal."

George shook his head. "We're not giving you any money."

"I don't want money. I want peace. Just a few hours of peace." He smirked at George. "Oh, by the way, are those grenades in your pocket or your testicles for safekeeping?"

"They're grenades."

"So why don't you throw one at me?"

"I'm here to talk, just like you," said George. That wasn't even remotely the truth, but if he was going to successfully use the grenades, he'd have to catch Ivan unaware. The last thing George needed was to throw a grenade and have it batted right back in his face.

Or he could shove one down Ivan's throat and pull the pin. That idea worked, too.

"We're two sides of the same coin, you and me," said Ivan.

"No, we're not."

"Yeah, you're right. Forget I said it. Just trying to connect. However, I really do think we can talk this one out, because you've got something I want, and I've got something you want. Those are the two elements in a successful deal, my friend."

"So what is it you want?" George asked. "For me to just let you go? That's not going to happen."

"I'm not asking for a permanent treaty. I just want you to tell me where the tracking chip is, and then I'll leave. Nobody else dies today."

"It's in your leg."

"Wrong. See, I can tell when you're lying to me. That's how close we've grown. They didn't tell you where it was, huh?"

"Nope. Sorry."

"Figures. So my next request is to watch you smash the tracking device. Take all of your frustration out on it. Pretend it's me. I know Bateman and Dewey can still follow me, but all I want now is to get you off my tail."

"You don't have a tail."

"Yeah, I know. I'm thankful for that."

George cleared his throat. "Well, Ivan, despite my appearance, I am indeed a businessman. You're right, we both want something from each other. My question is, how can I trust you? You can watch us stomp on the tracer, but if we're supposed to let you go, how do I know you won't turn the corner and start killing people?"

"Well, that's a tricky one. The answer is that I don't *want* to kill anybody else tonight." Ivan held up his arms, revealing a mostly healed but still hideous gash on each of them. "I'm tired. I've got all of those bullets in me that have to be taken out. I've murdered a lot of people today, more than you even saw, and it's like an Olympic athlete setting a world record—they don't want to jump right back in the pool and try for another one."

"I'm not sure that metaphor is correct, but continue."

"All I want to do is hide out and rest for a while. My promise to you is that I won't kill anybody else. I'm not even planning to stay in the country."

"Neither are we."

"Well, shit, let's just make sure we're fleeing to different countries and everything will be fine."

"Sorry."

"Then how about we settle this over a game of *Ms. Pac-Man*? You get high score, I'll surrender myself to you. I get high score, you leave me alone. Fair?"

"Now I feel like you're stalling."

"You know, George, I've tried to be friendly during this little discussion. Make a deal, go our separate ways, and end this in a reasonably pleasant manner. But I don't get the impression that you want to work with me."

"I wonder why?"

"Because you're a fucking idiot. If they can find me wherever I go, then I have nothing to lose. Do you think I want them to hunt me down in a cheap motel and take me out while I sleep? Fuck that. If you're not going to cut a deal, then I'm just going to go out in a big-ass blaze of glory and kill every fucking person in this place."

"All right," said George. "We'll destroy the tracer."

"Thank you. Call Lou."

"You don't want to see it in person?"

"I'm sure he's got video capability on his phone. Tell him to video himself stomping the tracer to pieces and then send it to you."

A little kid, maybe seven or eight years old, walked into the game room.

"The arcade is closed," Ivan informed him.

"No, it isn't."

"Are you really going to argue this with me? It's closed. Get out of here."

The little kid gave Ivan the finger and left.

"You know," said Ivan, "there was a time when kids would respect their elders. They don't even respect their parents anymore. If I'd flipped off an adult when I was that age, my middle finger would be in a cast."

"Mine, too."

"It's really sad where society has fallen. I mean, I'm not going to sit here and try to convince you that I'm helping society in any way, but compare the impact of me killing a few people to the overall damage done by the fact that our nation's youth no longer has any shred of respect for their elders. If you could trade my killings for a generation that doesn't give adults the finger in arcades, wouldn't that be a good deal?"

"What the fuck are you even talking about? That's like your whole vagina-with-teeth speech." Either the werewolf was having a mental breakdown, or he was trying to distract George from some sneaky plan that he was working out. George needed to cut this conversation short.

He took out his cell phone and punched in Lou's number.

Ivan seemed to visibly relax.

That was good. Real good.

George knew that Ivan could not be trusted. The second Lou trashed that tracing device, Ivan would change into his wolf-self and go on another slaughter spree, laughing the entire time. "Ooooops, sorry, George! I thought you knew not to trust a homicidal lycanthrope maniac! Better luck next time!"

Let him go, even without destroying the tracer, and Ivan could rack up another twenty, thirty, *fifty* corpses before they found him again.

He just needed a moment to catch the werewolf off-guard.

This looked like a good one.

George did not have the advantage of being able to transform into a literal wolfman, but he'd stored up a shitload of anger today. There was absolutely no reason to try to control it anymore.

"Lou? I'm going to need you to destroy the tracer and video it. Don't argue with me! Goddamn it, Lou, just do it! Send me the video the second you're done."

He hung up.

"How about a quick game while we wait?" George asked, stepping over to the video game. "I didn't think you could find *Ms. Pac-Man* anymore. That's pretty cool. I suppose you were a fan of that werewolf game."

"Which one?"

"That one from the 80's. With the werewolf."

"Never heard of it."

"It's that one where—" George grabbed Ivan and threw him to the floor. As Ivan transformed, George dropped onto him, knees landing on his stomach, and pulled the grenade out of his pocket.

He slammed the grenade against Ivan's mouth, breaking off another fang. Ivan snarled and twisted his wolf-head to the left and right, struggling against the attack, but George summoned every ounce of his rage and jammed the grenade in there.

George took a claw to the arm. He didn't let that distract him from his purpose. Ivan was much stronger, but George only needed to hold him down for a few more seconds...

The grenade was in there deep enough for the son of a bitch to choke on it, but Ivan's head was thrashing so violently that George couldn't get at the pin.

He grabbed for it, not even caring if he lost a couple of fingers in the process. Ivan's tongue slid over his hand as George's index finger curled over the grenade pin.

He yanked it out.

And at that moment, Ivan's rage surpassed George's own. He pushed himself up, sending George tumbling to the floor, then spat the grenade at him.

It landed on George's chest.

He scooped it up and tossed it. He was suddenly more concerned with getting the explosive off of his chest than taking out the werewolf, so his throw went wild. The grenade bounced against the console of a classic *Centipede* machine and exploded, shattering the screen and sending debris flying.

Ivan flexed his claws.

George quickly dug the other grenade out of his pocket.

Ivan ran out of the arcade.

George got up. His legs, burnt from the dynamite, now felt like they were actively on fire, but he pushed through it. He'd have plenty of time to wallow in agony later.

He ran out of the arcade after him.

Chapter Thirty-Two: The Final Fight

The explosion had already started a flood of terrified people fleeing for the exit, and the werewolf running out of the arcade added to the screams. George was right behind him.

Though he didn't want to waste his last grenade, if Ivan went for kills rather than escape, this might be George's last chance to use it before Ivan started slicing his way through a bunch of innocent people. If he could at least keep Ivan from going out the main entrance, the werewolf might try to run out the back, in which case Lou could take care of him.

A heavyset woman nearly knocked George over in her stampede to get out of there. Ivan was not going for the entrance—he was going for a crowd of people at the snack bar.

George had only a few seconds before a grenade would cause collateral damage. He pulled out the pin and lobbed the grenade at Ivan's back.

It came up short, but not *too* short. The grenade went off as it hit the floor, spraying Ivan with incendiary material. He stumbled, lurched forward, and fell.

George rushed at him.

The werewolf was back up before he got there, but Ivan changed direction, jumping down a few stairs to the actual bowling lanes. Every step felt like his legs were being pressed against a hot grill, but George continued to follow him.

George jumped down the five stairs. With the impact, he literally believed that his legs were going to collapse underneath him like an accordion, but they mercifully remained intact.

Ivan ran onto the lane.

Then he slipped.

He didn't fall, but the slip was all George needed. He scooped up a bowling ball and did an overhead throw, hurling it at Ivan's back.

Unlike the grenade, this throw did not come up short. The ten or twelve pound ball struck Ivan in the center of the back, knocking him down onto the shiny wooden lane.

George jammed his fingers into the holes of another bowling ball and ran onto the lane with the werewolf.

If he ever got to retell this story, George would enhance this portion, laughing gently as he told his grandchildren about how he rolled the ball down the center of the lane, bashing the werewolf in the face. *And then I shouted "strike!"* he'd tell them.

Instead, he adjusted his grip so that he held the bowling ball with both hands, and brought it down upon Ivan's head.

Though Ivan's skull didn't crack open, the force of the blow definitely left a dent.

George bashed him again. Then once more.

The ball popped out of George's hands and rolled into the gutter.

Ivan scrambled forward. George wrapped his arms around the werewolf's leg, forcing him to drag George along with him. George tried to rip off chunks of fur as they moved down the bowling lane.

He was losing his grip on Ivan. He couldn't let that happen. What if the werewolf ran back the way they'd come, rushing out the main entrance and hacking up new victims left and right?

Ivan got one of his legs free, and kicked George in the face. It definitely drew blood. George didn't care.

Several pins fell. Was some idiot really still bowling?

No, it was Lou, coming to the rescue.

Lou kicked away the remaining pins and crawled through the back entrance to the lane. Later—again, if he survived—George would thank him profusely for deviating from the plan. If Lou had been in here and George had heard explosions, he probably would've come in to make sure everything was okay, too.

Lou picked up a bowling pin as he got back to his feet.

George made another grab for Ivan's legs. Ivan caught George's wrists and gave them a powerful tug that sent twin bolts of pain all the way to his shoulders. Both of George's arms flopped uselessly onto the lane. He would've expected it to hurt twice as much as when he'd had one shoulder dislocated earlier, but it hurt a lot more than that.

Ivan ran at Lou.

Lou swung the pin, bashing it so hard across Ivan's face that the pin broke in half in a shower of wood chips.

George couldn't catch his breath. He felt like he might be having a heart attack. Considering the amount of pain he was in at the moment, that sounded almost relaxing.

«««—»»»

Lou slammed the broken pin into Ivan's chest, trying to use it like a broken bottle. The splinters wouldn't kill him, but Lou just needed to hurt Ivan enough to make him run away. If he ran away, Lou was confident that he could get him with the dynamite that was currently wedged into the waist of his pants.

Mostly confident, anyway.

He really hoped that stuff was stable.

«««—»»»

Ivan had no intention of running away.

He was going to fuck these guys up.

«««—»»»

George rolled onto his side, prayed that his shoulder was in the right spot, and bashed himself against the bowling lane. He thought he might be screaming louder than the blast of the grenades, but he didn't care. *God* that hurt.

He repeated the process with the other shoulder.

Lou seemed to be holding up…well, poorly. He'd gotten in some good hits, but the werewolf was nowhere near out of commission.

«««—»»»

Lou punched Ivan in the stomach. It was a solid, powerful blow, yet it did nothing.

What if he lit the fuse? Blew them both up.

He'd kill himself, but end the werewolf's rampage forever.

No. Fuck suicide, even heroic sacrifice suicide. He'd poke out the werewolf's eyeballs, kick him away, then blow his ass up, after which, he and George should probably make a hasty retreat for the exit. They were having good luck with the slow arrival of law enforcement agencies today, but that winning streak couldn't last forever.

He extended his thumb and jabbed at Ivan's right eye.

Ivan grabbed Lou's wrist, twisted it, and then shoved it into his mouth.

Lou shrieked as the werewolf's fangs tore through muscle and crunched through bone.

«««—»»»

He bit his hand off! Holy shit! He bit Lou's hand off!

George's arms still weren't working right, but he managed to push himself to his feet. His partner stumbled backwards, slipped in the gutter, and landed hard, blood spraying from his arm.

Ivan gulped down his hand and licked his bloody chops.

Then he frowned.

Shook his head violently.

Gagged.

"The cross!" Lou shouted. "He swallowed the cross!"

Ivan spat out some foam and clutched at his throat. George staggered over to the werewolf. He couldn't believe it. Lou had been right—that furry son of a bitch couldn't deal with a cross, at least one that was sliding down his goddamn windpipe.

If that cross was burning through his insides, George had to make sure it didn't take an efficient route.

Knowing that Ivan was an agent of Satan or something like that made George feel even better about the violence he needed to inflict. He punched Ivan in the face, sending bloody spew flying into the air. Ivan's lower jaw went off-center. A dime-sized hole formed in his throat.

No. That wasn't good enough.

George kicked Ivan's feet out from under him. The werewolf fell. George got down with him. Ivan's eyes were wide with fright as the tiny silver cross continued to do its damage.

Ivan's entire body began to shift from wolf to human and back again, a wave of transformation that ran back and forth from head to toe.

George punched him in the face, then grabbed him by the hair and pulled him to a sitting position. He didn't want the cross to burn out through the back of his neck.

Had to get the heart.

Ivan wailed and swiped at George, but they were weak efforts. Another spot of blood appeared on Ivan's chest, so George tilted him, hoping that he was aiming the cross properly.

Ivan's face became human. He tried to say something but couldn't speak. Probably trying to get in one last smart-ass comment.

Too bad for him.

With a sudden burst of strength, Ivan leaned his head forward and bit at George's arm. His human teeth scraped harmlessly across George's flesh.

Then Ivan gasped, loudly.

His eyes rolled to the back of his head.

Blood poured from his mouth as all strength vanished from his body.

George let him drop.

Ivan, his body half-human, half-wolfman, lay motionless on the bowling lane.

Dead.

Finally.

George tore off his shirt as he hurried over and pulled Lou to his feet. He quickly wrapped the shirt around Lou's bleeding stump, as tightly as he could.

"It's going to be fine," said George. "I promise."

Lou looked like a zombie, but he hadn't completely checked out quite yet. "Is he dead?"

"Yeah."

"Oh, good."

"Just come with me," George said. "If we can beat the cops, everything will be fine."

Chapter Thirty-Three: Wrap-Up

"The werewolf is dead," said Bateman. The phone felt like a live grenade in his hand.

"I know. I saw." Mr. Dewey's tone was hard to figure out. Bateman assumed that it was "tightly controlled rage."

"It wasn't my fault," Bateman insisted. "The guys we hired had an excellent reputation. It was just a simple transport job. He was in a durable cage. Nothing should have gone wrong."

"And yet we're left with a dead werewolf."

"I'm sorry. We did our best."

"I have a huge amount of resources at my disposal, Mr. Bateman. Resources that are no longer of any use to me. Therefore, I'm going to devote these resources to making the rest of your life extraordinarily unpleasant."

Bateman's throat went dry. "Are you threatening me?"

"Yes, I most certainly am. You have just made yourself the worst, and last, enemy of your life."

"Hey, you can't blame me! You want revenge, blame the guys who lost him! You can't come after me for this! I never had to offer him to you in the first place!"

"But you did, and you gave me false hope. I believe that responsibility always starts at the top. I have no interest in the lowlife thugs you hired to do your dirty work. This is all on you."

"Let's talk about this."

"We are talking. It's over for you, Mr. Bateman. Goodbye."

Mr. Dewey hung up. "Hey!" Bateman shouted into the phone. "Hey! You can't do this!"

He tossed the phone against the wall, shattering it. Oh, God, he was so very screwed. He threw up onto his new carpet, then ran out of his office.

"Dad, what's wrong?" Bryan asked. The dumb-ass was playing video games, right there in the living room where Bateman could see, even though he'd been strictly forbidden to do so.

"Pack your things!"

"Why?"

"Because I said so, you stupid fuck!"

"But I've got a date with Mindy tonight!"

Bateman ran across the living room and kicked the widescreen TV as hard as he could, putting a huge hole in the center of the screen. The satisfaction he felt was minimal, but Bryan did get up and hurry off to his room.

Bateman threw up again, then ran off to pack.

«««—»»»

Jonathan Dewey sat silently in his chair.

Helena put her hand on his shoulder. "It'll be okay, honey. We'll find another way. It probably wouldn't have worked anyway."

He pulled away from her hand. "Is that supposed to make me feel better?"

"I just meant—"

"Werewolves do not die of brain tumors, Helena! I had a *chance*, and now it's *ruined*!"

"But—"

"Shut up. Get out of here and leave me alone. I have to send some people off to bring me Bateman's head."

«««—»»»

"We got ripped off, bad," said George.

"Well, I'm sorry we weren't given the opportunity to seek medical care that would have been covered by my insurance." Lou poked at the heavy bandage over his stump.

"We needed that money."

"Yeah, well, excuse me for getting my hand bit off by a werewolf. If I'd known that it would cause problems with our financial situation, I never would have let him do that. I thought you were going to donate everything to charity anyway. Become a better person."

"I never said I was going to donate everything to charity. But I am going to become a better person. Deal with it."

It had been a rough two days. George had thought that Lou was indeed going to bleed to death as they sped away from the bowling alley. He pulled behind the next building, made a tourniquet out of a crossbow bolt and a rag he found in the van, and got the bleeding under control.

The process of cauterization had been ugly.

After a few panicked calls, they found a doctor of ill-repute who was willing to patch up their wounds and hide them away for a couple of days, in exchange for almost all of the cash in the briefcase.

"You couldn't have got us a car with more legroom?" Lou asked, shifting uncomfortably. "I can't make it all the way to Canada in this."

"Then we'll go to Mexico."

"Seriously, George. We need to steal something else."

"Yeah, let's steal a big roomy clown car with flashing lights that makes wacky sound effects. We certainly wouldn't want to be in a non-descript automobile when cops, bad guys, and the general public are all looking for us."

"I didn't say it had to be a clown car. Just something roomier."

"At least your arm takes up less room now."

Lou frowned at him. "Are you really going to make jokes about my hand? Seriously?"

"I'm just trying to make you laugh so you don't cry."

"I'm not gonna cry."

"Good."

"Do you think I'm a werewolf now?"

"Are you bringing that up again?"

"Is it really such a terrible thing if I want reassurance? I got bit. I got bit really, really bad." He held up his bandaged stump. "See?"

"You saw how quickly it affected Michele. It's been two days. Maybe it's a special kind of bite. An injection or something."

"I hope so."

"I told you, I'm going to watch over you. You start to feel wolfy, we'll put you in the trunk. Everything's going to be fine. I didn't get my throat torn out by Ivan, so I'm sure as hell not going to get it torn out by you."

"Yeah, you're right. I'm feeling optimistic."

"So am I."

Lou turned on the radio. Some hip-hop music blared over the speakers. "Do you like this song?"

"It's crap."

"Good. I think we'll listen to it." Lou began to move his head back and forth to the beat. "Groove with me, George."

"You look like an idiot."

"I'm an idiot with rhythm. C'mon, groove with me."

George watched him for a moment, then smiled. He cranked up the volume and the two thugs grooved off into the sunset.

Jeff Strand is the author of enough books that if you tried to cut off one finger for each of them, you'd completely run out of fingers, and then you wouldn't have anything left to hold the knife when you started on your toes. (You would not, however, run out of toes—at least for now.) Some of those books include *Dweller, Pressure, Benjamin's Parasite, The Sinister Mr. Corpse, and Graverobbers Wanted (No Experience Necessary)*. He's been a finalist for the Bram Stoker Award twice, and won zero times. He lives in Tampa, Florida, and thinks that it would be best for all concerned if you visited his website at:

www.JeffStrand.com